THE KILLER'S KID

A SUSPENSE NOVEL

ADELENE ELLENBERG

THE
KILLER'S
KID

ADELENE ELLENBERG

Woodhall Press | Norwalk, CT

woodhall press

Woodhall Press, 81 Old Saugatuck Road, Norwalk, CT 06855
WoodhallPress.com

Cover design: Asha Hossain
Layout artist: L.J. Mucci

Library of Congress Cataloging-in-Publication Data available
ISBN 978-1-954907-97-3   (paper: alk paper)
ISBN 978-1-954907-98-0   (electronic)

First Edition
Distributed by Independent Publishers Group
(800) 888-4741

Printed in the United States of America

To my beloved family. All of you have inspired this book to be born.

CHAPTER 1

Clarisse Quinn was tucked neatly into her satin-lined coffin. The sole funeral home in Longbottom, Massachusetts, was filled with townspeople ready to soak up the spectacle. Also in attendance was Darlene Bundt, who, unbeknownst to her fellow townspeople, was pregnant with the killer's kid.

My child has been conceived by Clarisse's murderer, thought Darlene. She shuddered. *Oh, my Lord. What have I done?*

Townspeople lined up for the viewing, murmuring how Clarisse Quinn had to so likable, so benign. But the consensus was that her murder was predictable, seeing as she had proclaimed her bold testimony in open court.

Against *him*. Mickey Quinn. A name usually whispered. Too many were still bound to him by circumstance, business, a lifetime of history. Ties that were impossible to sever unless one left the Town of Longbottom and the Commonwealth of Massachusetts. For too many, it was easier to stay where their families had always been. Even if it meant one had to self-censor for a lifetime.

Midway among the rows of seated spectators, the Jaston family stood to honor the dead woman. Robert Jaston, a dairy farmer, was on his feet, despite the wound he had just suffered.

We Jastons certainly got ourselves whammied by Clarisse's testimony, he reflected glumly. *But I can't blame her. I know she meant to help out.*

Robert's wife Maureen, his crutch in so many ways, held him steady and straight. At Maureen's side were her ten-year-old twin daughters, Layla and Shaina, who were flanked by their teenage brother, Jacob. The five of them stood in an unwavering line, in tribute to Clarisse's bravery.

A muffled sob emerged from the front row. There, an elderly couple leaned into one another, shoulders entwined over the folding chairs. They were clearly holding one another up in the face of their grief.

"That's Clarisse's parents," whispered a woman seated in the row behind the Jastons.

"How do you know?" whispered a second woman.

"The funeral director told me."

"Did he say where they're from? Not from around here."

"That's for sure." She sniffed. "I heard they're from somewhere out in western Mass., some little town."

Maureen Jaston turned slightly, enough to cast a stern shushing glance back at the two women. After meeting the eye of one of them, she turned forward again and resumed her vigil.

Poor Clarisse, she thought. *She certainly didn't deserve to die for coming forward with the truth. I pray there will be justice for her.*

The funeral home director was a fortyish, plump man, impeccably groomed and suited. All the correct sayings of comfort just slid off his tongue. He was anxious for this viewing and funeral to appear gracious and noncontroversial—a proper ceremony, with no drama. He decided to move things along.

"Now is the time we will remember the deceased, Clarisse Quinn," he intoned in his deepest baritone voice. "Anyone wishing to say a few words is welcome to approach the podium."

A hush fell over the room. People began to study their shoes. The funeral director gazed from one end to the other, but no one looked up.

The funeral home was stuffy and too warm from the wall-to-wall people packed in the oddly shaped rooms. Once a family home, it retained the odd sizes and ornamentation of a Victorian-era house, inside and out. Occupied folding chairs lined the center and filled the adjacent rooms. Still others, who couldn't find chairs, stood in awkward groups in the aisles and against the walls. The smell of lilies contrasted with the funeral home's people-mass, and there was a mix of cloyingly sweet perfume and mustiness.

The funeral director looked puzzled when no one came up to the podium. He cleared his throat tentatively, wondering whether to repeat his invitation to speak.

Still no one stepped up. The room was unnaturally quiet, as everyone waited for someone else to come forward.

This is ridiculous, thought Maureen Jaston. *The Longbottom townsfolk are such cowards. They don't dare say a word.*

She gently nudged Robert forward to let her pass. He gripped the chair in front of him, nodded, and let her go.

Maureen slowly and carefully parted the standing-room-only crowd and approached the podium. A whisper, a murmur, arose throughout the room. She stood motionless till the room quieted. Everyone's attention was fastened on her.

"Clarisse Quinn was an incredibly brave person," said Maureen in a soft voice. Despite standing back from the microphone, everyone remained utterly quiet.

"As you know, I wasn't born in this town. Neither was poor Clarisse. Maybe she thought she had the genuine option to choose to do the right thing." Maureen sighed. "Maybe she never dreamed that the consequences of doing the right thing would be so severe. That it would cost her—her life."

Maureen's mouth began to quiver. She lowered her head to gain control. Her auburn hair framed her sorrowful face.

"It was my privilege to meet her only a short time ago, when she was on the run. Normally our paths didn't cross; we traveled in different circles." She pressed her lips together in thought. "But when I finally did meet her, I thought she was a real lady, a person of integrity. She didn't need to die—she shouldn't have died! And she wouldn't've—if things had just gone differently."

Everyone in the room heard her sniff away her tears. She wiped a cheek, gave a sad smile.

"Of course, we all know who *actually* pulled the trigger!"

Maureen began to scan the faces in the funeral parlor, going up and down the rows. Her eyes landed on a tall, lanky fellow in an expensive suit who leaned nonchalantly against the wall. The crowd followed her gaze and saw Tobias Meachum, Longbottom's town lawyer. He smirked at the attention and mock-saluted Maureen.

"And we all know the devious lawyer who's defending Clarisse Quinn's murderer!" said Maureen, in a clear voice that carried to every corner.

The funeral director's face turned a curious shade of purple. He made a move to get Maureen Jaston away from the podium.

If that guy had had a giant hook, he would've used it on her, Robert realized. Seated next to his family, he sat up a bit straighter, trying to catch his wife's eye. He needn't have worried.

Maureen shrugged away the stout funeral director.

"I'm not done yet." She wiped her cheek, took a deep breath. "As you know, Clarisse Quinn went to great lengths to save this town—including my family's farm—from the ravages of our select-men. The Jaston family owes Clarisse so much. You townsfolk know how Jaston Farm was started by Robert's great-grandfather, way back. It was going to be taken from our family by eminent domain, by a mere vote of our three selectmen. Clarisse exposed the good-old-boy cronyism, the corruption behind it all. She was *incredibly* brave." Maureen swiped at her brimming eyes. "Now, all we can do is honor her memory, which is what I am asking from everyone today."

Tobias Meachum unexpectedly began to speak, loudly.

"My client—who's under indictment, *unjustly*—has done more for this town and its people than anyone else I can name." His thin, hatchet-shaped face thrust forward as he spoke. "Call Mickey Quinn a murderer again in public, and we'll sue you for slander! He's inno-cent until proven guilty!"

People swiveled their heads between Maureen Jaston and Tobias Meachum, horrified, appalled—and yet secretly excited—to see these longtime antagonists spew arguments at one another in such a public fashion.

Maureen Jaston's oval face flushed pink against the cloud of her auburn hair.

"I can't believe this nonsense I'm hearing," she said.

"Your precious little friend betrayed my client—her husband. She chose her path," Meachum growled.

"Your attitude is medieval and chauvinistic."

"Your sentimentality is pathetic."

"That's enough!" bellowed the funeral director. "This is not fitting or proper at this occasion. Everyone will cease—immediately!"

His round face was flushed and his eyes gleamed with annoyance.

Silence filled the room.

The funeral director continued, in a more even-toned voice.

"Does anyone else have anything to say—something *kind*—about the deceased?"

The elderly couple leaned into one another, silently weeping. The woman reached for a tissue and quietly blew her nose.

Maureen returned to her seat and sat between her twin daughters. Both girls clutched Maureen's arms, and she hugged them tightly, smiling over at her son, Jacob. He gave a slight nod of approval.

The funeral director went on. "Then we will continue with the service by asking Reverend Tim to say a few words."

He glared around the room, daring anyone to disrupt the proceedings.

Reverend Tim rose. "We are all here on this Earth for but a brief time, and it is for each of us to fulfill our God-given potential to do good . . ."

The roomful of people issued a collective sigh as they settled in for the standard prayers.

As Reverend Tim's voice droned on with its soothing intonations, Tobias Meachum left his place against the wall and began to sidle over toward Darlene Bundt. He moved noiselessly, placing his damp hand on the arm or shoulder of those in his way until they stepped aside. Eventually he stood over Darlene Bundt, who was seated in a corner, head down, listening.

Sensing a presence, Darlene looked up. She jumped in her chair, startled to see Tobias Meachum looming over her.

"So," whispered Tobias Meachum to her very quietly, "you think you can come here to pay your respects to the woman who betrayed Quinn?"

"What do you mean?" Darlene whispered back, unable to look away.

He held her terrified gaze for a long moment, then jerked his head to indicate Clarisse Quinn, lying in her satin-lined coffin.

"If you think you're gonna betray him, you'll end up just like her," he whispered.

Then he was gone.

———

Darlene shivered inwardly as she drove in the funeral procession. The hearse carrying Clarisse Quinn's remains was creeping forward, the line of cars that followed jerking along slowly. Darlene craned her neck over the wheel but saw nothing to explain the delay.

Suddenly she saw. She was astonished.

Deer lined the wooded patches along the road as the procession passed by. Darlene glanced to the opposite side of the road and saw more deer. What was going on? The animals stood utterly still, as if posed, while the cars rolled past.

It was when she saw the buck, antlers held proudly aloft, that she knew the deer were paying special homage to poor Clarisse.

Even the natural world mourned the passing of Clarisse Quinn. A righteous soul, on her way to heaven.

Darlene stared in wonderment as she slowly drove on.

CHAPTER 2

Anna Ebert had just left the county courthouse after representing her divorced client, which meant she'd missed the dramatic funeral of Clarisse Quinn. But no matter. She was hearing about it now, from her longtime friend, Sophie Parsons.

Juicy gossip was the spice of small towns. After this one-of-a-kind funeral, the town gossip mill raged on. Everyone was speculating about Mickey Quinn. Would he get charged for Clarisse's murder, or a lesser offense? And hadn't Clarisse looked beautiful, lying there, cut down in the prime of her womanhood? Such a pity . . . she had been such a generous and good woman.

Anna had been driving toward the town hall when Sophie called. Now she was stopped in a snarl of traffic. Slowly, she wove in and out of the meandering congestion at the rotary, which circled the historic Longbottom Common. An orange Kia pulled out in front of her, and Anna eased onto her brakes.

"Go on, Sophie—tell me what *else* people said," prompted Anna as she gripped the steering wheel.

"Well, after all the shouting back and forth between Maureen Jaston and that creepy attorney, Tobias Meachum, I saw him—Meachum— go over to Mickey Quinn's former employee, Darlene something or other, I can't remember her last name. Anyway, he was in the corner with her, where she was sitting, and he said something to her that made her look ghostly white."

"Huh!" said Anna, keeping her eyes glued to the road. "Do you have any idea what he might have said to her? Do you think he might have *threatened* her?"

"Probably. That's how Meachum does business. Always a threat— along with doing whatever his favorite mobster buddy wants carried out. I bet Quinn wants something from her." Sophie sighed deeply. "I can't imagine it'll work out in her favor."

"But what?" asked Anna.

"I'll tell you. I saw her in a corner, sitting by herself, and she looked like she had put on weight. She has this new plumpness to her. If I had to make a wild guess, I'd say she might be pregnant."

A silence fell as they considered this possibility.

Sophie snorted unexpectedly. "Come to think of it, maybe it's *his* kid! Heaven forbid. Poor thing!" She paused. "She *did* turn ashen-white . . . I'm probably wrong. Pure speculation on my part."

"It could be something else entirely," Anna said. "Like, she stole money from him, as an employee, and Meachum found out about it."

Anna braked again for a medium-sized landscaping truck that had pulled out in front of her. The diesel fumes were making her queasy, so she shut her car windows and put on the air-conditioning.

"Listen, gotta go. I'm on my way to Town Hall. Catch ya later!"

Anna hung up and started looking for a free parking spot around the Common. She eventually found one in front of the second-hand-clothing shop, a few storefronts down from Town Hall. She parked her old car, got out, and briskly walked in that direction, holding her briefcase.

Heaving open the heavy door, Anna entered the cool, dim hallway of town hall, her eyes still adjusting to the interior. She wore a summer suit made of baby-blue cotton, with a jacket and matching pants, striking against her black hair. These days, she dispensed with the formal lawyer's attire that had once been expected of all female Massachusetts attorneys. At least she could wear flat shoes with pants. She could move like a real person if she found herself in danger. These days, who knew?

To her right was the Town Clerk's office, the position currently occupied by Rufus Fishbane—one of Anna Ebert's least favorite people.

"Hello, Rufus!" she called out in a singsong voice. "Lovely day outside, wouldn't you say?" Anna stuck her head over the counter, trying to spot him.

Rufus Fishbane sprang forward. "What can I do for you, today?" Seeing Anna Ebert, his normally beet-red face turned an even deeper shade of purple. His hand-raked hair stuck out around his face as he vigorously stroked his short, pointed beard.

"Rufus, I'm here to challenge the election results you made public on Saturday night."

Anna plopped a sheaf of papers down on the counter, leaning against it as she spoke.

"I've got a petition here, signed by more than two hundred Longbottom voters. They question whether the people of Longbottom really wanted to vote away their Open Town Meeting form of government. I, for one, don't believe it's so."

She rattled the sheaf of papers again, deliberately, to annoy Rufus.

"Who are you here for?" asked Rufus.

"You know I represent the Jastons, specifically, Robert Jaston," Anna said, straightening up to her full height of five feet, three inches. She glared at Rufus Fishbane, her green eyes narrowed. "And you, as town clerk, just presided over this town ballot fiasco, with the question you cleverly and deviously posed with *three* alternatives. All of them written with deliberately confusing language, so people weren't sure *what* they were voting for."

She slammed her fist on the counter.

"And now you have the audacity to announce that the people of Longbottom voted away their Open Town Meeting? I don't *think* so."

Anna straightened, indignant. Her green eyes flashed. She bit back more words, waiting.

Rufus stood unmoving, arms crossed. He sneered. "Your petition is worthless!"

"Why? Why not date-stamp it, and send it up to the statehouse?" Anna countered. "They can reconsider the prior legislation, which abolished our Open Town Meeting. When a petition shows up within the time frame, they can vote to reconsider; that would restore it." She eyed him. "What? Afraid of townspeople who don't vote the way *you* want them to?" Her green eyes flashed again. "Imagine, people thinking and voting for themselves these days. We all know the pure democracy of Open Town Meeting is a horrible *danger*—"

Rufus cut her off. "Don't give me your stupid theories," he said. "Actually, your petition is of no effect. A ballot question that goes to a town referendum is superior to a paltry citizens' petition, signed by a couple hundred people. The referendum drew in over two thousand voters. It's over, Attorney Ebert."

Rufus chuckled, showing long yellow teeth.

"Your precious client, Robert Jaston, has only a few more months to woo the crowd to his side at Open Town Meeting—all of those bleeding hearts in town who want to save Jaston Farm. But your client is selfish and unrealistic. Dairy farms need to give way to something bigger, something that will bring lots of jobs to town."

He crossed his arms again, as if to signal, case closed.

Anna Ebert gazed up at his tall presence, defiant.

"Rufus, mark my words: You will be very sorry you disenfranchised the old-time voters who love their Open Town Meeting."

With that, she grabbed her sheaf of papers, and strode out.

CHAPTER 3

The cell floor felt gritty under Mickey Quinn's hands as he did his thirty push-ups.

His cell-mate watched him silently, sprawled on the lower level of the bunk bed. A highly tattooed twenty-four-year-old, his cell-mate refused to sleep on the upper bunk. He claimed he was prone to sleepwalking. Mickey Quinn had yet to see this walking billboard of street art tumble out of bed and smash face-first into the cell bars. He longed to wake in the middle of the night and witness just that. It would satisfy his simmering rage at having to heave himself onto the upper bunk repeatedly during the day. He was the senior jailbird of this cell. He deserved some respect. He deserved the easy bottom bunk.

Sweat trickled behind Mickey Quinn's ears onto his stinking cotton shirt. There was no air-conditioning in the county jail. The building, built more than eighty years ago, was outdated, crowded, and overrun with cockroaches and rats. Yesterday, a small rat had run over the back of his hand while he was resting on the floor after his push-ups. It dove into his sweat pooled on the floor next to his head and drank greedily. That had made Quinn jump up mighty quick. His cell-mate had howled with laughter.

Quinn stood up slowly after his thirty-second push-up. He must've lost count somewhere in the middle. He felt a bit dizzy in the suffocating heat. He was forty-six; too old for this.

"Move over—I gotta sit a minute," he said.

"Go sit on your own bed," said his cell-mate.

"Dooley—don't be a selfish bastard. Move over."

"I ain't movin' for you, old man. I don't want your sweat drippin' on my mattress."

Quinn almost launched a blizzard of fists at Dooley's smart mouth, but saw that his cell-mate was poised to counterattack, so he stood still until his haze of anger abated.

"Don't you respect your elders?"

"Nah. No old person ever did nothin' for me."

"Not even your mama?"

"Leave my mama outta this." Dooley's dark eyes flashed. He was a golden-colored man with short dreadlocks. He twisted them into shape with his fingers, till they formed a ring around his thin face. His jaw protruded, ending in rosy lips that looked strangely coquettish, almost feminine.

Quinn knew his own blond hair and blue eyes grated on Dooley. Dooley ignored him, generally. When Dooley bothered to speak to him, he mostly called Quinn "Old man."

"Dooley, don't you ever exercise?"

"If I want exercise, I'll start by poundin' your face in."

Quinn almost retorted, then decided he'd better shut up.

He climbed up the end of the bed to the top bunk. His sweaty body landed with a thump against the top mattress. The bed frame squealed under his weight.

"You trying to aggravate me, old man?"

"Nah. Just being old and feeble."

The silence between them stretched out till Quinn farted.

Dooley kicked the underside of Quinn's bunk twice, making it heave upwards.

"Knock it off!" Quinn said.

"Quit yo fartin', old man! I don't wanna smell yo ass-gas!"

"It's the jailhouse food, okay?"

"Stick a cork in it!"

"You gotta cork I can borrow?"

"My fist."

Quinn wasn't used to being the one to have to bite his tongue. He had always been the smart-aleck, the arrogant jerk. Being in a tiny cell with a young man who had no mercy was a new thing. Quinn sighed, and lay back on his top bunk. Time crawled.

"What's an old dude like you doin' in jail, anyway? What'd you do?"

Quinn was surprised by this sudden interest from Dooley. The two of them had shared a cell for three days now, and Dooley had never shown the slightest bit of curiosity before.

Quinn said: "My wife is dead."

"How?"

"She got shot."

Dooley squirmed sideways from the bottom bunk to eye him. "You do the shooting'?" His coquettish, pink lips were parted, awaiting an answer.

Quinn scratched his chest. "Nah. Not me."

Dooley waited. "So who shot her?"

"I don't wanna talk about it."

Dooley's golden face was impassive. His tattooed right hand lazily scratched his groin.

"She must've pissed somebody off."

Quinn grinned. "You could say that."

"You miss her?"

"Nah." He resumed scratching his chest. "She was a shitty wife."

Dooley was silent for a long moment. "Could she cook?"

"Barely."

"Spend your money crazy?"

"Oh yeah."

"Sounds like she bad news."

"You could say that."

Quinn wondered what Dooley was up to, with this sudden curiosity. Was he going to become a jailhouse witness in exchange for a plea deal? He'd better watch his own mouth, not brag about stuff.

"She got a lot of people coming out for her funeral?"

"I don't know."

"You don't know?"

"I don't care."

Glumly, Quinn reviewed the chain of events since his arrest.

He had been handcuffed and taken away in the Longbottom squad car without any special concessions, which should have been his due. After all, he was a "town father." Where were his people? He sure as hell had contributed enough to the town coffers—not only through taxes paid on his house and his business, but support for the town's Little League, soccer league, football league, the Lions Club, the Kiwanis Club, the Civic Club, the Chamber of Commerce, the Library Fund, the Town Democratic Party, the Town Republican Party, the Polish Club, the Italian Club, the Lincoln Club, and even the local women's shelter, Beacon House. He had spread enough money around to fertilize a friggin' bank, not to mention generate a measure of goodwill. So why had he been hustled into the squad car like a common criminal? Hell—he contributed to the annual Longbottom Police Association's fund-raiser for local kids. Didn't that count for a bit of consideration?

Sure, he'd shot his wife. But he was famously A Friend of the Kennedys, an FOTK, who'd been invited to their compound years ago. Everyone in Longbottom knew he knew the Kennedys. As an FOTK, he didn't expect to get foiled.

He had already endured a bench trial earlier on the public corruption matter. Everyone knew he held the Longbottom selectmen in his grip. Like, that was news around here?

The judge, who he had helped get on the bench of the Massachusetts Superior Court, had gone easy on him, found him guilty of only a misdemeanor. For the public corruption case—trying to screw a farmer out of his land, in order to put a casino there—the judge had given him community service. He snickered. Community service! That judge had done him a favor, being an FOTK and all.

Unfortunately, Quinn had only his own out-of-control temper to blame for his current predicament. He had shot his wife Clarisse in a rage. Now, he sat behind bars, awaiting yet another trial—this time for murder—sharing a cell with this lowlife.

The guard tramped down the concrete walkway, boot heels scraping with each step. He stopped at their cell. "Phone call for prisoner Quinn. From your lawyer."

Mickey looked up, surprised, and walked over to the front bars. "Look alive," said the guard. "Arms forward."

Mickey obliged, sticking his arms out through the bars. Once the guard had put the cuffs on his outstretched wrists, he unlocked the cell.

"Okay. Come with me." The guard pointed with his chin.

Quinn shuffled down the long walkway till they reached a central room with a wall of phones. The guard pointed to the phone on the end.

"Hello?" said Quinn.

"Mickey, it's Toby. Listen, I called to tell you that the question you got onto the ballot—it passed! Buddy, *it passed!* The Town of Longbottom is *done* with Open Town Meeting! We'll have a town council with nine councilors, one from each town precinct." Toby snorted. "That'll end all the nonsense."

"Hot damn!" Quinn said. He grinned and scratched his chin.

"It was posed as a three-choice question, so the voters didn't know what they were voting for." Meachum chuckled. "Good old Rufus."

"Yep. Good old Rufus." Silence on the line between them. "So, when d'ya think you can get me outta here?"

"Workin' on it, buddy." Meachum sighed.

"Well, hurry up! I got stuff to do."

CHAPTER 4

Quinn's Pub & Grill was having another terrible day of business.

What's going on here? thought Darlene.

She stood behind the bar, massaging the small of her back. She was a compact six months pregnant, just beginning to show on her slender, sturdy frame. She repeatedly tossed her long, straight blonde hair behind her with a flick of her hand. Standing all day was getting painful for her lower legs and feet. Oh, for a chair!

The heavy door of Quinn's Pub & Grill suddenly opened, letting a stream of sunlight into the dim room. A sharply dressed young man entered, followed by another carrying a camera. They walked up to Darlene, standing behind the bar.

"Hi," said the first stranger. "I'm a reporter down from Boston. I'm with WXB-TV, outta the Quincy office, actually. I'm tracking the wild rumor that's been trending all week on Twitter, about how this bar has become cursed?" He looked straight at Darlene. "What can you tell us about the curse on Quinn's Pub and Grill?"

Darlene began backing away, toward the mirrored wall of liquor bottles.

"I don't know what you're talking about."

"Wasn't there some kinda murder involved?"

Darlene rubbed her cheek before answering. "The owner, Mr. Quinn, did shoot his wife, Clarisse Quinn." She ducked her head.

"Why was that?"

"I wouldn't know." She pursed her lips and looked over her shoulder. The camera was running, pointed at her.

"Rumor has it that ghosts have been seen here. Have you ever seen anything out of the ordinary?"

The reporter extended his microphone across the bar toward her.

"Nope. Not a thing." Darlene looked down at the floor.

The reporter began reading from a card in the palm of his hand.

"I've heard that down here in Longbottom, you folks live on the edge of the Hockomock Swamp—a place sacred to the Native Americans for at least ten thousand years, where the English colonists fought Chief Ousamequin Massasoit in King Philip's War, a mere ten years after the Pilgrims first landed, back in 1620."

"Sounds like you know way more than me," said Darlene. "Why ask me anything?"

"The Hockomock Swamp is famous for its weird sightings and rumors of ghosts and such.

"Oh, we manage to get along all right in these parts," said Darlene, with the hint of a smile.

The reporter looked up at her again, as if noticing her for the first time. "Have you noticed any downturn in business lately? Any unusual sightings?"

Darlene cast him a wary glance before her blue eyes looked straight into the camera.

"I do know that receipts are down since my boss shot his wife. Maybe that's why. But I don't know anything about any kinda curse." She shrugged and looked away. "Maybe somebody else here knows." She pointed at a sole customer hunched over the far end of the bar, whose face was in darkness.

The cameraman paused his camera, lowered it, and walked toward the customer, followed by the reporter, who asked, "What can you tell us about the curse of Quinn's Pub and Grill?"

The shadowy figure rotated toward them slightly. "All's I know is, everything that Mickey Quinn has ever touched in our town has turned nasty. He was just a big, mean kid, originally, sent down from South Boston. He came here as a foster kid, and since then, he's bullied his way forward. He's brought nothing but trouble to all of us here," the man said. "*He* is Longbottom's curse!"

The reporter glanced at his cameraman, who shook his head.

"Can you explain that, sir?" said the reporter. "Can we get your name?"

The shadowy figure sprang up from his barstool, pulled the hood of his sweatshirt up over his head, and closed it in front of his face. He quickly strode out of the premises.

The cameraman started to follow, but the reporter called out, "Let him go."

The reporter, flustered, turned back to Darlene.

"Can you give us any examples of Quinn inflicting pain and suffering on this town?"

"I got nothing to say about it," she said, thinking, *If you only knew.*

Why should Longbottom spill its secrets out to the world, Darlene thought. The folks up in Boston think of Longbottom residents as just a bunch of know-nothing country folk, living among the ghosts and shadows on the edge of the Hockomock Swamp. If they only knew that this Swamp is actually a holy place, sacred to the Wampanoag Peoples . . . a place where, over time, evil-hearted spirits are brought to justice.

The reporter and his cameraman waited for more from Darlene, who remained stubbornly silent. After a moment, they shrugged, grabbed their equipment, and left.

If only they had seen the deer lining the highway, thought Darlene. *The Hockomock Swamp takes care of its own.*

CHAPTER 5

"Grandma, they shut down Quinn's Pub and Grill! Business is *so* bad. I barely made *anything* this week. Meachum—that lawyer who threatened me at Clarisse Quinn's funeral—he came in and told us that the place was closing. We had to get our stuff, 'cause *he was locking up!* Just like that, I'm out of a job!" Her fist clenched tightly on her thigh. "I'm six months pregnant now. How'm I gonna get another job at this stage?"

Darlene began patting her rounded stomach in a circling pattern.

"I'm naming her Bonnie, after Ma. Do you think that's a good idea? I wouldn't want any of Ma's bad luck to fall on her. Maybe that *is* a bad idea." Darlene looked toward her grandmother.

Luella's eyes, dark as olive pits, steadily gazed at Darlene.

"You're already calling the baby a 'her'?"

"You told me that."

The old woman's gleaming white hair floated around her face.

"We'll see, won't we? They say if you carry low and back, it's a girl."

"Who's they?"

The older woman flapped away the question with a thin hand. "How're ya feeling these days, sweetie?"

"I feel fine, Grandma. I'm past the morning sickness. But I'm worried about money. I've only got enough saved for a coupla months, and now I'm outta my job."

"Whatever you do, don't go on welfare. It sucks you right in, they say." Luella shook her head dismissively. "Apply for unemployment, girl!"

"Yeah, I'll figure it out. Never done that before. Always kept a job. Remember, Grandma? I started working, with a work permit, when I was fourteen. You told me to. But also, I'm paying some of this nursing home fee, too, Grandma. You remember that, right? I want you in a *decent* place, near me, here in Longbottom. And now that you're on dialysis, you need to stay put, especially now that this little one's coming."

Luella blinked. "You do what you need to do, for yourself and the baby." Smiling sweetly, she said, "Don't worry about me. I'm on my way out of this world, child—don't you see? I'll make do somehow." She stretched to pat Darlene's hand. "Just do what you intend to do for yourself, and for our baby."

"I got something to tell you, Grandma."

"What is it?"

Darlene took a deep breath. "When I was sixteen . . . I had an abortion."

Her grandmother looked at her, utterly still, and said, finally, "Tell me about it."

"It was over twenty years ago." Darlene couldn't meet her grandmother's eyes. A hot flush crept up her neck and cheeks.

"Who was the boy?"

"Just a boy. You don't know him. His name is Jonah." She looked down again. "He gave me the money for it, from his after-school job."

"How come you're just telling me about this now?"

"I've dreamed about that baby for years. The child would've been nineteen years old now."

Luella smiled ruefully. "The decision haunts you now, doesn't it?

"Sure does, Grandma. I feel guilty for what I did. I pray for that child's soul to forgive me." Darlene ventured a glance at Luella.

Luella sighed. "Thinking back, I wondered what made you so moody and sad back then. You were a skinny, pretty, sixteen-year-old, used to be so friendly to everyone. I *knew* something was wrong, but you turned away from me that year."

"I know."

"We coulda had another whole person in our family."

"So that's why I'm gonna have *this* baby. I'm thirty-six years old. This may be my last chance to have a kid."

Luella nodded. "Yes, I see. Too bad this child comes so late in my life."

Darlene looked down at the speckled nursing home floor, lost in thought. Her blue sneakers were totally worn out, nearly shredded. They needed replacing. In a week or two, she would need some maternity clothes. Her money would start going fast.

She bit her bottom lip and sighed again. "I just don't know, Grandma."

"The Lord will provide an answer for you."

"Thanks," she said, and reached over to pat Luella's hand. "Do you need me to bring you anything?"

"I'm good."

"Are you sure? A little treat or something?"

"They take good care of me here."

"Yeah, it's true. The nurses dote on you so."

"They like my little bits of Bible versifying and my country sayings."

Darlene smiled. "You are something else, Grandma. I wish I had your gift."

"You do, sweetie."

"So you say."

"So I *know.*"

Darlene grimaced, disbelieving. "Whatever."

"Wish I could have you and the little one, right here next to me at the nursing home." Luella's lean face, deeply grooved with age lines, softened at the idea. "That's impossible, of course."

"Yeah, that'd be a good one—the three of us crammed into your hospital bed! Think anyone'd notice?"

Luella chuckled, smoothing her tangled bedsheets. She began wiggling her toes rhythmically to a silent drumbeat.

"So, what's the news about that good-for-nothing father of your child?"

"Quinn?"

"He *is* the father, right?"

"Yeah. Unfortunately."

"So. Did he up and die on us?" Luella's face had an eager expression.

"No such luck."

"Then what?"

"It's just . . ."

"What?"

"He's in jail."

"*Ha!* Serves him right!" Luella cackled. "What'd he do this time?"

"Killed his wife."

"Lord have mercy!" Luella made a sign to ward off the evil eye. "What a worthless slimeball he turned out to be!"

"You got that right."

Luella waggled her head in disapproval, rolling her dark eyes. Her halo of pure white hair shook loosely.

"Wanna know what's even worse?" Darlene asked.

"Worse than killing his wife?"

"Worse for me."

26

"I can't imagine."

"He was supposed to pay me child support every month, for eighteen years, once this baby was born, you know? Well, now that Quinn is in jail, and Quinn's Pub and Grill is closed, he has no money to pay me."

"Oh, he's got money."

"How do you know?"

"Sweetie, look at his big house on the hill. His cars. His clothes."

"But wouldn't he have to sell stuff to get me money?"

"So he sells his stuff. So what. He made a baby on you. Now he needs to support it. Support *her*, that is."

"So you think I should hire a lawyer?"

"Probably."

"That'll be expensive. I don't have the money for that."

"Mmm . . ."

Silently, they held hands at the bed's edge. A full minute passed, both of them lost in their thoughts.

"It'd be easier for me to just get another job to support myself and the baby. I oughta leave him in the dust. Let him rot in jail!"

"Don't be bitter toward him," said Luella in a soft singsong voice. "You don't want bitterness in your child's essence." She grasped Darlene's hand more firmly. "Child, your daughter will be as sweet as clover honey if you clear yourself of bitterness. Concentrate on the deliciousness and sweetness of a newborn babe."

"I guess so."

"Be sweet with her, with the way you cradle her in your womb while she's growing inside you. You two are now sharing food, blood, oxygen, nerves. Let them all be sweet and smooth within you both. She'll be born smiling."

"That's all well and good, Grandma, but what about practicalities?"

"They'll sort themselves out, somehow. Have faith, sweetie. Faith in the Lord."

CHAPTER 6

Darlene returned home, climbing the stairs to her third-floor apartment in the brick building. A neighbor's golden-eyed brindle cat scurried away. Darlene wasn't sure where the cat belonged.

Reaching her apartment, Darlene turned the key and swung the door open.

Standing there, front and center, was Quinn's lawyer, Tobias Meachum.

Tall and stooped, he blocked the daylight from the windows in the opposite wall. His dark hulk in her own private space caused her to feel a sudden, gripping fear. She gulped heavily, then managed to growl, "How the hell did you get in here?"

"Your landlord. Or landlady, I should say." His face was in shadow.

Again she growled, "What'd you do? Bribe her?"

The lawyer smiled faintly. "She was a pushover. Didn't cost me a dime."

"Great! Good to know I can count on her for my privacy and my safety." She eyed him warily. "Now get the hell out, before I call the cops."

"I don't think so, little lady."

Darlene expelled a burst of air. The silence between them grew.

"What do you want?" she finally asked, stepping further into the room. Light slanted into the apartment, gleaming on Darlene's blonde hair.

"Let's talk."

"About what?"

"Your and Mickey Quinn's baby."

Darlene was silent. A chill run up her backside.

"He's gonna get that baby, you know."

"Like hell he is. It's my baby!"

"It's half his child," the lawyer responded smoothly. "You're gonna learn that his half counts for more." Malevolent energy surged toward her from his gleaming eyes.

Darlene could feel that malevolence in her gut, and cradled her pregnant belly. She was suddenly defensive. "What do you people want from me?"

"The kid. Mickey wants his kid," Meachum intoned. "Get used to it."

"He can't *make* me give my baby to him!"

Meachum smiled. On his way out of the apartment, he purposely jostled her shoulder. As he reached the threshold, he turned to face her.

"We're watching you. Your every move. You can't have that baby without us knowing."

"Who's us?" she whispered, trembling.

Meachum stood in the doorway, looking down at her from his great height.

"Wouldn't you like to know?" he said with a wicked grin.

CHAPTER 7

Darlene felt hunted. She stood in the center of her studio apartment, turning slowly in a circle. Her entire apartment was one large room, but for the kitchen alcove and the tiny bathroom. During each turn in the main room, she scrutinized the shelves and other flat surfaces. Could any of these nooks and crannies be sheltering a hidden camera or a hidden microphone? It was not inconceivable. Rich people spied on their nannies all the time, nanny-cams were available everywhere. Meachum had just shown her that he could enter her apartment at will, with the apparent consent of her landlady, which made it even worse.

She stopped circling, and stood still, thinking.

She had been a fairly new employee of Quinn's. She had known about his reputation as a mobster. But she had thought taking a job was just that—a job.

Looking back, she could see that he had been lying in wait for her, stalking her in a way—finding her weakness, and then taking advantage of the situation.

What was she at this point but a kind of surrogate, a breeder-mom for Mickey Quinn?

It was a revolting thought.

She flashed to the memory of that night.

———

There had been a sudden tapping at the window of her Volkswagen, where she'd been sitting in the driver's seat, smoking. She had jumped, jarring the lit joint in her hand. It burned the palm of her left hand as the marijuana smoke wafted out of the cracked-open window.

"Gotcha!" Quinn had said. "Didn't know my new bartender liked wacky weed."

"Jesus, Mr. Quinn," she had said. "You scared the shit outta me."

"So what'll ya do for me if I don't call the cops on ya?" Quinn had said, grinning.

"It's legal now in Massachusetts, Mr. Quinn."

"Not if a person is gonna be driving. It's illegal in all fifty states to be driving while high."

Darlene remembered still feeling defiant.

But he had been smoothly persistent. An image of a cobra, poised, getting ready to strike, crossed her mind.

Quinn's eyes had glittered in the moonlight.

"Did I ever tell you that you're a mighty good-looking woman?"

She remembered saying that she urgently needed to go home. But when she'd turned her key in the ignition and pumped the gas, her Volkswagen had just made a rasping noise.

She'd whirled toward Quinn. "Did you do something to my car?"

31

"Getting paranoid, are you, smoking that stuff?" he had answered, grinning like the Cheshire Cat. "Need a ride home? My chariot awaits."

Darlene had reluctantly gotten into his Cadillac.

Once she was seated, he'd locked the doors, saying, "How 'bout sharing some a' that with me?"

She'd handed him the joint. "When *you're* gonna be driving me home? That's rich."

"Soon enough. After a little of this."

He had suddenly leaned forward and kissed her full on the mouth.

"Jesus Christ! You're married!" she had said, shoving him away from her.

Mickey Quinn had laughed. "Like that's ever stopped me?"

He began pulling down the zipper on his pants.

"Pull your jeans down, Darlene, or I'll turn the cops onto you."

"For smoking a joint? You're smokin' it, too!"

"Yeah, but I don't deal it, like you do." Quinn had given her a squint eye precisely then. "Unlike you, I don't have two prior drug convictions. Third one, and it's mandatory jail time. But you know that already. I just wonder if your precious grandma knows about all of your troubles?"

Darlene had frozen then. *How did he know?*

As if he had read her thoughts, he said, "Of course I do a thorough background check on every employee I hire at my place. It helps that I'm friendly with our local police force. They looked it up and found your priors, with you trying to plead them down to misdemeanors.

Darlene felt trapped. "Jesus, Mickey."

"A search of your place might even turn up your stash."

"Why'd you even hire me then?" she had asked, suddenly very afraid.

Quinn hadn't answered. He had just begun tugging at the waistband of her jeans.

"I even know who sells you the weed. And who you sell it to, afterwards. All I hafta do is make a call to our local boys in blue." He had crouched over her to whisper into her ear. "Whaddya say, Darlene?"

"Okay, Mickey," she had whispered back. "You got me. Just make it quick."

When it was over, Darlene had wiped herself down on his shirt-tail. *Let him take that home to his wife*, she thought grimly.

———

There was absolute silence in the car as Quinn drove her home that night. The word "rape" floated on the tip of Darlene's tongue, but she bit it back. She had held back her anger, her tears, her total outrage, in the fifteen minutes it took to get to her apartment.

Once inside, she had begun to shake uncontrollably. She had felt cold, goose-fleshy, jumbled up in her guts. She had walked numbly to her bedroom, taken off her clothes, dropped them on the floor as if they were contaminated.

She had walked, utterly naked, to the bathroom, run hot water till the bathtub was half full. She had stepped in the water and begun to soap herself down with a loofah. When she had scrubbed every bit of herself, she lay back in the tub and let the tears flow.

The bastard. She *needed* this job, she had thought then. She remembered how she had been due back for another shift the next day, and she'd had to act like nothing happened. She had been goddamned stone-faced, never giving him the satisfaction of knowing he had wounded her.

The bastard.

She had turned up pregnant. Lucky her.

Why had she listened to Grandma about having the baby? If she'd just had another abortion like she'd originally thought she'd do, she wouldn't be in this fix. But no, she'd listened to her grandmother about the importance of blood kin. Everything was for blood-kin. Her child would be part Cree, like she was. Like Grandma was.

Too late now to change her mind. She was in her last trimester, and she'd recently felt a new fluttering presence in her belly. The only way forward, with full integrity, was to be aware of the spirit growing within her. She wanted to feel its essence in her heart and mind.

Darlene shook off the memory train. It only led to regrets. She needed to concentrate on the moments and days ahead of her.

Think! she told herself. If Quinn wanted to protect his future child, would he have gone so far as to have cameras installed in her apartment?

She shuddered. God knows what she had revealed here in the past months. She remembered the many times she had walked around her apartment at night, when the curtains were firmly shut, topless—or nude. She had falsely thought she was safe in her own little cocoon, behind the deadbolts. She squirmed as she remembered how occasionally she had danced in her underwear when the spirit moved her. Did they keep the footage? *Cringeworthy!*

The devices would have watched her come home from her bartending job, as she counted her tips. Spies would have watched her as she sat rolling her quarters, dimes, nickels, and pennies into coin rolls to take to the bank. Those same coin rolls that banks hand out to local businesses for their cash registers.

Peons like me do all the work of rolling the coins, and we only get paid their face value, she thought. *Heaven forbid we should earn a fee for our efforts.* Ain't that the way of the world?

Thank God she had not been caught on any kind of nanny-cam smoking weed. Not that she would've been. As soon as she found out she was pregnant, she had cut out the weed, pronto. No need to fry the baby's brain.

Actually, she had cut out the weed right after the rape. It had lost its allure, having triggered the awful event. By eliminating weed from her life, she hoped to avoid being busted or blackmailed.

Quinn will try to use that against me, to prove I'm an unfit mother. Then he'd be automatically awarded custody of the baby.

Thank God she had also given up her piddly weed dealing. Which was a shame, really. That had been the source of the extra cash to help Grandma. Darlene had been steadily eating away at her savings since then, helping to pay the nursing home bills.

Something was gonna hafta rescue her, financially. What a time to lose her job. And who would hire someone who was six months pregnant?

Darlene was tired. The small of her back ached.

She took four steps and plopped down on her nubby beige couch. Her thoughts swirled. When she thought of all she might have revealed to the hidden camera, she felt a rush of rage—followed by a chilling, sickening sense of shame. Shame that she'd acted the fool in a public way, albeit, unbeknownst to her. Shame at being the subject of town gossip. Rage, again, at being a subject of surveillance.

Then another wave of shame hit her, for having been so ridiculously naive. She had been a fool to think she could live her life free of Quinn.

Darlene rose from her couch and went to the kitchen, rummaging under the sink for a dust cloth. She straightened and shook it out over the sink. Twinkling dust billowed into the steel basin.

She began to wipe down everything in her studio apartment, inch by inch. She started at the television, then began dusting her books, most of them from her high school years. Her fingertips caressed the edges and undersides of every shelf, but she felt nothing out of the ordinary. She continued, doing each lamp, each chair, the table, until she had circled the room.

Still nothing.

She was back to the television, deeply frustrated.

She had another thought. Perhaps the spying was done *through* the television. She had heard that the audience, a targeted household, could be seen through its screen. Or was that one of those urban myths? She would google it.

There had to be *something* in this apartment. Otherwise, why would Tobias Meachum have told her "We're watching you?" Could he have said it as a way to control her? Or as a way to confuse her, or freak her out? If the latter was his intention, he had surely succeeded. She was definitely freaked.

She would open her laptop and see what she could find out.

Damn.

They were probably spying on her from the camera on her laptop! She usually left it propped open. She'd have to put masking tape over the camera eye. Why hadn't she thought of that immediately? If they were spying on her now, the camera would have picked up the image of her searching every nook and cranny of her apartment. They would know she was on to them.

Jeez. She was truly an idiot.

CHAPTER 8

Anna Ebert was back in her office, listening to the police scanner. She normally kept up with who had been in a car accident, and who had been arrested. This kept her apprised of likely upcoming cases. A lot of the lucrative legal business went to the more established attorneys in Longbottom—like Tobias Meachum. The establishment attorneys played golf with the local judges and district attorneys. And then there were the lawyers like her, who had to have their ducks in a row if they were going to win their cases—which she usually did. This caused immense annoyance to her fellow attorneys who opposed her in the courtroom.

Anna was a tiny woman with shoulder-length black hair and green eyes, known for the tailored pant suits she wore when she showed up at the courthouse, when she needed to even the odds. She fought fiercely for her clients, and they rewarded her with their loyalty, respect, and repeat business. Especially ever since she had dared to take on the Jastons' high-profile case.

What she was hearing today on the scanner was strange. Something about a Boston reporter coming down to Longbottom to check out Quinn's Pub & Grill. Whatever for? Everyone knew that Mickey Quinn had shot Clarisse dead as a doornail down at Jaston Farm—in their front parlor, to be exact. Poor Clarisse.

Something about a rumor, or a curse? *Some sort of nonsense,* she thought.

But now something was coming across the airwaves about how Quinn's Pub & Grill was being checked out by some reporters. Why?

Anna Ebert's cell phone rang. It was her best friend, Sophie Parsons. Again. Only two hours had passed since they'd last talked.

"Hey, Sophie! What's up now?"

"You heard that Quinn's Pub and Grill is closing up, right? You know why?"

"No. Why?"

"There's a rumor going around town about the 'Curse of Quinn.'"

"Ha! And what's this supposed curse about?"

"That Clarisse's ghost, and the ghost of her grief-stricken lover, are haunting the place."

"Really?" Anna was incredulous. "I didn't think Clarisse had a lover. She was married to Quinn, who kept her on a pretty short leash, as I recall."

"Whatever. I don't think she had any lover either. I think the rumor is just an excuse for people to stay away from his place, since they disapprove of him now."

"Actually, some people, like me, have disapproved of him for years. It's just that disapproval of Mickey Quinn is more *fashionable* now."

"Yep." Sophie snorted. "Let's all jump on the local 'Curse of Quinn' bandwagon."

"Well, if it puts the kibosh on Quinn, that would be great. Unfortunately he does have quite the staying power."

"He sure does. Not to mention all his connections you know where." Sophie sighed.

"Mmm . . . We shall see. Keep me posted. Love ya—bye!"

"Bye, sweetie."

Anna kept her scanner on for a while longer till she reluctantly turned to her legal work.

CHAPTER 9

Maureen Jaston peered through her kitchen window, wondering who was approaching their farmhouse. It seemed to be yet another young woman. Maybe a teenager. Somehow the word had gotten out about their place being a haven for troubled girls on the run. She had nothing to do with it, really.

"Whatcha staring at, honey?" asked her husband.

"Looks like another teenager making her way up the incline, heading for our driveway."

"Come sit beside me for a few minutes, before she gets here," Robert said. He took another sip of coffee. "You're such a good woman. Rest a moment." He stretched his wounded leg out under the kitchen table and massaged the sore spots.

Maureen sat. "I don't mind them showing up at our door occasionally. But it's getting to be more than that. I don't know what it's all about."

"I do, sweetheart." He grinned. "You're becoming a local folk hero to the women in town, the way you took Clarisse into our house to protect her."

"Yeah, but that's just it. I *didn't* protect her. She ended up getting killed! Right *here*, in our house!" She shook her head. "Thank God the girls didn't see it. I'm still having nightmares."

"You? I'm the one who shot the guy."

"Thank God you did!"

There was a knock at the kitchen door.

Maureen walked to the door and opened it to see a willowy teenager with green hair falling over half her face. Maureen willed herself to smile, be sweet.

"Hello," she said. "Welcome. Come on in. You've walked a long way, I'm sure."

The teenager smiled shyly, gratefully, and nodded. She stepped up onto the stone steps at the farmhouse's kitchen door. She stood still, waiting to be summoned forward.

"And who might you be?" asked Maureen gently, indicating the girl should take a seat at the kitchen table.

"I'm Faith," said the girl. She gulped hard, then blurted out, "My parents found out I'm pregnant, and now my dad's ashamed of me. Ashamed to admit it to his friends. And to his sister, my aunt Sally. He wanted me to get rid of it, but I don't want to. He got so mad at me, he threw me out of the house. My mom's in my corner, but she always folds to my dad."

"Why did you end up coming here?"

Faith peeked out from behind her screen of green hair. "I heard from my girlfriend's older sister that Jaston Farm is a place where girls and women who are in trouble can go."

Maureen looked at her speculatively. "Anything else?"

The girl hesitated. "Just that Mr. Jaston is a fair guy, and you're a nice lady." She nodded to them both. "And that this is where Clarisse Quinn ran to, for safety."

Maureen grimaced. "Yeah. But things didn't exactly turn out happily for her."

"Yeah, *horrible* for her. But I don't have someone else after me. I just got kicked out."

"I see." Maureen brushed back her auburn hair. "Well, no doubt you're hungry and thirsty after that walk. How far did you come?"

"From the center of Longbottom. My parents' house is near Town Hall."

"My word! That's almost four miles!"

"I hitched part of the way."

Robert Jaston snorted, slowly stood up with his cane. "Gonna do some chores." He dragged his leg behind him as he left the kitchen.

Maureen eyed Faith. "Want a sandwich?"

"Sure."

"You'll be staying in our attic tonight, by the way. You'll sleep up there, on a mattress on the floor. That's where all of our wayfarers stay, till we get them on the way to where they need to be."

Maureen started making a peanut butter and jelly sandwich.

"Dinner will be in about four hours, after evening milking. All our visitors, whether pregnant or not, are expected to help with farm chores while they're here."

She put away the sandwich fixings and poured a tall glass of milk.

"Our son Jacob has been managing most of the chores ever since my husband was injured during all of that unfortunate business back then."

Maureen handed the sandwich and the full glass to Faith.

Faith began to eat hungrily.

"We're glad you're here, Faith. We'll figure things out, somehow, make some calls. Okay?"

"Thanks," said Faith, shoulders dipping slightly as she began to relax. "I've been wicked scared."

CHAPTER 10

Darlene peered into her grandmother's room at the nursing home. The older woman's hair formed a cottony-white helmet that framed her face as she dozed. Sleeping, her face was unlined, although her mouth drooped toward the pillow, which made her look disapproving.

As she slept, her glasses rested on the tip of her nose, attached by a braided cord around her neck. When Grandma gazed through her specs, her nearsighted eyes shrank to hard little olive pits, brown and penetrating. Darlene always felt she had to tell Grandma the truth, because those eyes would spot any floating falsehoods waiting to burst forth.

Darlene looked sideways to see if anyone was near. No aides were in the vicinity, and Grandma's roommate was gone. The relentlessly cheerful wallpaper, featuring open-faced children cavorting amid colored wildflowers, only emphasized the sad decrepitude in the nursing home. Patients seated in their wheelchairs lined the hallways. Darlene still wasn't used to that nursing-home smell of stale airlessness inside the overly heated building.

Ignoring her queasiness, Darlene sidled into her grandmother's room, intending to wake her up. Luella still had her wits about her, if not her physical strength.

When Darlene reached out a hand to jiggle her arm, Luella abruptly opened her eyes.

"Hello, sweetie," she said, in a low voice. "What brings you here? I didn't think I was going to see you today."

"Hi, Grandma. Do you want to go for a walk?" Darlene bent her head closer. "I need to talk to you privately. Let's go into the garden."

"Sure, honey. You'll need to help me get into my wheelchair."

———

Cockscomb, fiery red and sunny-gold, spiked up boldly among beds of spreading emerald vinca around the building. Dew sparkled on the crew-cut lawn. The morning was quiet and sweet; the more talkative residents had not yet come outside. Concrete paths curved along the sloping lawn, heading toward the distant, narrow river.

Being six months pregnant made it difficult to push the wheelchair along the paths. Her arms ached with the exertion, but she didn't notice. She was intent on reaching a place beyond any listening ears.

Grandma sat hunched in her wheelchair, a blanket covering her from chin to shins, thin ankles exposed, wearing fuzzy slippers on her feet.

Darlene suddenly veered from the concrete path, onto the sparse lawn. She pushed the wheelchair under the swaying embrace of a weeping willow, put the brakes on, and turned her grandmother to face her.

"What's happened?" asked Grandma, her face alight with curiosity.

"They broke into my apartment."

"Who? Quinn's people?"

"His lawyer."

"Meachum?"

"Yeah."

Luella's lips tightened. "Never could abide him, or his father. Nasty lawyers, both, who never hesitate to break the law."

"Old news."

"Still relevant."

"Got a more immediate problem."

Luella blinked, gestured to the lawn. "Siddown. Tell me everything."

Darlene lowered herself gently onto the thin grass, careful not to stir up the dirt underneath. She didn't want to dirty her jeans today, or else she'd have to do laundry tonight. Slowly, she settled herself cross-legged on the lawn.

"Grandma, they're watching me," she whispered, craning her neck. "All the time. Wherever I go. Whatever I do. Whoever I see."

"How do you know?"

"Meachum *said*. While standing in the middle of my securely locked apartment. I had locked both the door lock and the deadbolt, like I always do."

"How did he get in?"

"According to him, my foolish landlady let him in."

"Hmmm." Luella pursed her lips. "A lot of help she is."

"That's not the worst part. He told me they're watching me—who knows how. Maybe he's put a listening device on my phone. Or a nanny-cam in my apartment. Maybe he's got people following me—I don't know exactly."

Darlene's eyes were welling up, and she pressed her lips together firmly.

Luella sighed. "How will you find out if any of this is true?"

"I'm not sure." Darlene dropped her head. "All I know is, I can't live like this."

"Sweetie, what does it matter if they're all over you? You're not doing anything wrong."

"You don't get it, Grandma!" Darlene reached up to squeeze her grandmother's hand. "It's all for a very bad reason. They're going to try to take this baby away from me!"

Luella's gaze hardened behind her glasses. "Who's *they*?"

"Quinn and Meachum," said Darlene. "Meachum's working it, since Quinn's in jail."

Luella tightened her jaw.

"Sweetie, now listen to me. Don't get yourself all worked up. You say Quinn's in jail, which is a good place for him. But it's a stupendously bad place for someone who wants to claim a baby." Her wrinkled hand gave Darlene's a reassuring squeeze. "It simply ain't gonna happen. Don't make yourself crazy—it'll all work out."

"I hope so, Grandma," Darlene whispered, rocking in place, still cross-legged.

"I know so. Now please take me back to my room. The van will be here to take me to the dialysis center soon, and I have to comb my hair before I go. And remember, my sweet girl. *Have faith in the Lord.*"

CHAPTER 11

Footsteps slapped on the concrete floor of the hallway.

A guard appeared at the cell door. "You got a visitor, Quinn—your lawyer," he said. "You know the drill."

Cuffs clicked, the guard unlocked the cell door and Quinn stepped out, chin up. His blond hair was greasy, and he had a scruffy, three-day beard. His blue eyes shifted from side to side, eyeing the premises. A wan light filtered in through high-up glass-block windows. The guard shoved Quinn toward the locked steel door at the end of the hallway, where he signaled to his colleague on the other side.

The door swung open. They walked through, the first guard a half-step behind.

Quinn saw his lawyer, Tobias Meachum, standing in the small, barely furnished meeting room. The walls were painted institutional green—supposed to be pastoral. Jailers wanted the lawyers and their clients very calm.

"Have a seat, Mickey," said Tobias.

"I'll stand. Feels good to even walk down the hallway."

"You doing okay?"

Quinn gave him a long look. "I've been better."

"You know I'm working on getting you out."

"When is that likely to happen?"

"I've already filed a motion for a 'dangerousness hearing,' " said Meachum. "You know that's what they do in Massachusetts, to determine bail."

"Any chance we can judge-shop?"

"Unlikely."

"Why not?"

" 'Cause that newly elected district attorney—you know who I'm talking about, Buster Perkins? He's a real law-and-order guy, and he's gonna steer the case toward a law-and-order judge."

"What about our guy in the DA's office, the assistant DA?"

"I doubt O'Hara will be assigned the case."

"Why?"

"Don't you know, Mickey? This case has garnered tons of publicity." Meachum fingered his collar. "I expect that old Buster will want this one for himself."

Quinn was silent, thinking. Then he looked up. "Whaddya mean, tons of publicity?"

"Oh, the whole 'Curse of Quinn' thing that's been going around town. It was bad for business, so I closed the pub down, sent the employees home. No need for your place to be bleeding money."

Quinn scratched his chin stubble. "*Shut down!* This is the first I'm hearing about it! You gotta get me back out there, Toby." He looked rapidly from side to side, as if he could find a way to escape.

"Hey, remember—the ballot question passed, thanks to Rufus. Since then, he's turned away a citizens' petition brought by Anna Ebert against the ballot question. Told her the petition was totally invalid.

Refused to accept it." He chuckled. "That's the end of unruliness and disrespect toward you at those rowdy Town Meetings."

"Yeah. Pissed me off, the first time I got booed at Town Meeting." Quinn's mouth was twisted. "Did you ever figure out who did that?"

Toby shrugged. "Nope. But never mind. At least Jaston and his buddies in town can't block us anymore, so we can finally get that land."

Quinn glanced over at Meachum. "Do you think the new nine-member council will vote to take the Jaston Farm by eminent domain?" He smirked. "I might get my Longbottom gambling casino after all—just as soon as you get me outta here!"

"Buster Perkins has said he wants a showcase trial and conviction on this killing."

Quinn's sea-blue eyes were fixed. "Could you put in a discreet call or two, to some high-placed friends? You know . . ."

"Ah." Tobias touched the tip of his nose in thought. "There's an idea."

"I'll bill you for my time." Quinn snickered.

Tobias gave a ghost of a smile, clearly still thinking.

Quinn watched him. "So when will this dangerousness hearing happen?"

"Tomorrow." Tobias looked down at the sheaf of papers on the table. "I've been reviewing your records in preparation. Your criminal record is clear, except for some traffic tickets. The juvenile stuff was sealed long ago—that's so old, I would argue that it's irrelevant anyway. Of course, you *were* just tried, found guilty of a misdemeanor, and convicted of election fraud in Longbottom. Coming off one case right into another, aren't we?"

"Whoever said life was dull?"

Tobias flung his hands in the air.

"There's just the minor problem of you shooting your wife dead, in a room full of witnesses. Other than that, no problem!"

He stared at Quinn, eyebrows raised.

Quinn sighed. "So, you got this?"

They locked eyes.

"You know I do."

"You better! I only got a short window of time, see?"

"Till what?"

Quinn smiled. "You'll find out."

CHAPTER 12

Maureen Jaston was tending stew on the stovetop. As she stirred, she peeked over at the latest girl to wash up on the farm's doorstep, wondering, *What was her story?*

Faith was straddling a kitchen chair, bent over at the waist, rummaging through her backpack on the floor.

"Got a change of clothes with you?" asked Maureen.

"Yep. Packed up as quietly as I could before I broke the good news to my parents today, at breakfast." Her face crumpled. "My dad almost choked on his toast." She swiped at her nostrils. She finally said evenly, "I packed last night, actually."

"Sounds like you expected your father to react the way he did."

"Yeah." She flicked her green hair away from her cheek. "He's an asshole."

"I know he acted unkindly, and you didn't deserve that treatment. But because I have youngsters here in this house, I ask you not to use that language here, please."

"Okay."

"Thank you." Maureen paused. "Your green hair looks good, by the way. Glossy." She grinned at Faith. "My son, Jacob, will be down soon to start afternoon chores. He'll probably stick you on his least favorite—shoveling manure. Do you have another pair of shoes, other than the ones you're wearing?"

Faith's mouth, downturned, showed clear distaste. "Yuck," she said. "Can I ask him for a different job?"

Maureen chuckled. "I doubt he'll agree. He really hates shoveling manure! Anyway, we've got muck boots for you." She grinned. "Our visitors have feet of all sizes, so we've got plenty to fit everyone." Maureen laughed. "That way our visitors get to experience the reality of farming, not just the reality-TV version."

She waited, arched eyebrows framing her steady stare.

Faith was silent.

"You can go and sit in the parlor—the front room—if you want, until Jacob comes down from his bedroom. He's fourteen. Do you know him from Longbottom High?"

"I'm a senior. I don't think so."

"You'll meet him soon enough."

Maureen turned back to her stew.

———

Faith heard him before she saw him. He rattled his way down the farmhouse's old staircase, making the wooden railings creak as he rounded the corner.

He stopped when he saw her sitting in a rocking chair on the far side of the parlor. He paused, looked at her for a moment. Took in the green hair, that she was older than him.

"Hi. I'm Jacob. I go by Jake at school." He looked down shyly, then back at her. "Welcome."

She smiled a tiny smile.

"Who are you?" he asked.

"I'm Faith. Thanks for letting me crash here. My dad kicked me out." She looked at her lap, then back at him. "Your mom is nice."

"Thanks." He smiled lopsidedly. "I guess she probably told you about chores and stuff, huh?" He grinned. "Bet they didn't tell you about that part in town, did they?"

"Not exactly," said Faith, with obvious chagrin. "I guess I'm in for it now." She tossed her green hair back as she stood up. "I don't know how good I'll be. I'm not very strong, or athletic—I'm like the worst one in my gym class." She made a face.

Jacob eyed her and slowly scratched his elbow.

"Whatever. Follow me. I'll show you where the gloves are, so your hands don't blister. Then we'll get you muck boots from the shed. You can try some on till you find the size that fits. Then after today, you can set that pair aside, so it'll be quicker next time."

Faith sighed and followed. No getting out of it, apparently.

———

Faith carefully stepped in Jacob's exact footprints in the mud as they approached the barn door, though why, she didn't know. Wasn't that why she was wearing these big, awkward, and ridiculous-looking boots in the first place?

Faith was town-raised, and seeing the inside of a huge dairy barn for the first time was wild. Her eyes swiveled in all directions, taking in the sights and sounds. And yes, the smell, which was all around.

Inside the barn, the heat rising from the cows' bodies attracted circling flies, as their tails flicked listlessly to and fro. Faith stood transfixed. Motes of hay floated golden, effervescent, in shafts of sunlight.

"Pay attention, Faith."

She watched, fascinated, as Jacob first wiped down the cows' swollen teats with disinfectant, one by one, before attaching the suction devices. Soon, the milking machine was pumping the pure white milk through the hoses into the holding tank.

"Some of that will be made into pizza cheese," Jacob said.

"Cool."

Jacob looked at her. "Okay, now comes your job." He pointed to the barn wall. "Over there is the shovel. Next to it is a four-wheeled wheelbarrow." He grinned. "All's you do is shovel the shit into the wheelbarrow, take it outside, go left, and empty the load onto the pile that's already there."

"That's it?

"That's it. It ain't rocket science." He hitched up his jeans. "I'll be back to check later. Have fun."

"Yeah. Sure. *Lots* of fun."

"Hey! Haven't you heard the latest farm slogan?"

"No. What?"

"No Farms—No Food."

CHAPTER 13

Darlene lay across her bed, still dressed, except for her discarded shoes. She was exhausted from her six-hour shift behind the counter at Dunkin'.

After having worked as a bartender for more than a decade, making decent money, Dunk's was a big step down. The day Darlene interviewed, after having filled out the application, the manager took a sympathetic look at Darlene's gently swelling belly, saying, "As long as you can keep up with the high school kids, the job is yours."

Darlene broke into a wry smile, and nearly lurched forward to give her a grateful hug.

"Thank you," she said fervently.

"Here's your shirt," said the frazzle-haired manager, who abruptly turned away.

The interview was over. Darlene was left fingering the shirt, and soon resorted to following her coworkers to learn the procedures.

Darlene wondered if she would last at Dunk's all the way to her due date. Her legs throbbed. Her swollen feet ached. She felt too tired to get up off her bed and make herself supper. Plus, she was also nauseated by spending six hours next to Dunk's fast food. And she was aware that her hair smelled of coffee. She could always try to claim it was her new, organic hair conditioner that was *supposed* to smell this way.

Darlene's eyelids drooped and she slid into sleep.

Mickey Quinn's leering face hovered over her, mouthing incomprehensible words with a muffled, underwater sound. His yellow, curved teeth grinned from the Quinn-face at the top of the undulating snake's body. She desperately tried to curl herself away from him, but the snake, somehow sprouting arms and groping hands, fumbled at her private parts while she recoiled. He became heavier and denser till he squashed her, pressing air out of her lungs, pressing the spark out of her. She lashed out, a fist, a curse word.

She awoke, trembling. She lay across her bed, holding her mounded belly, shivering with revulsion. She detested knowing that the child she now carried had been conceived through rape. She wished she had lashed out for real with a fist, or a curse word. She wished she hadn't knuckled under the way she had. She cringed at the memory of how she had feared his influence, his money, his power.

She wondered again, for the umpteenth time, if she had been wildly foolish to not abort this baby. But she had wanted a child. Especially since her first baby, a love child, was now no more than spirit and memory for her. She *wanted* a child. And even more than that, her grandma had wanted her to have this child. That was the heart of it.

The truth was, she hadn't had a chance of having a child, with no relationship at the time; she was getting close to forty. There had been a nagging feeling that this might be, for better or worse, her last chance to have one. But she couldn't help but wonder: Had she just been a damn fool?

In a perverse way, Mickey Quinn was a good candidate to father a child. He was good-looking, charming, intelligent, well-off, well-connected. *If only he hadn't been married.*

She rolled her eyes. Was she really thinking this? How about, *If only he hadn't shot his wife!* However she tried to shirk the truth, this cold fact would forever be part of her child's personal history, even though it wasn't the child's fault. Her child's father had killed Clarisse. She had to face it. He was a stone-hearted devil! Or a sociopath, as the fancy shrinks would say.

She awkwardly sat up on her bed and gazed out the window of her apartment, willing herself to think through her situation.

Was she crazy to want a child so much that she'd accept a rapist's child—a murderer's child? Was she insane?

She closed her eyes and began to rub her forehead, her blonde hair spread unevenly behind her head. She was getting a massive headache from all of these thoughts, memories, and feelings swirling in her heart and mind.

Maybe she *was* crazy.

But still.

Maybe it was because she longed to reconstruct the family she had lost.

Another memory she longed to keep buried.

Ah, words. *Buried. Burial.* Even simple words and phrases triggered deep feelings. At age eight, Darlene had had to watch as two pine boxes, supposedly holding her dead parents, were lowered into the dense earth. She had smelled the tart, sandy soil under the towering pine trees along the edge of the cemetery. The long sprays of green needles had shivered in response to the prayers uttered by the minister.

At the time, Darlene wasn't entirely certain that her parents were even in those boxes. Maybe they had run away, instead, and left her behind. A crowd of grown-ups had gathered together. Did she dare voice aloud her suspicion that they had run away? Uncertainty glued Darlene's tongue to the roof of her mouth. Her grandmother Luella stood next to her, keeping a gentle, firm hand on her shoulder. As the minister droned on, Grandma bent over to whisper to Darlene, smelling of lavender soap. The lace flowers on Grandma's black veil puckered against her doughy cheek; a single tear hung on the end of her nose. Darlene watched the teardrop shine, barely listening to what was being whispered. Darlene watched as two grown men shoveled spadefuls of rocky loam over the boxes set deep in the earth-holes. She concentrated on the thought that her parents had driven away somewhere for a time. They would be back.

Darlene had always been an obedient child, so she followed Grandma Luella along the cemetery's brick path to the parking lot. They got into Grandma's brown Dodge Dart. Grandma let her sit in the front seat, opposite her. She and Darlene were going to become a team, said Grandma. That meant Darlene got to ride shotgun. Darlene didn't understand what those words meant; she pictured herself straddling a long, metal gun, running around the yard with it between her legs like a hobbyhorse.

Grandma was still talking. Darlene began to listen.

Grandma said Darlene would live with her in the same house where Darlene's mother, Bonnie, had grown up. That Darlene would always have a home with her.

Darlene's face suddenly felt hot and raw. Her throat hurt too much to utter a sound. All she could do was give a solitary nod that she understood. She knew then, at that moment, that her parents really were dead; they were never coming back. But a part of her kept on hoping, anyway, for years to come.

———

Darlene did have a loving home with her grandmother, but a lemon-sour sadness hovered over the small house. Her parents, Bonnie and Grady, were rarely spoken of. But sometimes Luella would tell Darlene, out of the blue, that she was very much like her girl, Bonnie; Grandma claimed a similarity in the way they played games, or stirred cookie batter, or sang. Or the way Darlene looked. "Like sunshine breaking through the clouds!" Grandma would say, with an indulgent smile.

Then the child Darlene would feel lonely all over again, and would wander off to her markers and paper, where she drew her dreams in color. Or she'd skip down the back steps to go to the tiny creek in their parcel of woods, where she could catch tadpoles. She never could capture the wily, slippery salamanders, though she tried.

On the few occasions when the teenaged Darlene dared to ask about her parents, Grandma grew silent, pondering. Once, she said only a single sentence: "They worked hard, and they played hard."

"What do you mean?"

Grandma would say no more, just tightened her lips in a grim line.

Another time, Darlene asked why she had no brothers or sisters. She got only a heavy sigh for an answer.

Still later, when they were driving around Longbottom, doing errands, Grandma Luella and Darlene had watched a beat-up sedan swoosh by, with heads, torsos, and tattooed arms dangling out of the open windows. Loud music radiated out into the street. Shouting from the riders mingled with the thumping music. Bumper stickers with attitude and esoteric philosophies adorned the rusted chrome.

"Silly fools!" Grandma muttered. "They'll end up like Bonnie and Grady."

"What do you mean?"

"I'll tell you when you become a parent."

Those words had echoed in Darlene's memory like a mantra.

Grandma will finally tell me when I become a parent.

Darlene suddenly felt a glimmering bubble of laughter rise up through her well of grief. She had discovered another ridiculous reason why she was so stubbornly having this kid, by a connected Boston mobster!

Really? she thought. Against all common sense. Against all practicality. Against society's conventions.

Of course. She was having this baby because she wanted Grandma to bring her closer to the essence of her mother and father.

No more thoughts about death or burials, she vowed to herself.

From now on, I will be brave and forward-looking, focused on the new life growing inside of me.

CHAPTER 14

Darlene's labor pains started before she knew what they were. She was only eight months along when she woke up on a Sunday morning with a backache that she couldn't out-stretch. Her body had an alertness to it that surprised her. It was as if her body had been busy making plans while she had been busy sleeping. Moving with her huge belly was an ordeal. She shuffled to the bathroom to pee and brush her teeth.

Since this was her first pregnancy, she didn't know what to expect. She considered calling her grandma, but then thought better of it. Darlene figured that her phone was tapped, and that a phone call would alert her watchers. She decided she would take a few things with her in a backpack, like her toothbrush, her hairbrush, and some clean underwear, for when she went to have this baby.

The only problem, as Darlene saw it, was that she didn't know *where* to go to have this baby. Of course, she had no health benefits.

She hadn't managed to get herself signed up for MassHealth in time, and her savings were running low. They would certainly empty out once the baby's needs kicked in.

Did she dare just show up in the emergency room of the local hospital? She knew emergency rooms were required to treat anyone who came through the doors, but that seemed a sorry way to do things. Maybe the neighborhood clinic could help her. Or would they freak out when she started having her baby there?

The right side of Darlene's abdomen went rigid. This was getting more uncomfortable by the moment. She would have to get herself to a facility of some sort, and soon. She wasn't about to call an ambulance; they were damned expensive. Who could she call at eight o'clock on a Sunday morning?

She decided she would knock on her neighbor's door, across the hall.

Darlene stripped off her nightgown and began putting on her loose-fitting big T-shirt and elastic-waisted pants. She sat on the edge of her bed to put on her socks and shoes. She began adding the contents of her purse to her half-filled backpack, dropping the emptied purse on the floor next to her bed, its strap askew.

She went to the bathroom to put on a bit of makeup and comb her hair. She wanted to look decent. She tried to ignore her belly, stiffening into a cramp.

Darlene's next-door neighbor in the apartment building was a fellow called Nathan Green. He worked as a drag queen during the summers, in Provincetown, Massachusetts. But that was a deep, dark secret up here in Longbottom, where he worked for nine months a year as a guidance counselor at Longbottom High School. He was about fifty, medium build, with thinning light brown hair and a twinkle in his almond-shaped eyes. He was strangely popular with the high school students, who generally thought all teachers, counselors, and adults in general were lame. Maybe the students somehow sensed that beneath the still waters of his quiet demeanor raged the wild currents of a vibrant life.

One day, several years ago, Darlene's toilet had backed up, and she'd stepped across the hall to ask if she could borrow a plunger. She knocked on the shiny, dark door and saw a shadow pass behind the peephole. She heard jazz music suddenly playing lower in volume.

"Hey!" she called out. "I know you're in there! It's an emergency!"

Reluctantly, it seemed, the door slid open a crack and a brown eye peered out. Darlene caught a whiff of weed. She smiled widely.

"Thank you, kind neighbor. I'm Darlene, and I live across the hall from you."

"I know," said the voice belonging to the brown eye.

"I'm in dire need of a toilet plunger."

"And why would you think I'd have one?"

" 'Cause you're so neat and tidy. You're the only one who bundles the recyclables. And you have flower boxes, filled with flowers, hanging from your windows. You must have an awesome apartment."

The eye looked bored.

"And you have the best air freshener ever!"

"Do I, now?" The brown eye looked directly into hers.

"Yes, indeed! And when I solve my toilet difficulties, I'll be utilizing some air freshener myself." Darlene winked. "I'll even lend you some of mine."

"In that case, my dear, I might just have the tool you need."

The door closed again in her face, and she stood in the hallway, waiting. A half a minute later, the door reopened, this time much wider. Darlene saw Nathan Green in his purple, embroidered silk robe, his hair tousled, his grin wide and welcoming. His outstretched arm held a red rubber plunger.

"It even looks obscene, doesn't it?"

"Totally. Back in a jiff."

That evening had been the start of a friendship grounded in mutual respect and relief that neither person was going to be judgmental. Though several months would pass before Darlene discovered the blingy outfits drip-drying in his shower. She wasn't going to say anything when she came out of the bathroom, but curiosity overcame her.

"Taking to the stage, are we?" she ventured.

"Precisely, my darling Darlene. As soon as I'm released from my day job at Longbottom High School, I head down to the Cape for the summer."

"Oh? Where?"

"To Provincetown."

Darlene ducked her head in embarrassment. Of course.

She faced him, smiling. "Silly me. Of course. What part or parts, do you play?"

"Mostly Joan Rivers, with my thin face."

"Yes, I can see the resemblance."

"Thank you, darling."

"Darlene."

"Whatever, pumpkin. Will I see you down in P-Town this summer?"

"Probably not. You know Mickey Quinn keeps me busy at the bar all summer," she had said. Little had she known at the time that that would be the fateful summer.

Although Darlene had eventually told Nathan that Mickey was her baby's father, she'd never told him that she had been coerced into having sex—that she considered it to have been a de facto rape. Nathan had watched, without comment, as her belly grew. She had shied away from asking him for help, because she was embarrassed by the circumstances.

But now the day had come, and, being in full denial, as she was, she'd failed to make any definitive plans for the delivery of her child. She was going to have to throw herself on the mercy of Nathan Green, school counselor. Maybe he had already done this sort of thing as part of his job.

Lord help me. I'm a damn fool, she thought.

Darlene waddled about her apartment, having put on a comfortable outfit. Her purse lay askew on her bed, her wallet now in her backpack. She locked the door and dropped her keys in her backpack, too. She hesitated for a moment, then rapped sharply on Nathan's door. It was eight-thirty on a Sunday morning. Was he even up?

Nathan's door opened quickly. "Ah, hello, darling. Feeling all right?"

"Not really. That's why I'm here." She looked up at his almond-shaped eyes, which were watching her closely. A spasm tweaked her left side, and she gasped.

"What do you need?"

"I need a ride somewhere."

"Where?"

"I don't know. Somewhere I can deliver this baby for free, or almost free."

"No insurance, pumpkin?"

"Nah. That ended when my job did."

"You mean, when you lost your job after that bastard closed his business, leaving you high and dry?" Nathan's hand touched her hand sympathetically.

"You mean Quinn, right?"

"What other bastard could I mean?"

"You could mean this out-of-wedlock child I'm about to have."

"Never mind that. It surely isn't your child's fault. No, I meant that bastard of a father. Maybe I should call him the bastard father of a bastard baby."

Darlene almost laughed, but was in too much pain from the next contraction.

"Well, he had to close his business when he was arrested," she muttered.

Nathan rolled his eyes. "Well, of course he was arrested! Making excuses for him, are you? He killed his wife!"

"These contractions are killing *me*," she said, and squeezed her eyes shut.

"Okay, should I take you to the Orangeville Neighborhood Clinic? I think they take everybody there."

"Let's go. I've got my stuff. And let's try not to tip off Quinn's people that I'm about to have this baby, okay?"

CHAPTER 15

"Put on this baseball cap, and tuck up that blonde hair underneath," said Nathan. "Here, put on these sunglasses, and this raincoat of mine will hide your belly. Try to walk like a guy. A guy who's kinda stout."

"No way I'm gonna pass," said Darlene.

"You have to," said Nathan. "You want to be followed by that goon lurking in his van out front, on the street corner?"

"You noticed him, too?"

"How could I not? He's as obvious as a drag queen."

Nathan and Darlene took the inside staircase down to the apartment building's musty basement. The washer and dryer for the tenants were there, but no one was using them at this hour on a Sunday morning.

"I don't think anyone saw us," said Darlene.

"Shhh," cautioned Nathan. "We don't want anyone to hear us, either."

Nathan slowly opened the door to the back alley. The rough brown bricks of the building's back side were mottled with age. The alley between buildings was scarcely paved, with large potholes in the tarmac.

Nathan gazed to his right, then his left.

"Looks clear," he whispered. "Follow me to my car, and keep your head down."

At the precise moment she stepped through the doorway to follow Nathan, she felt a sharp wrench in her lower belly. She gasped, and held herself protectively.

"Steady as she goes," murmured Nathan.

"I can't hurry," moaned Darlene. "I've *got* to walk slow."

Nathan sighed, his mouth a grim line.

"I'm doing the best I can," muttered Darlene. "How far is the car?"

"Just around the corner, in the lot. You know my car, don't you? I park right next to your Volkswagen most of the time."

Darlene didn't answer. She took one deliberate step at a time, head down, arms at her sides, doing her best to appear to be striding toward the car.

"We're here," said Nathan. He beeped his key fob and the locks on his Toyota sedan sprang open. "Get in the back, and lay down on the seat. You'll feel better, and you'll be less visible."

"Why did you get a purple car?" asked Darlene. "Don't you feel conspicuous in it?"

Nathan smiled. He gazed up into the rearview mirror and started the engine. "Me, conspicuous? Nonsense." His head swiveled as they backed out of the parking space. "Head down, remember?"

The ride to the Neighborhood Clinic was a kaleidoscope of traffic sounds, snippets of swaying tree crowns and ornate building tops, and the uneven motion of stop-and-go traffic. The sky was streaked with faraway, fluffy clouds. The silver-cloth upholstery scratched her cheek.

The Neighborhood Clinic was a large, brick building that took up most of a city block. Nathan had pulled up to the drop-off area. He came to a stop and faced Darlene.

"We're here, pumpkin. You go in and I'll park the car. I'll be inside in a minute. You'll be all right."

Darlene strained to rise from her prone position on the backseat. She clutched her backpack and managed a lopsided smile of gratitude as she groped for the door handle.

"Nathan, you're the greatest. Ever."

With those words, she waddled across the pavement to the clinic's front doors.

The employee at the front intake counter took one look at her swollen belly and said, "Prenatal care, second floor, to the rear."

Darlene clutched her belly as another spasm took hold. She groaned deeply. She didn't need to explain that she was already in labor. The clinic worker picked up her loudspeaker phone and called for a wheelchair.

"Thanks," Darlene managed, leaning heavily against the intake counter. She concentrated on holding herself together until the wheelchair arrived.

Upstairs, the premises were overflowing with patients and their families, all crowded into a large, central waiting room. Darlene was wheeled into a corner, facing offices that ringed the waiting room. Opposite her, a very pregnant Hispanic woman with two children at her knees gave her a weak smile. Her little boy ran his Matchbox car up and down the legs of his mother's chair, while her older daughter combed her doll's hair repeatedly.

Darlene managed to peer around the room in the letup between contractions. She had no appointment, no doctor. How was this going to work? She longed to see Nathan, who had a way of cutting through red tape. She had no choice but to wait here, in this wheelchair. Either Nathan would arrive first, or her baby would, simple as that.

Meanwhile, the clinic personnel seemed to have forgotten about her.

Darlene was hungry, but she knew not to eat now that she was having this baby. A huge wrench overcame her, and a groan escaped her throat.

"You okay, honey?"

Darlene turned to her right and saw a formidable-looking Black woman sitting two rows away.

"Not so good," admitted Darlene.

"You gonna have that baby in this here waitin' room?"

"I hope not." Darlene's eyes squeezed shut at the thought. "That'd be quite the scene."

The woman chuckled. "You better believe it, honey." She swiveled her head toward Darlene. "So whatchu gonna do about it? You gonna sit there, or are ya gonna speak up?"

"I guess I gotta be brave."

"Reckon so. Just tell 'em—or else you gonna have that baby right here in front of ever'body."

Darlene felt another fiery contraction start low down and rise up her abdomen. A long moan emerged from her throat that she couldn't stop. She was aware of many curious eyes watching her.

Suddenly a nurse appeared in front of her.

"Excuse me," groaned Darlene. "I'm having a baby."

"Of course, dear," said the nurse in a soothing voice. "That's why you're here.

"You don't understand!" Darlene yelled. "*I'm having it right now!*"

CHAPTER 16

Tobias Meachum and Mickey Quinn stood shoulder to shoulder in front of Judge Cole, who was seated on his high bench in the front of the courtroom. Quinn was aware of being garbed in wrinkled, faded jailhouse gear, while his buddy, Attorney Meachum, wore a tailored Italian suit that fitted him precisely. Also there was a lawyer from DA Buster Perkins's office.

Judge Cole refrained from scowling at them as he reviewed the court file, his expression inscrutable. Through the legal grapevine, the judge knew who these two were, and what roles each had played in the recent notorious Longbottom election-fraud corruption case. He sighed. A local scandal had resulted, in which both of their names had become fodder for gossip. They were becoming outright notorious.

His judicial colleague had presided over the case, which had featured Clarisse Quinn's tell-all testimony. That testimony, which had blown the election-fraud case wide open, had resulted in Clarisse's death. Had been the cause of her death.

Actually, her murder, he corrected himself. Tsk, tsk. A murder case now, on top of the election-fraud case? This Mickey Quinn character was a walking, talking disaster of a man. Now he must decide, in this dangerousness hearing, whether or not to keep this guy locked up until his trial. *He deserves to stay in jail,* thought the judge. *But I'll listen.*

"We're seeking a release for Mr. Quinn from the custody of the county jail," said Attorney Meachum. "We all know that Mr. Quinn has deep ties to Longbottom." He gestured grandly at Quinn. "We are here to plead for the release of my client under the court's dangerousness hearing." He turned back to the Judge. "Mr. Quinn is not a danger to anyone in the community, Your Honor."

"And how can we be assured of that? Apparently, he was a mortal danger to his wife."

"Your Honor, he poses absolutely no danger to anyone *else* in the community. Mr. Quinn has substantial property, both real and personal, that he wishes to preserve, that he does not want to forfeit." Meachum paused. "Therefore, we *also* believe that Mr. Quinn is not a flight risk." He smiled brightly, his lean face taut. He craned forward, trying to meet the judge's eye.

Judge Cole kept his eyes firmly on the paperwork. "I'm trying to decide whether to let your client out of jail. Remind me of his assets."

"Mr. Quinn's primary residence, a luxurious home in Longbottom, has been valued at eight hundred thousand dollars, house and land together. And, of course, he is the owner and manager of Quinn's Pub and Grill, which employed a number of people, until such time as my client was incarcerated. That business is valued at a million dollars, including land, building, and business operation."

The lawyer from the DA's office stepped forward. "This man, Quinn, is a repeat offender. I *strongly* urge this Court to deny bail."

Judge Cole rubbed his closely cropped gray hair briskly as he considered. Eyes narrowed, he turned his gaze from Meachum to Quinn and back again.

"Counselor," he said, "granting your client bail runs against my gut instincts. I think he's a bad actor. This entire configuration of cases stinks." Judge Cole pursed his lips. He swiveled his head to look down at Quinn, who stood before him, silent and watchful. "But you—you've been a model jailbird, they say, and I have to take that into consideration, according to the guidelines."

He scowled again.

"Mr. Quinn, mark my words," said Judge Cole. "If you ever even *think* about fleeing the Commonwealth of Massachusetts ahead of your trial, like the notorious Whitey Bulger, I will personally sic the FBI on you. They will dog you till they bring you in, just like they got Whitey." He pointed his thick index finger at Quinn's face. "You understand?"

Quinn kept his face expressionless. "Yes, sir."

"Yes, Your Honor," corrected Meachum quietly.

"Yes, Your Honor," parroted Quinn, adjusting his stance slightly.

Judge Cole gazed unrelentingly at Quinn, as if he could read the man's character from his outward appearance. Quinn kept his eyes carefully lowered.

The judge finally sighed. "Against my better judgment, I set bail at five hundred thousand dollars."

"Five hundred thousand, Your Honor?" Meachum asked, surprised.

"Five-hundred-thousand-dollar bail, Counselor."

The judge turned away from them to hand the court file to the clerk, and reached for the next file. He was done with them.

Meachum and Quinn looked at each other wordlessly. Meachum put a steadying hand on Quinn's elbow and began to steer him toward the rear of the courtroom.

Quinn's blue eyes hardened as he looked back once at Judge Cole. His mouth clamped tight to hold back the words trying to burst from his throat.

"Not now, Mickey," whispered Meachum. "Outside."

They emerged from the high-ceilinged courtroom into the tall, narrow hallway.

"Mickey, you want out of the clink, right?"

Mickey said nothing for a moment, just scratched his stubbled chin. Then he exploded.

"Bastard! That guy oughta find another line a' work real soon." He snorted. "Where'm I gonna come up with that kinda cash? Huh?" Quinn's blue eyes blazed. "He's pretty much consigned me to jail, until I finally get to trial. And I won't *ever* see my kid!"

"You take out a loan against your house to get the cash," said Tobias. "That secures the bond until you go to trial. I'll take care of arranging it for you. 'Course, if you skip out on us, you lose both—money *and* house." Tobias smiled grimly. "But you won't do that, right?"

CHAPTER 17

Oblivious to everything but the band of fiery pain encircling her middle, Darlene huddled in the wheelchair. She breathed deeply, trying to stay ahead of the next wave of pain.

It was fierce—too fierce—and she let loose another deep groan, which turned into a throaty scream.

"Get her into Dr. Morel's office, now," said the nurse. "We don't need this happening here in the waiting room."

An aide approached Darlene to wheel her into the inner offices.

"Good luck, honey!" the Black woman called out.

Darlene was wheeled into an examination room with stirrups on the table. As she climbed on, the paper underneath her buttocks crackled.

"Let's get your pants and undies off, for now," said the nurse, already grappling to remove them. She tossed a patterned johnny onto Darlene's legs. "You can throw this over yourself in the meantime."

Darlene groaned. Her innards were splitting open; her baby would be spit out like a peach pit. Where was this doctor? Couldn't someone give her something for the pain?

"Catch you by surprise, did it?" inquired the nurse, peering over Darlene's bent knees and heels perched in the metal stirrups.

"Kind of. I'm only eight months along."

"Who's your regular doctor?"

Darlene hesitated. Another contraction overcame her; she gritted her teeth.

"Your doctor?"

"Don't have one," she gasped. "No insurance."

"You never signed up with MassHealth, for low-income women and children?" The nurse pursed her lips. "You're going to have to do that, so your baby can get all the basic vaccinations."

Darlene nodded, gritted her teeth. Her insides were being torn apart. She screamed as another terrific wrench swept over her.

A huge man dressed in blue scrubs burst into the office. "I heard screaming."

"You're just in time. Her baby's coming any minute."

He grinned. "Let's get this baby born!"

"This is Dr. Morel," said the nurse from across the room. "He'll be delivering your baby, and I'll be assisting him."

The doctor stood at the sink, washing his hands with soapy water. He donned latex gloves and reached over to lift up the edge of the johnny.

"No episiotomy—so you'll tear a bit—which might be a mess, sewing you up."

He stuck his hand deep inside to feel around. His gray eyes met her tired, miserable gaze.

"Hope you're tough. You're in for it."

She squeezed her eyes shut as another wave of pain overtook her, then opened them to look at Dr. Morel. He was tall, broad, and almost as hairy as a bear, watching her closely from gray eyes overshadowed by bristly eyebrows.

Another contraction overwhelmed her. She began to howl.

"You're too far along for any pain medication," said Dr. Morel. "But the good news is, you're almost there. Any other children?"

"No," Darlene gasped.

"You're at ten centimeters, which means your baby will begin to descend. The baby's already in the correct position."

He wiped off his gloved right hand with a paper towel. His arms were massive—looked like he was a former athlete. The better to yank this baby out of me, she thought, barely rational under the encircling pain.

"At least this didn't happen in a taxi," Darlene muttered.

"Well, this exam room is hardly a proper place to deliver a child."

"So I screwed up?"

"Yep."

Darlene felt her abdomen go rigid with yet another mighty contraction. She felt a powerful urge to expel the foreign object that was ripping apart her insides. A deep-voiced growl emerged from the back of her throat. She was a lioness.

Dr. Morel bent over to take another look. "The baby is crowning."

"So?"

"It means your baby will be born after a few more pushes."

"About time."

Dr. Morel stood motionless, his eyes unwavering.

In a sudden gush of bloody floodwaters, the baby swooshed out into Dr. Morel's waiting arms, slithering and wiggling, leaving bloody stains on Dr. Morel's forearms. The umbilical cord dangled between mother and baby like a live wire, still attached.

"Kathy, cut the cord, please," said Dr. Morel in a calm voice.

The nurse reached for the scissors and gave a snip.

"A fine boy! Can you clean him up a bit at the sink, then wrap him in a towel?"

Dr. Morel handed the bloody bit of a new person over to the nurse, then turned back to Darlene.

"A *boy*?" asked Darlene.

"Yes—congratulations!"

The baby gave a piercing cry.

"But I expected a girl. That's what my grandmother predicted."

"She predicted wrong." The doctor's gray eyes twinkled.

"No way. My grandmother's *never* wrong."

"She was this time." He openly grinned.

Darlene blinked. "When can I hold my baby?"

"As soon as we get him cleaned up."

Dr. Morel looked down at himself. "Me, too. Can't look like I just came out of surgery. Excuse me—I've gotta change into fresh scrubs before I see my next patient."

And with that, the bear-like man exited the room on silent feet.

Over at the sink, Darlene's son was wailing.

The nurse, Kathy, gently soaped him clean. His scrawny legs kicked the air and his tiny hands grasped at nothing as she washed his full head of blond hair.

"He'll be needing a proper haircut soon," said the nurse, smiling.

She rinsed his hair, then deftly dried him off, putting a diaper on him and wrapping him in a towel before handing him over to Darlene.

Darlene looked down at the small bundle in her arms. His wrinkled, red face peeked out of the towel wrapped around him.

My little gift, she thought. A sweet gift, despite how he came into being.

Never mind. I'm not going to dwell on that.

"I've got another diaper for now," said Kathy, "and a dozen more for the next couple of days. Are you going to nurse your baby?"

"Yes. I guess I'll start now."

Darlene lifted her shirt, placed her son at her breast, and nuzzled his face. He opened his mouth and immediately latched on.

Darlene smiled. "I guess he's a natural."

"Good. I'm going to leave you two alone for a bit. Then we'll have to clean you up. Do you have a ride home?"

"Yes. My friend, Nathan Green."

"Is he the father?"

"No. Just a friend."

"I see." The nurse's face was carefully expressionless. "Who shall I put on the birth certificate as the father?"

"Nobody."

"Are you sure? Your child will be half-orphan, coming into this world, with only one parent."

Darlene shrugged. "It's best that way."

"Are you married?"

"No."

Kathy's mouth clamped shut into a thin line. "We'll put down just your last name, then?" "Better that way," said Darlene, as she caressed the small head of her nursing baby. "Much less complicated."

"Okay. Do you have a first and/or a middle name for your son?"

"Nope. I thought I was having a girl."

"Okay." Kathy looked up, pen in hand. "He arrived real quick! Does that inspire you?"

"Maybe."

Darlene shifted the baby from one breast to the other, and began looping his hair around her forefinger. She laid back and stared at the tile ceiling.

She could name him Grady, after her father. But that would upset Grandma, who had never liked her son-in-law. She wouldn't do that to Grandma, who was so looking forward to the family being continued for another generation.

How about David? His whole life would be like that of a David battling a Goliath.

David Bundt didn't sound bad. Dave Bundt. David Jonah Bundt— Jonah, after that boy I was sweet on in high school.

Darlene turned to Kathy, who was wiping down the sink and counter area with disinfectant soap.

"I've decided on a name."

"Good. That didn't take too long. What is it?"

"David Jonah Bundt." Darlene began to spell out each name.

The nurse sat at the small desk opposite the sink and completed the birth certificate form.

"We'll file this with City Hall."

"Thanks.

"That'll be a twenty-five-dollar filing fee."

"I have some money in my backpack, if you'll hand it to me. It's on the floor, in the corner."

Kathy lifted the backpack and placed it alongside Darlene on the examination table.

"Can you hold him while I get my wallet?" asked Darlene.

She gave the baby to Kathy and started to stir through the contents of her backpack till she found her wallet. Opening it, she found fourteen dollars and some change.

Tears sprang to her eyes. She was so broke she didn't even have enough to pay for David's birth certificate to be registered.

"Can I speak to my friend, Nathan Green?" She fought to keep her voice from quavering.

"I'll go to the waiting room and see if he's there. If he is, I'll bring him back to see you."

The nurse handed David back to Darlene, turned on her heel, and left.

Darlene clutched her son, unable to think of anything beyond just holding him.

———

"Hey, pumpkin, how goes it?" Nathan said. "And who have you got there with you?"

"I'd like you to meet my son, David Jonah Bundt."

Nathan came over to see the new baby and congratulate her.

"I'll admit," he said, looking amused, "this is the first time I've ever been in the gynecology wing of a medical facility."

"You were in this kind of place on the day you were born," said Kathy, who'd followed him in. "You just don't remember it," she added, with a laugh.

"Those metal things there look like instruments of torture," Nathan said, gesturing to the stainless-steel stirrups.

Darlene chuckled. "The real torture is actual childbirth," she said. "Everything else is gravy. And these people here were an unbelievable help."

"I'm glad," Nathan said. "Now, how can I help you, darling?"

"Well, I need to register David's birth certificate, and there's a twenty-five-dollar fee. I didn't bring enough cash with me." Darlene grimaced at Nathan, ashamed.

"Not a problem, darling. We'll get the little fellow legitimized—legalized, whatever."

He reached for his wallet and took out a twenty-dollar bill and five singles and handed them to the nurse.

"I'll take the birth certificate and the fee to our intake desk," said Kathy, holding the bills gingerly.

They waited until the door was fully closed to turn to one another.

"How are you really feeling, pumpkin?"

"Pretty exhausted—but I'll make it."

"And you have this beautiful baby to focus on."

81

"I know. I adore him already."

Nathan's face lit up. "Restores my faith in motherhood."

"But I don't know what kind of mother I'm going to be," Darlene said, her voice quivering. "With no job, no one to watch David if I get one—I won't be able to pay my rent."

Darlene wondered if Nathan would want to be her friend anymore if she turned into a horrid, whining, clinging woman. She struggled to control her voice.

"I don't know what to do. I don't want to become a welfare mother. I've heard that once you start down that path, you can never get off of it. It's like jail."

Nathan pursed his lips, thinking.

"You've got few options." He scratched his head. "I don't know. I'm going to think, make a few phone calls, see what I can rustle up on your behalf."

"Thanks, Nathan. You're a true friend." Darlene smacked her forehead. "Dammit! I should've named him Nate, after you. You've helped to shepherd him into this world more than anyone else I can think of." She gestured to the door. "Can you catch the nurse, have her change the birth certificate?"

Nathan smiled and took her hand.

"It's okay, darling. Let it go. David is a perfectly fine name. Anyway, if his name were Nate, people might suspect I was the father—and we wouldn't want to ruin my reputation as a gay man, now would we?"

CHAPTER 18

It was Monday night, and Town Meeting was starting in a few minutes. Townspeople were greeting each other and chatting as they took their seats in the high school gymnasium. People looked around, gauging where to sit in the steadily increasing crowd. Some chose to sit up in the bleachers that lined both walls of the gym. Others chose to sit on either side of the center aisle, at floor level.

Article Six on the Town Warrant—to rezone Jaston Farm into "an industrial zoning district"—was the gossip of the town these days. The Jastons were at Town Meeting, with Anna Ebert at their side, intent on her notes.

"Looks good for us so far," Anna murmured to the Jastons. "Looks like people are coming out in force to support you."

"Yeah," said Robert. "At the very last—*ever*—Town Meeting in Longbottom. A truly terrible day. My father would be sad and outraged, at the same time. As I am." He sighed. "This'll be the last time my friends and neighbors, the people of our long-standing community, will be able to come out in force to support our farm." He paused. "And not just Jaston Farm! This is the last time we can come together to protect all of us from nasty businesses—to protect our countryside . . . what's left of it, anyway." He shrugged. "We'll see tonight, won't we?"

"Funny how there's no quorum required for any Open Town Meeting in Longbottom," said Anna. "Not that that'd be a problem. There must be over six hundred people here."

"They're just here 'cause it's the last Town Meeting. It's a nostalgia thing," said Maureen.

"Let's try to be optimistic, shall we?" said Anna.

The town moderator stood behind a podium. A retired businessman who had lived and worked in Longbottom for decades, he was short and stocky, with a bristly mustache that was half-ginger, half-gray.

He banged his wooden gavel on the podium. It echoed in the microphone.

"Town Meeting is called to order," he said. "We begin by saying the Pledge of Allegiance."

The moderator placed his hand on his heart and began reciting. The crowd stood and joined in, rumbling through the Pledge.

"You may be seated."

Everyone sat, noisily.

"Article One is before us. Anyone wish to speak about the town acceptance of streets?"

Anna Ebert was ready. She stood at the middle-aisle microphone.

"Mr. Moderator, I move to bring Article Six forward first, for discussion and a vote. I believe many folks are here for this particular article."

A buzz arose in the crowd.

The moderator banged his gavel. "All in favor of discussion on Article Six right now, say 'Aye.' " He paused.

"Aye!" The room rumbled in response.

"All opposed?" the moderator said.

"Nay!" yelled a thin group of voices.

"The 'Ayes' have it. The town clerk will record this voice vote to take up Article Six first." He looked over at Rufus Fishbane, who nodded. "Article Six is open for discussion."

The moderator looked out at the jammed gymnasium, saw a few townspeople lined up at the microphones. He banged his gavel again.

"Please state your name for the record."

"I am Anna Ebert, attorney for the Jaston family. I'm also a resident and registered voter of Longbottom. I am here to speak out *against* the Article Six rezoning, as y'all can see on your copy of the Town Warrant."

Papers rustled across the room. People whispered while they read Article Six on their Warrant.

The Moderator banged on his gavel. The gymnasium went silent.

"I'm here to speak on the merits—or in this case, *the demerits*— of rezoning Jaston Farm into industrial land." Anna Ebert paused, looked at the crowd. She waited for total silence. Anna continued, "It's up to this very last Town Meeting vote to protect Jaston Farm, which is a family-owned business. Jaston Farm was originally started by Robert Jaston's great-grandfather, after the Civil War. The 1880s, actually. It should probably qualify for Historical Landmark status, something for the Jastons to look into."

She turned away from the moderator, to whom she had been speaking, and scanned the crowd for a reaction. The room was silent.

"Regardless, in this time of supply-chain issues, high fuel prices, food shortages—like the recent shortage of baby formula—we should all be supportive of a good, clean, dairy farm right here in Longbottom, producing milk for those babies, helping them grow into strong children!" She paused. "But there's more to this, really. The Jastons have been good and *smart* farmers. They should be rewarded with

85

being able to keep their independent farm in operation. I believe it's one of the oldest family businesses in our town. Good and *smart* business, involving our food supply, needs to be supported by voting *no* on Article Six!"

The gymnasium erupted in applause.

The moderator banged his gavel. "Any further discussion?"

A thin, hunched woman who looked to be in her late thirties had walked up to the microphone, behind Anna, who stepped aside for her. The woman ducked her head to speak into the microphone that Anna had preset to accommodate her own five-foot-three-inch height. The woman's face was hidden behind her hair. Her speech was slurry.

"We need to bring more businesses to town—ones that pay more in taxes, and will provide some decent jobs!" She nodded at the moderator. "More than just a farm," she muttered to herself. She drifted back to her seat toward the front, to the sound of dutiful applause.

Anna Ebert, away from the microphone, leaned in close to the Jastons. "One of Mickey Quinn's people," she whispered. "I think she might be drunk."

A tall, ruddy-faced man with a shock of white hair spoke next.

"John Rutherford, from Vine Avenue. I'm speaking *against* the rezoning. The Jastons are dear friends and colleagues of mine. I knew Old Man Jaston, Robert's father, back when he was a Longbottom selectman."

John Rutherford paused and looked at the crowd before speaking again, to the moderator.

"You heard the Jastons' lawyer, Attorney Ebert, talk about how the Jastons have maintained their family farm for generations. Family farms are getting rare. We have a chance to stop the tide of big agribusiness, right here, with Jaston Farm!" He gestured toward the podium. "I make a motion to call the question, and to then call for a standing vote on Article Six."

"I'm calling the question." said the moderator. "All in favor of rezoning Jaston Farm to an industrial zone, please stand."

A cluster of eleven people in the front stood up. A few individuals scattered about the gymnasium also stood. The crowd was silent, looking around at who was voting for the rezoning.

"There's crazy Rufus Fishbane standing, along with all three selectmen," said Anna. "Isn't it wonderful that *he's* the one who gets to tally the votes!" Her voice was quietly scornful. "How he gets away with it . . ."

"All opposed to rezoning Jaston Farm, please stand."

A thunderous noise arose as nearly everyone in the gymnasium stood. The counters roamed the aisles, counting standing voters in each section. Anna watched closely as they reported each section's tally to Rufus, who added them up, then walked over to the moderator with a slip of paper.

"He couldn't possibly claim that we lost!" murmured Anna to the Jastons.

"The vote is 571 opposed to 19 in favor," announced the moderator. "Article Six, to rezone Jaston Farm, is defeated!"

The gymnasium erupted in applause and cheers. Spontaneous conversations blossomed throughout the crowd.

The moderator banged his gavel again. "Order, please! Everyone, please come to order!"

Anna Ebert hurried back to the microphone. "I make a motion to reconsider, in hopes that it will fail!"

The townspeople gazed at her questioningly.

Anna paused, looked around. Her voice rang out. "If you're against the rezoning, vote 'No' on the reconsideration."

"All in favor of reconsideration of Article Six?" intoned the moderator.

A few voices yelled "Aye!"

"All opposed?"

"Nay!" roared the gymnasium of townspeople. Cheers rang out again, along with renewed bursts of conversation.

The moderator banged his gavel. "Come to order!"

Maureen and Robert Jaston hugged one another.

"We got through it, honey!" said Maureen, tears streaming down her cheeks. "Let's go home and tell the kids the good news." Maureen's face was flushed pink, and her eyes shone through her tears. She hastily swiped at her cheeks with the back of her hand.

Maureen and Robert began to make their way toward the closest exit. They heard "Congratulations!" repeatedly out on their way out. Robert, smiling, nodded his thanks to all, as he hobbled along with his cane. Finally, the Jastons reached the foyer of the high school.

John Rutherford was waiting for them. "Congratulations! Your old man is smiling down on you today!" He grinned and clapped Robert on the shoulder, making him lurch sideways a bit.

Robert grinned, nevertheless. "Thanks for your support! My father would have loved your speech!" He placed both hands on the handle of his cane and leaned onto it.

"And you've got that gutsy lady lawyer," John continued. "She was quick to close it all down with that motion to reconsider. Sharp move! That puts an end to it—at least for now."

"Thanks, Mr. Rutherford," said Anna, overhearing his comment as she approached the group. "It's a good day for me when I've been useful! I like to protect my clients from unscrupulous people."

"Well, you've certainly done that, Anna," said Robert. "But we can't count on any more rescue votes by Town Meeting, now that it's been abolished . . ." Robert's voice trailed off. Maureen, her arm linked in his, nodded.

"Well, at least Jaston Farm survives to fight another day," said Anna, as she turned to leave. "I'm exhaustred, so now I'm off! I'm heading home to bed. Town Meetings have always gone on too late for me. I'll call you guys tomorrow," she said, looking at Robert and Maureen. "Good night!"

And with that, she strode off into the night.

CHAPTER 19

Darlene dozed off and on in her deeply sagging armchair. It had once belonged to her parents, but had found its way to Grandma Luella's house, and eventually, to Darlene's apartment. Now it was covered with an Indian paisley coverlet, wrinkled and askew.

Rather like me, she thought.

She was barely functioning. David required feeding every few hours, and she hadn't had a full night's sleep in days. She was delirious from extreme fatigue.

She nuzzled David's head, with its surprisingly thick curls of blond hair. They tickled her nose, and she sneezed. David shifted in her arms but didn't wake. Her neck ached; she had zoned out while nursing, and now a wiry tension stretched from her right shoulder to her right ear. She twisted as she tried to ease the discomfort without waking David.

Nathan had been a life preserver in her ocean of troubles. He regularly brought her food and supplies in the afternoons, when he got home from work. He waved off her offers to reimburse him.

"I'm not going to have a child of my own, so this is my contribution to the next generation," he would say.

"You could always adopt," Darlene suggested once.

"Darling, I would need a partner for that. As you know, I'm quite the eligible bachelor," he said, twirling his index finger in the air.

Darlene laughed. "Let's hear it for eligible bachelors!"

"Especially eligible drag-queen bachelors!"

They laughed in unison.

Darlene closed her eyes, took a deep breath, and said, "Thank you, Nathan. I truly don't know what I'd do without you. You know my grandma's on dialysis three times a week, so she's not exactly able to pitch in to help me." She opened her eyes again, as she sat up. "I need to at least *talk* to her, but I'm scared to use my cellphone. Could I use yours to call her?"

"Of course, pumpkin." Nathan dug his cellphone out of his pocket and handed it to Darlene. "Let any calls that come in, go to my voicemail. I'll catch 'em later. Now I'll go back to my place for a bit... give you some privacy."

———

"Grandma, it's me——Darlene. I'm using my friend's cellphone for this call. I'm too nervous to use my own." Darlene placed David on a blanket on the floor. "How've you been, Grandma?

"Never mind *me! What's happening with you and the baby?*"

Darlene's laughter rang out. "Grandma...I've already had our baby! The newest Bundt baby is a *boy—-not the girl you predicted*—-called David Jonah Bundt. He was just six pounds—at birth —-cause he

90

came early—-at eight months. But he's okay. He's nursing with vigor, so that's a good sign. I sure wish I could bring him to you, but I'm afraid to visit. There's a creep hanging around the neighborhood—-in some kinda beat-up car—-and I'm afraid that creep may work for Mickey Quinn. I don't know. I've just got a funny feeling about him."

"You do what you've got to do, sweetie. Don' worry about me—-protect yourself and our little David. That's a good, solid name you gave him, too. Take care, you two! I love you and little David——all the way to the moon!"

Nathan knocked gently on her apartment door. "Everything alright with your grandmother?"

"Yeah, everything's alright with her. She's *so* curious to see me and David. I *so* want to see her, and bring David, so she can meet him. But I'm just not ready. I can't deal with stalking. I can't deal with trying to creep out of the building with David in my arms, wondering if Quinn, or somebody else, will *pounce* on us"

"Wait a bit. Get your strength back."

"I wish I had more family. But Grandma's all I've got. And now David, too, of course."

"Your little family just doubled in size!"

Darlene smiled, teary-eyed. "You always see the bright side of things. That's what makes you so special."

"Oh, I'm special all right," Nathan said, grinning. "So, moving right along—what can I bring milady for dinner tonight?" He bent forward, eyebrows raised. "A grilled cheese sandwich and some cut-up fruit?"

"Sounds marvelous," said Darlene, her mouth watering at the thought of it. "Keep me company for dinner, Nathan."

"Of course, pumpkin."

David woke suddenly and raised his little head. He blinked and looked in Nathan's direction. His head wobbled as he unabashedly stared at Nathan.

Nathan gazed back, a tender smile on his face. The two of them didn't move, didn't make a sound.

"He knows you. You're the only other person he's seen, so far," Darlene said, in a near-whisper. "I imagine he's looking at you like you're his father."

"Darling, as much as I sympathize with your plight, I'm not going to step in as his substitute father." Nathan bowed his head for a moment, then looked up at her again. "I'll be his godfather—how about that?"

"No one has a bigger or sweeter heart than you, Nathan. It would be an honor to have you as his godfather." She smiled, eyes brimming. "That's why the high schoolers of Longbottom flock to you. You are so real, and so caring."

She blew him a kiss.

Nathan ducked his head and chuckled softly.

"I'll be in charge of his spiritual and moral upbringing. Who better than me?"

CHAPTER 20

Outside Darlene's apartment building, the trees had sprouted new, pale springtime leaves. The sun dappled the pavement and sparse lawn.

At the end of the block, an old blue van that sported a barely readable inscription had been parked for more than six and a half days. Inside the tinted windows, the driver waited for Darlene to emerge from her apartment. He was highly annoyed; he had been on this assignment for far too long, already. All this time, she had not come outside once. How was he supposed to check out her situation, when he could never see her?

Xavier Baccara had been hired by Quinn's lawyer, Tobias Meachum, to tail Darlene. Baccara called himself a private investigator, but unofficially he was willing do whatever was needed to get the job done.

Baccara wore a nondescript grayish jacket in all weather, with pants to match, that looked like a uniform. He wore a dirty baseball cap pertaining to whichever team the locals would support—in this instance, the Red Sox—that covered his hair and cast the top half of his face in shadow. His three-day beard growth disguised his jawline, and he generally kept his head tucked down, anyway. He was utterly forgettable, which is precisely what he wanted.

Right now, he was irate. The fact that his target had not set foot out of the apartment in a week was bogus. He knew she was home. Her lights shone from her windows at night and went on and off at odd hours. It clearly was not a timer working the lights; they were too erratic. So what was she doing inside for a week straight? Frustrated, he lifted his baseball cap to scrape his oily, long dark hair behind his ears. He crammed the cap back down on his head and bit his lip, thinking.

The answer hit him like a bolt of lightning.

She had had her kid, and was resting up in her apartment.

Anger flushed his limbs with newfound energy. She had fooled him! How the hell had she slipped out of the building, had the kid, and then slipped back inside?

Of course! He was an idiot. There had to be a back entrance. He should've used a helper—then they would have had it all covered. They would've known the moment she'd snuck away to have the baby, and the moment she'd returned. He scratched his stubbly chin, realizing then he would've had to split the juicy fee, which he was inclined to keep all to himself.

He wondered if a helper would have made a difference, anyway. And what was he supposed to do now—kidnap the kid and deliver it to Quinn?

He shook his head. No way. That was pure craziness. He wanted no part of kidnapping, which would get him serious time.

Think, he told himself. Your assignment is to report her status, so you just need to verify that the baby has been born. That should be easy enough. Just calls for some ordinary stalking.

Piece of cake.

Xavier Baccara was a meticulous planner. He knew he needed to see Darlene in person to get the facts.

He began to consider various scenarios. To be disguised as a mailman or UPS man required an actual uniform, but they didn't get inside people's homes, so why bother? No need of an electrician or plumber in her apartment, unless he figured out a way to shut off her utilities, which was a long shot. He didn't want to be fiddling with things in the bowels of the apartment building. Cable guy? Nah. She probably couldn't afford cable.

Baccara pulled at the brim of his Red Sox cap and ran his fingers through his hair again. He would have to go with the tried and true: pizza delivery guy. He grimaced. Anyone'd be suspicious of a pizza they hadn't ordered. How to make it seem legit, he wondered.

He watched the apartment's front entrance from afar, his fingers tapping on the steering wheel of the van. He was bored, waiting for someone to go in or out. The afternoon sunshine slanted against his windshield. Shadows of tree leaves danced over his van in the spring breezes.

A tall, thin man carrying two grocery bags rounded the corner and approached the front entrance. Baccara glanced at his cell phone: 4:30 p.m. He'd seen this guy the day before, carrying groceries. Come to think of it, the day before that, too. It was around the same time each day. The man sure bought a lot of groceries.

Dinnertime was approaching. Pizza at this time of day would be welcomed by most people. The question was, was this Darlene like most people?

Time to find out.

Baccara dialed the nearest pizza joint in Longbottom. He waited the requisite twenty minutes before leaving to pick up the pizza. It was a nuisance having to give up his prime parking spot, but if he got his answer today, he'd be done with this bogus assignment.

When he returned, his parking spot was taken. Natch.

He parked around the corner and walked the extra distance. He had avoided double-parking in front of Darlene's building, where she could spot his van and possibly identify it later.

He scooted along the sidewalk with the pizza box clutched in his left hand, head down as he approached the building. He slowed on the front walk, then opened the heavy front door and went inside the foyer. Above the individual mailboxes were buzzers for each apartment. He randomly tried two, in hopes of being buzzed in.

Bundt was her last name. He looked for her apartment and found it: number 18, third floor. Naturally, the damn third floor. Suddenly, one of the two people responded, buzzing him in without even knowing who he was. Hardly a secure system, unless maybe they had been expecting someone, other than him. Good thing he wasn't a murderer—just a stalker.

Baccara held the pizza box up high in front of his face, in case anyone encountered him by surprise. Before he knew it, he was standing in front of Darlene's apartment. He hesitated, then rapped on the door, keeping his face lowered under his Red Sox cap.

He heard the safety chain being pulled back, and the front door opened an inch. He spotted long blonde hair through the crack.

"What do you want?" said a woman's tired-sounding voice.

"Pizza delivery."

"I didn't order pizza."

"Is this the Bundt residence?"

"Maybe."

"Well, I've got a pizza delivery for someone named Bundt."

"I just told you, I didn't order any." Behind her, the thin cry of a newborn baby arose.

"You don't want it?"

"No. I didn't order it, and I'm certainly not paying for it."

The baby's cries grew louder.

"Aw, come on, lady."

"I said, I'm not paying for something I didn't order!"

"Okay, okay. I'll take it back. Shame, though. My store'll make me pay for it, 'cause they'll say I screwed up the order."

"Then *you* eat it, if you're gonna be charged for it."

The door clicked shut.

Baccara headed down the stairs, walking briskly down the sidewalk to his van, holding the pizza aloft. He got inside and put the pizza on the passenger seat next to him. His pizza would ride shotgun. It was his favorite—onion and bacon.

He opened the cardboard box and reached for a slice. He was hungry, and it tasted greasily good.

He started the engine, cradling his pizza one-handed, and slowly drove away.

A chunk of bacon fell off and left a stain on his pants as it fell to the floor.

Damn. He hated mess. One good thing, though. He could finally report on Darlene's status: She had had her kid.

CHAPTER 21

Maureen Jaston had recently noticed an increase in traffic on their off-the-beaten-track road. Their farm encompassed one hundred acres, located in outermost Longbottom. Ever since the whole trial, that whole mess with Clarisse, their obscure country road had become somewhat busier. And some of the cars came down the road slowly—too slowly, as if they were checking out the farm. Were Quinn and his people still after their land? Or was she just imagining it all?

I've had enough of this foolishness, Maureen thought. Didn't the Town Meeting vote settle all of this? My husband has been through enough. He won't ask for help; that's not his way. My children have been through enough. And these stray girls keep showing up on my doorstep. *Enough!*

Maureen was alone in the kitchen. She looked around to see if anyone was in earshot. Jacob and Faith were out doing the morning milking. Faith had made a sour face when she'd heard she needed to muck out the barn after milking, too. Maureen had stifled a hearty laugh. The poor kid was a town girl, after all, facing a heart-rending situation. Her baby would be born in five more months. What was to become of that child? What would become of the young mother, her own chances cast aside so young?

Maureen sighed. She needed to think about this girl's chances in life. Faith was far enough along that she needed to be steered toward considering adoption. She would make some calls, see what she could find out.

In the meantime, she needed to call the Longbottom cops. There was entirely too much traffic down their road, which made a long loop around the perimeter of Longbottom. There was no need to be traveling it unless you were visiting Jaston Farm or the few other houses that straggled along the road.

Somehow, things didn't feel right. There was a watchfulness in the air that put her on edge. Made her cast her eye over her shoulder. She sniffed. Time to make that call.

"Town of Longbottom," said the dispatcher. "Is this an emergency?"

"No, this is an inquiry," said Maureen. "May I speak to the officer in charge?"

"Is this Mrs. Jaston? I'll transfer you over to the sergeant."

In a moment, Maureen heard the sergeant on the line.

"What is this about?" he asked.

"It's about getting more patrol cars down our way, by Jaston Farm."

"What seems to be the problem, Mrs. Jaston?"

"Well, we seem to have all sorts of cars and trucks going by these days, an inordinate amount of traffic. Some of them are going very slow, in an almost *menacing* way. You know I've been very sensitive to menacing situations ever since what happened . . ."

"Mrs. Jaston, you have every right to be upset, considering what you've been through, but our department has suffered budget cuts.

There's no way we can send patrol cars to your road every time some creepy car or intimidating truck comes crawling down your way."

"So what do you suggest, then?"

"Hire a private detail, Mrs. Jaston—I don't know."

"Hmmm . . . Could I put up a flyer in the station?"

"*Really?* Let me ask you straight out: Could you guys really afford that?"

"Probably not."

"Okay, Mrs. Jaston. In the meantime, I'll tell the officers to keep an eye out."

"Thanks. I'll come by in a day or so to bring my flyer, if that's still okay."

"Sure. Coupla guys have been laid off. Who knows? Have a good day, Mrs. Jaston."

"You, too."

CHAPTER 22

Darlene needed to find a safe haven for herself and David, before she found herself unable to pay her monthly rent. Otherwise, she'd be unceremoniously evicted, her belongings lining the street curb. She shuddered, thinking of the two of them posed like frozen dolls among the boxes, bags, and rickety furniture on the sparse lawn, waiting to be scooped up or pounced upon by who knows what. It was unthinkable.

Darlene put David in his cardboard-box crib. While he slept, she would go on her computer for some serious job hunting. She brushed back her hair into a no-nonsense ponytail and started googling various job sites. There were so many jobs she wasn't qualified for; it would be almost laughable, except that she felt like crying.

What had she accomplished in life, other than learning how to mix drinks?

She sighed. If only she could take another bartending job. If only she could have David strapped to her back while she scurried from one end of the bar to the other.

Get real, she told herself.

She knew David couldn't come with her. She had to find a real job.

Something secretarial? No way. Her typing was miserable. Waitress? Worse than bartender; less tips. Housecleaner? A truly thankless job, cleaning up other people's messes.

Wait. Here was one: *Companion to elderly lady. Live-in position.*

Darlene clicked on the ad to read the details. It was here in Longbottom, on the fancy side of town.

She printed out the contact information. She'd buck herself up with a cup of coffee, then make the phone call. Darlene peered over at David. Still asleep, thankfully. She would have to step into her tiny bathroom to make the call, so as not to wake him. Nothing worse than a squalling baby to sour the phone call.

The phone rang four times before a quavering voice said, "Hello?"

"Hello, ma'am," said Darlene. "I'm calling about the online ad for a live-in companion. Might you be the one who placed it?"

"I might," said the thin voice. "But my nephew is handling all the details. You'll have to speak to him."

"Is he available?"

"No. He's not here at the moment. But let me give you the phone number to reach him."

"Thank you."

"If he likes you, I'll meet with you."

"Thank you so much, ma'am."

"Well, at least you were raised with manners."

"Yes, ma'am."

"While I've got you on the phone, I might as well ask you a few questions myself."

"Go right ahead."

"Why don't you tell me your name and age."

"I'm Darlene Bundt, and I'm thirty-six years old."

"Ever married?"

"No."

"Any entanglements in your life?"

Darlene hesitated. "Well, I have a son. A newborn. That's the main reason I need to look for this kind of job situation."

"I see." There was a pause. "In my day, that would've been a scandal."

"Yes, ma'am." Darlene took a deep breath. "I hope that won't disqualify me from this position."

"Nonsense."

"I can promise you, I'm of good character."

"Okay. Call my nephew, and he'll check you out further."

"Thank you, ma'am. May I ask the name of your nephew?"

"I suppose I can tell you." Coughs erupted on the other end of the line. "Excuse me." Darlene heard a throat-clearing sound, and then, "My nephew is Nathan Green."

Darlene gasped. "No *way!* Does he happen to live on Linden Street, here in Longbottom?"

There was a pause. "How would you know that?"

"He's my neighbor, and my personal friend!"

"Oh!" There was a longer pause. "Well, I suppose I'll have to give you serious consideration now."

Which means I wasn't under serious consideration before, thought Darlene. *Let's see if I can turn this situation around.*

"Thank you so much, ma'am. I have a feeling that when we finally meet, it will turn out well."

"Let's hope so, young lady. I'll talk to Nathan about setting something up. And why don't you bring your son along when you come? I want to see what sort of baby he is."

"Of course. I'm really looking forward to meeting you, ma'am."

"Likewise. Good day."

Darlene was still standing there holding her phone when David suddenly wailed from his makeshift crib.

Darlene swiveled to look at him.

"Your timing is impeccable, son. Now let's see if you behave on the day of the interview."

———

"Maybe you can tell me why your aunt's got an ad for a live-in companion, right here in town, and you never even told me? You *know* I desperately need a job!" Darlene's blue eyes flashed annoyance at her longtime friend.

Nathan's face reddened, and he looked at the floor. He was silent.

"And don't tell me that *she* put the ad online. I can't imagine she would know how!"

Nathan looked even more embarrassed.

"Are you going to tell me what's going on?"

"I'm not entirely sure why I haven't told you about it," he said in a quiet voice.

"Oh, come on. What is it?"

"It's not you, it's me." He pursed his lips.

"Famous last words of every breakup artist."

"Really?"

"Yeah, right. So what is it, Nathan? Are you ashamed of me? Am I too low-rent for you to spring on your precious aunt?"

"Darlene . . ."

"No. I wanna know the *truth*." Darlene hitched her fists on her hips.

Nathan smiled slightly. "If you could see yourself right now."

Darlene narrowed her blazing blue eyes at him.

"Actually, it's my aunt," said Nathan. "Auntie Joy. Joy Green."

"Her name is *Joy?*"

"The name doesn't quite fit, I agree."

"You got that right!"

"Anyway, she's a real bear. I believe the proper term is 'old battle-ax.'" Nathan scratched his head bemusedly. "I guess I didn't think it would be right to put you through the hell of dealing with her."

"Sounds charming."

He grimaced, looking her in the eye for the first time. "I'm sorry, pumpkin."

"I need this job, Nathan. Let me try, at least. I promise you, I can deal with her."

"Are you sure?"

"I'm sure. I'm tough."

"I guess so."

"You know my grandma raised me. Believe me, she was no piece of cake. I'm used to tough old broads. Your aunt will just be one more."

"Okay, then. Tomorrow's Saturday. We'll go meet with her then."

CHAPTER 23

Rufus Fishbane was feeling expansive, so he was throwing a cookout at his property, a century-old colonial-style house along a busy main road leading into Longbottom.

Nearby, the old cemetery's thin, slate gravestones stood like jagged teeth. On the other side was a new hairdressing salon. While the stream of traffic at rush hour was unrelenting, Rufus was undaunted. His property went deep behind the house. He and his ex-wife, years ago, had put a large, enclosed porch onto the house, along with an outdoor patio, where Rufus now stood, adding charcoal to his grill. He liked the taste of well-smoked meats.

Rufus stood with a beer in one hand, spatula in the other, grinning at his buddy.

Denton Clay was a bank officer at Longbottom Savings Bank. Not too long ago, he had been roped into Mickey Quinn's social orbit. A bout of drinking one evening had led to an unfortunate car accident on the Longbottom Common. A young girl was killed—the governor's niece—and Denton Clay had panicked.

He had quickly called Mickey Quinn for the name of an auto-repair shop that would be suitably discreet about the damage to his vehicle. And that was that. He found himself indebted to Quinn. For life.

Now, Denton was here at Rufus's cookout. The purpose of the gathering was to discuss the ramifications of Longbottom having jettisoned Open Town Meeting. Was it going to affect how business decisions were made? Was it going to mean that zoning changes would be far easier to enact? Two of the three selectmen were present. Nary a Jaston to be seen with this crowd!

Like that would've happened, Denton thought. He blinked rapidly and brushed back his white, Albert Einstein hair.

"So, what's cooking?" inquired Denton.

"On the grill? Or in Longbottom?" Rufus grinned again, his reddish face sweaty from the heat rushing up from the coals. "Good news! Open Town Meeting has been replaced by a town council, which will have nine members."

Denton sniffed, casually sipped his beer.

"I've already got people, Quinn's people, lined up to run for the council."

Denton said nothing, eyes lowered. He sniffed again. "How did you manage that?"

'Twas easy, me lad," said Rufus, affecting an Irish persona. "Put a twinkle in me eye!"

"No, really—how exactly did you manage it?"

Three townspeople were in earshot, getting beers out of the cooler. Rufus's back was turned to them, so he didn't notice they were listening.

"Town Meeting had to go. That's a given. So the question was put before the voters of Longbottom." Rufus grinned. "Two ballot options would not have worked. I specifically put *three* ballot options for them to choose from, which made for maximum division in the vote." He chuckled, sipped his beer. "Maximum division is the secret—divide up the vote as many ways as possible, and the desired result is achievable!" Rufus rubbed the spatula on the grill. "Worked like a charm!" He took another hefty gulp of his beer and returned to his grilling.

"Giving away all the in-house strategies, are we?" murmured Tobias Meachum, sidling past the listening townies. His thin, hatchet face was glaring at Rufus, who didn't notice.

"Guess so," said Denton, turning toward Tobias. " 'Loose lips sink ships!' " His fluffy white hair drifted, dandelion-like, around his face. "I believe that's the relevant quote for this occasion."

"So do ya think we can still land a casino here in town?" said selectman Danny Tripiano.

Danny was a short, scrappy fellow with a prominent nose who had joined Denton near the grill. Holding a plastic glass of wine with one hand and a wine bottle in the other, he was known for his rough edges.

"I mean, once the council takes over, Jaston can't count on his friends to save him. He'll be just an ordinary citizen again. A plain old dairy farmer."

"Yeah," said Denton. "But he's still got a lot of support in Longbottom."

"Yeah, but there's plenty of people in town who were looking forward to the treasure trove of jobs from the casino," Danny countered. "What about them?"

"What *about* them?" asked Denton.

"People like that, what—they don't count? Why should a dairy farmer count more?" Danny Tripiano set his jaw, ready to argue.

"Maybe because milk production matters more than tossing gambling chips," said Denton.

"Pah! You're a banker, not a developer! What do you know about it?"

"Are you going to run for councilman?"

"Nah, I'm moving to Florida soon. Unless this casino gets off the ground—then I'll stick around," said Danny Tripiano. He reached for a nearby plate of appetizers, took a few olives. "If we're lucky, we could get rich off this."

The townspeople there were all cronies, or a members of a crony family, and thus, on the town's payroll.

A group of town secretaries were clustered around the table with the cookout supplies. Denton left Danny and Rufus by the grill and went to join them. As a slight, elfin fellow, Denton slipped in and out of crowds effortlessly.

"Hello, folks," said Denton. "How're things?"

"That remains to be seen," said a woman from the assessor's office. "Let's hope the new town council doesn't try to cut our jobs—or consolidate them. Couldn't they just leave well enough alone?"

"Guess not," Denton said mildly. "Open Town Meeting was getting too rowdy. The townspeople kept asking questions about the budget. They had the funny idea that they should control their taxpayer funds." He smiled slightly, sniffed again, lips pursed.

"What's gotten into you, Denton?"

"Can't you take a joke—see the irony of it all?" Denton tilted his head to one side, stuck out his tongue waggishly. "Where's your sense of humor, ladies?"

"Just so things don't get all mixed up," said an older woman. "We got a system, and it's working fine. Leave us alone, and we'll get the job done."

At glacial speed, thought Denton.

Everything in this town moved slowly, except when someone got trampled on. Then it seemed like things suddenly moved at lightning speed.

CHAPTER 24

The clear sky today must be a good omen, thought Darlene.

Baby David was bundled in his one "going visiting" outfit she had for him, a gift from Nathan. She wore a modest, non-bartending outfit, one of the few dresses she owned.

She knocked gently on Nathan's door. He opened it and welcomed her in.

"Take off your coat. I want to see your outfit," said Nathan.

"What? Are you a member of the fashion police?"

Nathan smirked. "Yes, actually. Every gay man is, didn't you know?" He gestured for her to turn around in place. "Very good. You pass."

"Thank you."

"FYI, Auntie Joy is a charter member of the fashion police. I'm checking you over to be sure you'll pass *her* scrutiny."

110

"Ah." Darlene put on her coat again. She lifted David up off the low-slung couch where he lay in wide-eyed silence. "Let's go."

"The goon who's been lurking on our street for the past couple weeks seems to be gone—for now," said Nathan.

"Thank goodness."

"Don't know what he's up to, exactly," said Nathan, "but it can't be good."

"I've been thinking he's gotta be one of Quinn's people," said Darlene. "He scares me, hanging around out there. Let's try to go without anyone seeing us."

***

Nathan rang the doorbell of the brick mansion, which chimed like church bells. It went on for an unreasonable length of time.

Darlene had to suppress a laugh when she noticed an eye, magnified in the peephole lens, rotate from side to side.

Joy Green took a very long time to open the door, fumbling with the complicated, heavy locks.

"How would she get out in a fire?" Darlene whispered to Nathan.

Nathan chuckled. "Any moment now . . ."

The door finally swung open.

"Good afternoon, Nathan, and welcome—friends of Nathan," said Joy. "Why don't we go into the front room for our chat." She gestured for them to precede her.

Darlene bit her tongue. The place was grand, fabulous, awe-inspiring. She stood there, enthralled.

The furniture was carved dark wood, with brocade and velvet upholstery. A massive, intricately patterned Oriental rug muffled their footsteps as they entered her front room. The high walls were densely hung with paintings, some of them, no doubt,

111

portraits of rich ancestors. Other canvases, landscapes and still-lifes, were dazzling.

Darlene could scarcely keep her eyes from skittering about, trying to take it all in. She was truly amazed by it all.

She forced herself to turn around and face Joy Green with a smile.

"Thank you for agreeing to see me today. I hope I won't disappoint you."

"I hope so, too." The elderly woman sat in her armchair, book and Kleenex at the ready.

Darlene continued to stand, clutching David to her left shoulder.

Joy Green was clearly arthritic. Her hand, resting on the back of a chair, was as bent as a twisted piece of ginger root, thought Darlene. She was not more than five feet tall, with one shoulder markedly higher than the other. Her face was lean, with an arched nose and dark, penetrating eyes. Her hair was snow white and carefully styled.

"Take off your coats and have a seat," she said.

Darlene sat, and perched David against her stomach, so that he faced Joy.

They'd do this interview together.

"So, you need a job." Joy Green laced her knobby fingers upon her crossed knees.

"Yes," said Darlene. "I noticed you had a bit of trouble with your front door. I could help you with that."

Joy looked over at Nathan, who sat wordless and watchful. She cackled unexpectedly. "I see you brought me a live one. That's a start." She tilted her head. "Tell me about yourself, young lady—Darlene, isn't it?"

"Yes, I'm Darlene Bundt, as you know from our brief phone call." She edged forward in her seat, clutching David. "I'm Nathan's neighbor—he can vouch for my good character. He knows I worked for many years as a bartender in various clubs here in Longbottom, most recently at Quinn's Pub and Grill, until it closed down. After that, I worked for a bit at Dunkin', until I had my son, David. Since he was born six weeks ago, I haven't worked."

Darlene met Joy Green's direct gaze with her own.

"This is the first time in my life that I haven't worked, since I was fourteen, when I started with a work permit."

"Admirable."

"Thanks."

"So, why do you want to work for me?" She smiled thinly. "I'm ancient."

"To be honest, I want a job where I can keep my son close."

"Most mothers use day care these days."

"I prefer not to."

"And why is that?"

"I guess you'd say it has to do with family history." Darlene scratched her cheek. "My parents were killed in a car crash when I was just a kid, and I grew up with no siblings, no cousins—just a grandma who did the best she could, but who's now in a nursing home, 'cause she's really sick. I want to keep what little family I have together, for better or worse."

Nathan and his aunt exchanged a glance. A smile played on his face.

Joy's white hair gleamed as she shook her head. "Where are my manners? I never offered you two any tea or coffee."

"A glass of water would do for me," said Darlene. "Actually, why don't I get it myself, rather than trouble you?" She stood. David stirred against her, yawning. "Nathan, could you show me where the kitchen is? I can make a pot of tea while I'm at it, if Nathan shows me where everything is."

Joy nodded her agreement. "That's fine."

Nathan and Darlene headed down the long corridor that led to the kitchen, which was immense, with old-fashioned appliances from sixty years ago. They stood together on the black-and-white-checkered tile floor, looking around.

"I haven't been in here for a while," said Nathan. "Being with you makes me see it with new eyes. It truly is an anachronism."

"More of your fancy words again, Mr. Smarty Pants." She nestled David across her shoulder, and into her neck. "Where's the kettle? Time to boil some water."

Nathan handed her the kettle, which she filled at the sink and placed on the burner.

"I think she likes you," Nathan said. His dark eyes grew serious. "She might even hire you."

"Good to know I've got a chance."

"She's rejected everybody else she's ever interviewed."

"Oh."

"You're doing better than all the others."

Darlene made a face. "Great. My chances have moved from zero to slight."

"You see why I hesitated to tell you about the job? Believe me, I was trying to protect you."

"Nothing ventured, nothing gained."

Nathan gathered a tray and some tea cups, poured some milk in a little pitcher. He added an assortment of tea bags, a sugar bowl, and some spoons to the tray. "You're having tea, now?"

"Yep. Let's get back in there."

The two of them headed back to the sitting room, where Joy was reading her book.

In silence, each made a cup to their own liking. Darlene noticed that Joy took her tea with milk, but no sugar. Darlene having decided to have tea rather than water, added two sugars to her cup.

After taking a sip from her steaming cup, Joy spoke first.

"In terms of what I'm looking for in a companion, I'd expect some cooking, some shopping, light housework, that kind of thing." Joy Green folded her arthritic hands together. "And of course, assisting me, with things like answering the front door." She gave a wry smile.

114

"That all sounds fine," said Darlene. She shot a look at Nathan. "I'm sorry, I have to ask. Would my son David and I be able to live in this house, rent-free, and have our meals here?"

"That was the thought." Joy glanced at Nathan, but he remained expressionless.

"How much are you offering?"

"Not much. I'll pay for twenty hours a week, minimum wage, plus room and board. As I'm sure you know, Massachusetts has just raised its minimum wage, so you'll be costing me a pretty penny, even at twenty hours a week." She smiled, then turned somber. "Nathan, here, has been telling me to get someone for a while. But I like my solitude, and my peace and quiet." She gazed directly at David. "I must admit, he's a remarkably good baby."

It's now or never, Darlene thought. *Be brave.*

"So . . . what do you think? Do I have the job?"

There was an agonizingly slow moment as Joy Green stared openly at her and David. It was as if she was trying to read the future, seeing the two of them in her life. She pursed her lips.

"I guess I'll give you a try. You and your little one."

Darlene felt a rush of warmth toward the elderly woman, and then remembered Nathan. He was the one who had helped to engineer this for her. She grinned hugely at her friend, then at his aunt.

"You won't be sorry—I promise you both! *Thank you!*"

Nathan smiled crookedly.

Joy's expression was inscrutable. "When do you think you might start?"

"In a day or two, if that's okay with you. My lease is month-to-month, and it's almost the end of the month now. I'd like to start as soon as I can get my things packed and moved into storage."

"No need to pay good money for storage. There's plenty of room in the cellar."

"Really?" Darlene gasped. "Wow! Thank you—again!"

"Well, let's see how it all works out, shall we?" said Joy. "I'm afraid your tea has gotten cold." She gave an accepting smile toward David, who wiggled his arms in her direction. "We'll see how the little one and I get along, won't we?"

CHAPTER 25

Maureen wondered where Faith should be when she gave birth. Surely not living in her attic. That was ridiculous. Probably unlawful.

She and Robert could probably get in big trouble for housing these young girls who kept walking up to their farmhouse. She hadn't told the sergeant about them when she had called for extra security on their road; it probably would have triggered a major investigation, the *last* thing she and her family needed.

No good deed goes unpunished, she reminded herself. She would just keep her mouth shut. She decided to call Attorney Ebert to get some advice.

Faith was in her second trimester. She would be showing soon, and it would be harder for her to help with the farm chores. Maureen didn't want Faith risking any harm to her baby by lifting heavy loads, like shovelfuls of manure. She'd have to stop the heavy work soon.

117

Maureen chuckled. She suspected it had been a useful lesson for Faith; not only had she seen a dairy farm up close, but she'd been forced to work for her room and board here. A useful life lesson, indeed.

She'd put Faith on kitchen duty, peeling veggies.

The question still remained, about where she should go to have the baby. She'd have to call her usual contacts: St. Mary's Home for Unwed Mothers in Dorchester. The Covenant House. She'd also call Longbottom's women's shelter, Beacon House, to see if they might be able to take Faith.

Maureen didn't want to be housing her right up to her time of delivery. Besides, Faith needed appropriate prenatal care. She sighed heavily. She had a farm to run, a family to raise, and a husband to heal. She didn't need to be a nurse and a social worker, too.

She needed to talk to Faith. Would she really give up her child for adoption? Or was she going to raise her child herself, as a young, poor mother, probably going on public assistance, living in public housing? That would mean a quick downward slide for young Faith's life trajectory, and her child's life as well.

She wondered about the young man who had gotten her pregnant. Was he in the picture at all? Maureen hadn't heard Faith mention the father. Was he unreliable? Probably broke. Maybe a schoolmate. Could be living in his parents' basement.

Maureen snorted in frustration.

Maybe Faith's mother could be persuaded to raise her grandchild. Faith had said her mother always buckled to her father's wishes. Maybe the prospect of blood kin would soften their hearts. Would they allow their own grandchild to be put up for adoption—to go to complete strangers?

Only time would tell.

CHAPTER 26

Darlene and David were given the guest room next to the master bedroom, which had a great view of the river. From the mansion's proud stance on the hill, the river was easily visible, in wintertime, when the trees had shed their leaves. Now, in early springtime, the trees were beginning to leaf out, but Darlene could still see the glittering waterway that flowed swiftly toward the sea.

She had never lived in such elegant circumstances before—which made a certain incident all the more embarrassing. She had brought David's cardboard-box crib into their new bedroom, along with several suitcases containing their clothes. She had set the cardboard box down next to her new bed, folding the blankets that would provide padding for him within it. David lay on the floor, alongside the box, waiting, pedaling his legs in the air.

"Whatever are you doing?" said Joy.

119

Darlene looked up. "I'm sorry?"

"What is that?"

Darlene realized she would reveal her destitute circumstances if she admitted that this was David's crib. *Will she hold it against me, that I'm down-to-the-bone poor?* wondered Darlene. Will she think I'm not good enough to be her personal caretaker?

"I . . . umm . . . I was just going to store David's bedding in this box."

Darlene paused, realized she couldn't hide the reality.

"You wouldn't happen to have a crib, would you?"

"You didn't bring yours?"

Darlene pursed her lips, kept her eyes averted.

"No . . . Well, actually, I hadn't gotten around to buying one yet."

Darlene looked at the floor where David lay, pawing the air.

"And where has your baby been sleeping at night?"

"With me—because I've been nursing him, you see. I don't want him to have any allergies. He's exclusively on breast milk for that reason."

"*With* you. Day and night." There was a long pause. "We do have a cradle. It's an old-timey thing. I suppose it'll do. You'll have to haul it up from the cellar and dust it off."

"Thank you so much."

"Nathan slept in it."

"Huh." Darlene tilted her head, smiled. "Well, now Nathan's godson will be sleeping in it."

Joy coughed sharply.

"Nathan is going to be your son's godfather?"

Darlene snuck a sideways glance at Joy. "Yes." More silence. "I hope that's okay."

Again, a long moment.

"You're religious?"

"Somewhat," said Darlene. "My grandmother's influence."

Joy tapped a gnarled finger against the guest bed's corner post. "I suppose it'll be all right. You do realize that this will make you practically family. I thought I was hiring an employee. I didn't know I was acquiring *family*."

Darlene knew that her next words would determine her future, and David's. She had to say just the right thing.

She paused to gather her thoughts, her energy, her spirit. She stood up, straightened, and raised her chin. She looked directly into Joy Green's eyes, securing the old lady's attention.

"Our family-to-be connection will only make me more loyal, more dedicated, and more devoted," Darlene said softly.

"Yes," Joy Green replied. "I could use some loyalty."

"And we hope we'll bring a youthful sweetness and blessings to you," added Darlene. "With faith in the future."

"Yes. It *is* nice having a youngster around. Let's see how I feel when he gets to the terrible twos, shall we?"

———

Even though the queen-size bed was lumpy, Darlene was not about to complain. She slept soundly all night, despite the mattress, and woke early the next morning.

The guest bedroom, painted sky-blue, sparkled in the morning light. She was jubilant in the radiance. As her grandma had promised, the Lord had provided. "Thank you, Lord!" she whispered.

David still slept next to her. She'd haul the cradle up this afternoon She stood up, dressed quickly.

David was still nursing at odd hours, which kept her tired. Fortunately, Joy Green was a late riser. Darlene needed a chance to get herself and David going before tending to the old lady, but she'd go and see if she was up.

Darlene took a deep breath before knocking gently on Joy's bedroom door. "May I come in?"

"Enter!" Joy was still in bed, a slight figure under thick, creamy quilts. She was sitting up on a massive wooden bedstead under an arched lace canopy.

"Did you sleep well?"

"I slept surprisingly well, for a change." Joy brushed back her disheveled white hair with a gnarled hand.

"Can I bring you anything? Coffee, tea?" Darlene asked.

"I'll eat downstairs, thank you. I'm not an invalid—yet. I'll be down in a bit. If you'd have a pot of tea ready, along with some well-done toast and jam, that would be splendid. Never could abide crumbs in bed."

She put her legs over the edge of the bed.

"You're excused while I get myself dressed."

Darlene returned to her room and retrieved David from the bed, where he was safely against the wall. She was going to have to get some sort of sling to wear while she worked. Grandma Luella, who was part Cree, would have known of an ingenious solution. Darlene would have to, or get herself to a fancy baby shop with those fancy baby slings.

As Darlene entered the spacious kitchen, she glanced out the small windows perched over the double sink. A furtive movement caught her eye. She halted and stared fixedly. She waited a long minute for whatever or whoever it was to reveal itself. Nothing. Only the branches of the scrubby trees along the lawn's border stirred in the spring chill. She remained motionless, David cuddled in her arms, as her eyes carefully scanned the landscape.

Nothing.

She turned back to the stove, thinking about her move to Joy Green's mansion.

Little went unnoticed in Longbottom. She and Nathan had attempted to be discreet, waiting till their apartment building had emptied, as it usually did on a Monday morning. Nathan had taken a personal day, and they had loaded her stuff in Nathan's sedan and her Volkswagen, loading from the building's back alley. They drove over to Joy's mansion that afternoon, pulling around to the service entrance in the back, where their cars were out of sight.

But had they been observed? Probably. Did Tobias Meachum know where she was now? Probably. This put a knot of fear in her stomach.

Again, she scanned the landscape for signs of a trespasser on the mansion grounds. A large crow swooped down onto a low-slung tree, cawing. Thin white sunlight shone. The crow cawed again. Was it announcing the presence of someone?

"Darlene?"

Darlene jumped.

It was Joy's voice, coming from deep within the house.

"How's the tea and toast coming?"

"Water's almost boiling. Be ready in a minute or two."

Darlene stopped scanning the outdoors and began hastily filling the teakettle with water. She turned the burner on high, and placed the kettle on.

"I hope water boils quick in this kitchen," she muttered.

She turned to the refrigerator and began searching for bread to toast. Frustrated by doing everything one-handed, she placed David on a kitchen towel, on the floor.

"Sorry, son. I'll have to figure out how to better handle everything, including you."

She rummaged in the fridge, retrieved the jam, laid out teacups, and waited for the water to boil. Joy Green and David, both, would keep her hopping.

CHAPTER 27

Toby drove Quinn back to his house after the bail release hearing.

Toby was unusually quiet for much of the ride. Finally, he said, "You do realize that I put my legal reputation on the line for you? If I were to ever step outside of the law for you, it could—and probably *would*—mean I would be disbarred."

Quinn was silent. He breathed in and out, thinking, then scratched his eyelid. "Yep."

" 'Course, we go back a long way."

"Yep."

Toby continued to pick his way through traffic.

Quinn reached over and clapped Toby on the shoulder from the passenger seat. "Plenty'a bored and lonely men back in the county jail. They'd advise you to chill."

124

Quinn gazed out his window as they passed by a series of small bungalows; their efforts to "pretty up" were pathetic, he mused.

Back at his huge house on the rise, alongside the pond, Quinn felt a burst of pride. *Land and home*, he thought. The landscaping looked a bit raggedy, but nothing so bad that it had to be torn out and replaced. The wild geese were still hanging around.

He and Toby went inside. They halted in the foyer, getting their bearings. Beyond, a spacious living room was furnished with blue leather seating. Between the L-shaped couch and two leather arm-chairs was a blue-and-white Oriental rug, spread over a hardwood floor. Mickey headed straight for the long couch. Toby took an armchair, his lanky legs stretched out in front of him.

Quinn looked up, noticed Toby staring at him.

"Ya wanna talk about anything?" Toby said.

A long pause.

"Nah," said Quinn. He smiled lopsidedly, ducking his head to one side.

Another long pause.

"Just . . . before you make any moves . . ." Toby brushed the tip of his nose, then pushed up his glasses. He waited.

"Yep. Got it. I'll call ya." Quinn rubbed the palms of his hands together, staring at Toby.

Toby stared back, waiting.

Quinn was silent, still rubbing his hands.

Toby blinked. "Okay. I'll trot along. Call me for any damn thing, and stay the hell outta trouble!" He slowly rose from his seat and walked to the foyer, turning to look at Quinn once more before leaving, shaking his head with chagrin. He waved good-bye, then hustled away from the angry geese.

———

Mickey stretched his body lengthwise on the couch. He flexed his legs, then his arms. It felt *so* good to be in his own house again. Better than lying on that thin, hard mattress in the jail. Sleeping on that thing had made every ache in his body burn. This leather couch felt cool, smooth, and firm. Nice. Back on this couch, he was in control of his life again.

It him like a thunderbolt. He was now all alone in his big house. His third wife, Clarisse, wasn't next to him anymore. He couldn't reach across and fondle her soft breast first thing in the morning, while she was still asleep in their big bed, or here, when she dozed off on the couch.

Never mind those two women he had married before her. Clarisse had been the best of the bunch, the one he missed the most, despite his recent tough talk with his cell-mate.

Now, she was dead—stone-dead—and he had been the one who killed her.

He felt his brain sizzle. He jiggled his head, as if by doing so he could shake the vision of his hand pulling the trigger, watching the red bloom spread across her chest.

He groaned in an agony of guilt. "The bitch deserved it!" He smothered his face with his right hand, rubbing his chin with its morning stubble. "The bitch deserved it," he repeated, in a hoarse whisper.

He sat up. He was so tired of this memory. He had the rest of his life to live, and his dead wife Clarisse was not gonna screw it up for him. He willed himself to lie down again.

In fact, he thought, my life has taken an unexpected twist. A screwy, wonderful twist. He could hardly believe it. Three wives, and not one of them had gotten pregnant with his child.

126

I am finally a father, he thought. *No thanks to my dead wife, the barren bitch. Now, I focus everything on Darlene.*

He scratched his scalp, remembering her. A scrappy, thirty-six-year-old bartender from Longbottom's hard-luck crowd. Never mind that their kid's conception had been a bit on the funky side. To say the least. When she had told him she was pregnant, he had coaxed her to have the child, rather than abort it. That had taken some fancy footwork. Some promises. Some money. It was always about money, wasn't it?

Damn women, he thought. *Only ones that can give us our sons and heirs.* The Big Man upstairs must be laughing his ass off at that one.

Now the question was, how to get ahold of his kid. Any future Quinn's gotta be a winner in life. There was no way he'd put the future of his child in the hapless, hopeless hands of Darlene Bundt. Not gonna happen.

Thoughts about Darlene, and how she was so close to her grandma, made him jealous. He longed for blood-kin he could call his own. He was beleaguered by a profound hole in his heart.

While my kid grows up, I'll take him under my wing. I want real family, since the shell of the family I left behind is erased, he thought. *I've got plans for my son. If my child is a son.*

He stood up abruptly and headed for the kitchen. He needed coffee, immediately. He set up his coffeemaker and stood there, watching the coffee drip.

He was already thinking this kid was gonna be a son. His bloodline. Quinn had never revealed his sorry family life to anyone, except Toby, his best friend. His only real friend. Toby knew Mickey had been raised rough on the streets of South Boston, with a father who was a drunk, and mostly gone, and a feckless, kinda-crazy mother who had a series of boyfriends that slapped him around. Heartless bastards, one and all, who coulda cared less about him. He hadn't been their kid.

Well, I'm different from those bastards, he thought.

127

His kid wasn't gonna be raised up like that. He'd be sent to the best schools, meet the best people, be raised smooth instead'a rough. His kid wouldn't hafta brawl his way forward, be a bar-owner like me. I Ie could become a lawyer, like Toby, maybe even a judge someday!

He grinned at the thought.

Quinn had been sent out of South Boston, taken away from his so-called parents, and placed into the foster child program. At age thirteen, no less. He had landed with a well-meaning but clueless foster couple, here in Longbottom. The Hammonds. She had baked good pies, he remembered. But the Hammonds had had no idea that he'd managed to furtively terrorize his fellow classmates within the first week of arriving in Longbottom. After Southie, the country town of Longbottom was a laughably easy nut to crack.

Quinn thought back to when he and Toby had become friends. They had met in Longbottom High, freshman year. *My first friend after a long, lonely year in Longbottom.* He and Toby were in a history class together when their teacher had made an especially asinine remark. He and Toby had happened to catch each other's eye and smirked simultaneously. After class they joined up in the hall. Quinn had been big, blond, and tough at age fourteen, while Toby had been small, skinny, and sallow. No matter. Their attitude matched, their humor bounced off each other easily. Quinn didn't mind his first follower in town. Everybody else in Longbottom was an enemy, a rival, or just a patsy yielding up lunch money. Pah!

Toby's parents had discouraged his friendship with Mickey Quinn. "A foster kid from Southie is a bad influence," Toby's mother had said to him. But Toby was a deeply curious guy; he liked knowing people from all walks of life. He found Mickey fascinating. Dangerous, but fascinating. He admired Mickey's stone-cold bravery in all situations, not to mention his sheer brawn in a brawl. Toby had stuck close to Quinn, and Quinn had finally begun to trust him.

Their friendship had proved useful to both of them in the long run. They had become almost like brothers. He grinned. They were kinda like the new Bulger Brothers, Billy and Whitey. Billy Bulger had been the president of the Massachusetts State Senate for eons, while his brother, Whitey, had run the Irish Mafia, which had infiltrated the New England Italian Mafia, and brought them down, working with the FBI. Heck, the FBI had even tipped off Whitey as to when he needed to skip town! Whitey had had another ten years of freedom out in California till the law had finally caught up with him. Until he got hauled back to trial in Massachusetts, was convicted of those nineteen gruesome murders, and was sent to prison in West Virginia. Where he got iced within two days of his arrival.

Not such a happy ending, after all, thought Quinn.

He and Toby had taken very different paths as adults, but had stayed close. As Mickey had hustled to acquire Quinn's Pub & Grill, he had used Toby's legal talents to steer his way through the local politics of Longbottom. Together, they had the Town of Longbottom in a powerful grip, he thought, especially when Toby had become Longbottom's senior town lawyer!

He and Toby were a good team. Toby covered the legal angles, while he rode the soft psychological edges of adversaries. Quinn, a charming enforcer, savored the sweet victory of an adversary buckling. Together, they'd made a lot of money, and climbed the hierarchy of the Massachusetts crowd who mattered.

He grinned again. *His kid was gonna go to the top.* He'd get a fancy English nanny for him, till he was of school age. His blood-kin was gonna grow up powerful, shrewd, and adept. No do-gooder crap from Darlene and her screwy grandmother.

Quinn shuffled toward the bathroom, carrying his cup of coffee. He began his morning routine in front of the mirror. He paused while shaving, looking for signs of aging on his lean face. Still intact. Although his beard was going white in places.

His hair had grown long in jail. Having a full head of hair was a miracle at his age. In jail, he had taken to hooking his straight blond hair behind his ears, and wearing the rest of it in a ponytail. He needed a haircut badly before being seen around town.

Quinn's sky-blue eyes stared back at themselves in the mirror. He'd used them to confound plenty of people through the years. Eyes were supposedly the windows to the soul, but his were more useful, showing no mercy to an adversary.

His eyes sharpened, as he thought about his Pub & Grill. He'd certainly had his share of adversaries over the years.

"Which one thought up the 'Curse of Quinn' stupidity?" Mickey muttered to himself. Thinking about it made him angry and careless, and he nicked himself shaving. "Dammit!"

He reached for a square of toilet paper to apply to his chin.

"It's probably some cowardly idiot I've dealt with before—trying to get back at me in a sneaky way." He realized he was saying this out loud.

Keep your mouth shut, he told himself. *No use bellyaching.*

―――

The Longbottom police had been keeping an eye on Quinn's Pub & Grill since it closed down, making sure vandalism didn't strike. Toby was in charge of the premises, even though he now lived outside of town. He saw to it that the water, lights, and phone service had stayed connected. The idea had been to maintain the premises just enough to keep it viable, without costing Quinn a pretty penny. Anyone who called heard a recorded message that announced Quinn's place was closed for repairs.

After he'd finished his morning routine, Mickey decided to drive over to the pub. The building was all closed up, shutters in place, massive front door, bolted shut. The parking lot was empty. A plastic bag skittered across the pavement in the erratic breeze.

Mickey scanned the condition of the premises. Windblown trash on the periphery of the parking lot, caught on the taller vegetation. Splash of yellow paint near the entrance where someone had flung a can of paint against the siding. Spiderweb of cracks, gaining ground in the parking lot.

All closed down. Customers gone. Fled. Vanished. His former clientele had found new bar stools on which to roost. Dollars and cents gone, gone, gone.

Quinn grimaced. He needed his business back.

That Clarisse. This whole mess was her fault. If only she had kept her mouth shut. If only she had been a *loyal* wife. Where had she gotten the idea of testifying against him in court? No wonder he'd shot her.

Damn. All this trouble flowed from that testimony.

Now his business was shut down. He'd hafta work like a demon to revive it. He *needed* his business—and the cash flow—if he was ever gonna get his kid away from Darlene.

Quinn decided to park behind the building, out of sight from the highway. No need for everyone in town to see his car parked there, all by itself. That just looked pathetic.

He got out, locked his car, and leapt up onto a three-foot-high, pitted concrete loading dock. *No liquor deliveries these days*, he thought. He disarmed the alarm, entered the steel door. He peered down the hallway toward the kitchen, the restrooms, his office, and the cavernous public area with its shiny, rectangular bar. It was eerie being here when it was so utterly quiet.

He stiffened, anticipating something unpleasant coming at him. As a kid, he had hated dark places that were big and empty. Still hated them.

Noiselessly, he walked to his office. He waited for his eyes to adjust to the darkness, pushed open the door, and felt for the light switch. The fixture over his desk buzzed to life, gradually emitting a yellow glow. Much better.

His desk was its usual mess. He didn't remember what papers he had left strewn about. His tall, swivel-backed chair was turned toward the wall safe. As he swung the chair around, a tiny mouse scrabbled down a chair leg and disappeared under the desk. Yikes. What was it doing in his office? He didn't keep any food in here.

Damn. This meant there must be more of these nasty vermin, all over the premises, probably thick as thieves in the kitchen. He'd have to call the exterminator first thing.

At least his safe appeared all right, not breached or blown. Thank God for small favors. Hopefully, his cash was still inside, untouched. He'd need it to live on, now that he was out of jail. One thing about jail: You got three squares a day, courtesy of the taxpayers.

Quinn walked behind his desk and gingerly sat down in his chair. He reached sideways, turned the combination lock on the safe, feeling the numbers click into place. After the third number, the safe door was released, and he swung it open. His stash was there. Hallelujah.

Quinn had another thought. He leaned over to look deeper into the safe, reached in, and pulled out his passport. He checked the expiration date. Still valid for another year and a half. He chortled. That would be more than enough time, thank God. The safe also held his big envelope of extra get-outta-town-in-a-hurry money. He could still make plans while hanging around, pretending that he'd wait for his murder trial.

Quinn dialed Toby on his cell.

"What's up?"

"You've done that bail thing against my house, right?"

Meachum sighed heavily. "Yeah. Why do ya think you're walkin' around a free man today?"

"You did good. Now I need you to look into that agreement thingie I signed with Darlene Bundt. I need to find out my rights concerning my kid."

132

CHAPTER 28

"Attorney Ebert, I've got a problem. These girls keep showing up at our farm, and I don't know what to do with them," said Maureen, running her hand through her auburn hair in exasperation. She was on her cell phone, sitting on her bed, upstairs, in search of some much-needed privacy. Anywhere but the farmhouse kitchen, the family's nerve-center. "Won't I get in trouble for harboring these girls if they're minors?"

"I'd advise you to get the girls to an accredited facility of some sort," said Anna Ebert. She was sitting behind her huge desk, twirling a straw in her Dunkin' coffee cup. "There are agencies that help these girls, you know. You just have to refer them on to the right place."

"Easier said than done," said Maureen, lying on her back while she talked. "I'm like an unpaid social worker with these girls."

"You are our local hero in these parts!"

"Hmph. Something I never asked for."

"Yep. Welcome to the club, my friend," said Anna Ebert.

———

Maureen had sat Faith down by the kitchen table to talk about her plans. Would Faith really give up her child for adoption? Would she go about getting herself some prenatal care? Where was the child's father? Could he provide for this child? Did she love this boy? Did he love her? Did they have dreams of marrying? She was just a high school senior—how old was he?

Faith had buried her face in her hands, her green hair providing another layer of protection. "I don't know," she moaned. "I've made a mess of everything."

"Have you been in touch with your parents at all?" Maureen asked.

"My mom."

"What does she say?"

"She wants her grandchild to stay with our family."

"Of course. A normal grandmother's reaction." Maureen closed her eyes in thought. "Is it possible that you and your family—I guess I mean you and your dad—might reconcile?"

"How do you mean?" Faith poked one eye out from behind her hair.

"Do you think you could go home again, get the help of your family in raising your child?" Maureen leaned in toward Faith. Their shoulders touched.

"Maybe."

"Should I make a phone call to your family, on your behalf?"

Faith nodded. Maureen patted her back.

"Okay, sweetie. I'll do my best."

Maureen timed the phone call for after the dinner hour. The voice that answered was gruff and deep.

"Hello. Is this Faith's father?"

"Yes. Who's calling?"

"I'm the lady who's been feeding and housing your daughter these past few weeks."

Silence, then a sharp exhalation. "What's going on?"

"You know what's going on." Maureen kept her voice calm. "Your daughter will give birth pretty soon. She needs prenatal care. I can't get it for her—she's not my child, not on my family's insurance plan—but she could get the necessary care for herself and your grandchild on *your* family's health-care plan." She paused. "Faith is feeling lonely, away from her family and friends. She especially misses her mother."

"Who are you—*where* are you?"

"I'm interested in whether you and your wife will take responsibility for your daughter and your grandchild."

"*Lorna?*" he called out loudly. "I'm calling my wife to the other extension," he explained.

A rattle, and Faith's mother was on the phone.

"Hello?" she said breathlessly. "Do you have news about Faith?"

"I do. Faith is fine, and so is her baby—at least it seems so. She needs prenatal care, and a doctor should check her over. Please come and pick her up. Once she's home, take good care of her. She's a sweet girl."

"Bless you! Thanks for watching over our daughter for these weeks. We've—I've been so worried," said Faith's mother.

"Where are you located?" Faith's father asked again.

"Actually, I think I'll drive her over to your house, in town. I've got a few errands to run anyway. No need to come all the way out here," said Maureen.

"I heard a rumor . . ." Faith's mother said. "You wouldn't happen to be Maureen Jaston, would you?"

Maureen paused, wondering whether to admit it. She rubbed her lips. "Yes—I am."

A grunt came from Faith's father.

"Bless you, again, Mrs. Jaston," repeated Faith's mother, adding, "You and Mr. Jaston have been through so much. And you're still doing so much for others—even while you run your dairy farm!"

"We all do what we have to in life," said Maureen softly. "I'll bring your daughter home tomorrow afternoon."

CHAPTER 29

On his second day out of jail, Quinn woke up and grinned hugely. He was finally home. His two-story, colonial house on the hill hadn't suffered in his absence, thanks to the vigilance of his buddy Toby, who had actually done right by him.

As for getting ahold of his kid, there was more than one way to go about it, he'd been told. Toby would scope out all the angles.

Holding that comforting thought in mind, Quinn got out of bed to begin his day. He dressed in jeans and a comfortable turtleneck. It was great, rooting through his dresser drawers and closet again, seeing all his choices of clothing. Sure beat the jailhouse garb.

He shuffled to his living room and plopped down onto his blue leather couch, put his feet up on the coffee table, where there was a stack of local papers six inches deep. Toby'd been telling him he was crazy to still get actual newspapers, but he liked the smell and feel of real newspaper. Nothing like dozing off on a Sunday afternoon under a newspaper.

Now I get to see what happened while I was in jail.

Quinn picked up his cell phone, cradling it in his hand. He thought about Darlene and her new baby. He knew the child was his. Darlene had told him she was pregnant, by him, one afternoon in his office. It had been a strange occasion. It was midafternoon, between the lunch crowd and the after-work crowd. She had walked in with a funny, tense look on her face. She told him she'd thrown up in the bathroom three days in a row. She'd finally bought a pregnancy-test kit, and it had come up positive. She was pregnant. With *his* child—" 'Cause I've not had sex with anyone else in a very long time," she added.

Right then, he had begged her not to abort the child. She had given him a dirty look and walked out of the office.

Quinn had had Toby draw up a document that said he would support the child until age twenty-one, just so she'd agree to have the kid.

She'd agreed. *Must've been the prospect of the child support money that convinced her*, he thought. *Money. Always money with women.*

He couldn't believe his luck. He was no longer fated to go through life childless and alone. Hallelujah! Not that he was religious or anything, although he was kinda superstitious. He had always felt untethered, unmoored. Something about not having *anyone*—any live person on this planet who was linked to him—rendered him deeply sad. If he admitted the truth, he had been grieving his lack of family for most of his life.

Now, he felt a spark of optimism within his heart, a physical expansion of his chest that he'd never felt before. It felt good, and very unnatural. He didn't really trust it.

Better he should trust his inclinations and get real. As if he and Darlene would ever work out some friendly situation between them? Better he should just take possession of this child—especially if it was a boy—and proceed with his instincts to build his own family.

If that child is a son, I will absolutely secure custody. This child will be my legacy.

First thing he needed to find out was whether it was a boy or a girl.

Even more importantly, he had to figure out how to get the kid. Did he dare out-and-out take his child? Wouldn't he be seen as a kidnapper?

He'd put his feelers out, see what he could find out.

First stop, Beacon House, Longbottom's women's shelter across town. It was supposed to be off the grid to the public, but he was on the board of trustees, which gave him the freedom to pay a visit.

And while he was there, he'd see his longtime buddy, Martha the Whisperer.

CHAPTER 30

Lenny Starbird, a former cop, was working as a security guard at Beacon House. He had previously worked for the Town of Longbottom, but, as one of six of the newest cops on the force, he'd been laid off as part of the political rush to "defund the police." He was one of six. Now he and another ex-officer were covering shifts at Beacon House, along with two of the original guards. The pay was nowhere near what cops made, and the benefits were a joke.

Lenny's worthless ex-wife, Mary Beth, had gotten their bungalow in their divorce. Not that he'd cared much for that tiny house. He just preferred to pay a mortgage rather than rent. Thank God they hadn't had children; she would have been a terrible mother..

After Lenny had been laid off, he had continued to show up at the police station. He was mostly waiting to see if the town budget was going to be restored by Town Meeting voters, and he could be reinstated. The budget discussion was put off to the end of the fiscal year, and then the referendum had taken place, abolishing Town Meeting. Lenny knew his chances of rehire were slim with the nine town council members. That's when he'd seen the notice put up by Maureen Jaston, and decided to take a chance.

———

Lenny Starbird stood on the stone doorstep of the Jastons' farmhouse and knocked on the kitchen door. It was a sunny day. A set of eyes peered at him between the curtains. Finally, the door opened, on the door chain.

"Hello," he said in a gentle tone. "I'm Lenny Starbird, formerly of the Longbottom Police Department. I'm here to inquire about the security detail needed at your farm."

"Lenny? Is that really you?" Maureen said. She took the door off the chain and opened it fully. "Haven't seen you in an age! You're the answer to my prayers. I just hope we can afford you. Come in—let's talk."

Lenny crossed the threshold and entered the kitchen.

"Have a seat," said Maureen. "I'll pour you some coffee."

Lenny sat at the kitchen table, leaned back in his chair. This kitchen smelled wholesome. Like cinnamon. He inhaled the scent deeply and smiled.

"Smells nice in here. Hope you've been alright—-since your family's troubles."

"We've been managing. How've you been?"

"Maybe you heard that my wife and I have split up? And that I've been laid off of the police department, too? I'd rather not go into details. I'm forward-looking, these days." Lenny sipped his hot coffee. "What can I do for *you*—now?"

141

Maureen sat down at the kitchen table, so as to speak to him in a low voice. She glanced around to see if anyone was in earshot.

"Ever since the horror of a killing taking place in this house," explained Maureen, "I've been skittish, having my twin girls and my teenage son here, virtually unprotected, since my husband, Robert, is still recovering from his gunshot wounds. I don't know that he would be in a position to protect our family . . ." Her voice trailed off uncertainly. "I've been going crazy with three youngsters underfoot and a farm to run, especially now that Robert can't do as many farm chores as he used to."

"Of course," said Lenny. "You need some protection after what you and your family have been through." He cleared his throat. "I gotta tell ya, everyone admires your husband, Mrs. Jaston. And you, too."

"The thing is, we don't make a lot of money on this farm, as you can imagine. We don't really have enough to pay for an official security detail. I'm not sure how to go about all of this."

Maureen frowned in frustration.

"I have a proposition for you," said Lenny Starbird.

"Oh? What is it, exactly?"

"Well, I have an RV I can live in, if I can find a place to park it. All I need is water and electric hookup, and I'd be set. If I could park it on your land, and you have the necessary hookups—without charging me for them—then I'd be happy to be your part-time security detail on the farm, for no salary. Just giving me a rent-free place to live would count as my pay. I'd rather live on Jaston Farm than in a trailer park."

"Really?" Maureen was stunned into silence. She looked down, pondering.

"Really. The nearest place to park my RV is three towns away from Longbottom, and I'd rather stay in town."

"Where're you living now?"

"I'm in Fletcher Park, over in Linnville. Takes me about forty minutes to get over here, or to where I work."

"Where do you work?"

"Well, these days, I'm working thirty hours a week at Beacon House. It'd take me only five minutes to get there from here. You familiar with it?"

"Oh yes, I know it well."

"I bet you do, with the various folks who find their way to you out here."

Lenny grinned, tried to meet Maureen's eyes.

Maureen was silent, wondering if she'd invite trouble if she admitted to anything.

"No worries. You and your husband are admired for what you do." He paused. "So, what do you think? You realize I wouldn't be here all the time. I'll be absent when I'm on duty at Beacon House."

Just then, Robert Jaston walked in, leaning on his cane.

"Hi, honey," said Maureen. "This is Lenny Starbird, come to talk to us about a security presence on our farm."

"I heard most of it from the other room. Sounds like a good deal. No out-of-pocket for us, except for electric and water. Sounds pretty reasonable to me. You don't take crazy-long showers, I hope? Or run your television all day and night?"

"No, sir."

"I've heard from a few people that you're a straight-shooter. Should I believe them?"

"Yes, sir. Can I ask who, sir?"

"Never you mind. Reliable people."

Robert Jaston paused, lips pursed in thought. He nodded, as if to himself.

"Let's do this," he said, reaching out to shake Lenny's hand. "It's official."

Lenny grinned. "When should I start?"

"Just as soon as you can get your RV over here. Let's go for a walk, see where'd we situate it on our land."

"I'm ready if you are," said Lenny, rising from his kitchen chair.

He stood back to let Robert pass.

Robert turned and said, "This'll be very good for the farm. Gotta put a lid on craziness these days."

Robert opened the door, swung onto the granite doorstep, and down onto the rough lawn surrounding the farmhouse. He glanced back to see if Lenny was coming, too.

"I'm right here, Mr. Jaston. Gonna have your back from now on."

CHAPTER 31

Quinn, sprawled on his blue leather couch, was aggravated by Xavier Baccara's hefty bill. He'd called up Baccara and asked him to come over and give him an update on Darlene's doings.

Quinn scrutinized Baccara's bill in his left hand.

"You spent this many hours on her street, just watching her apartment?"

"Yeah. She never came out of her place—*ever*."

"So, whaddya got for me?"

When Baccara told him that Darlene had recently moved out of her apartment, Quinn felt his blood pressure rise. *Stay calm*, he thought.

"Where's she gone?"

"To some old lady's big house, on the rich side of town."

"Do you have an address?"

"Yeah. I wrote it down on a slip of paper somewhere."

Baccara patted his pockets to see if the paper was somewhere on his person, shrugged, then said, "It's in my truck."

Quinn rolled his eyes, then re-focused on Baccara. "Why'd she move?"

He noticed Baccara's black hair was in a short thick ponytail at the base of his neck. Middle-aged men wearing ponytails, too? Quinn restrained himself from further eye rolling.

"Beats me." Baccara rubbed his nose. "Who can explain women? Oh, yeah, I meant to tell you. She had the kid."

Quinn blinked. "Boy or girl?"

"Don't know. Didn't get close enough to see."

Quinn snickered. "It's okay. Didn't expect ya ta check out the kid's equipment or nothin'. Wasn't like you were up in her apartment changin' the kid's diapers, right?"

"I meant . . . well, you know," Baccara stammered. "I never saw what the kid was wearing, I mean, boy or girl clothes . . ."

Quinn's lip curled slightly. "As if she'd have money to buy special baby clothes."

"Actually, she had some guy helping her, back at her old place, before she moved. Bringing her groceries and stuff."

Quinn sat up, suddenly attentive. "Who?"

"Her neighbor."

"Who's that?"

"According to the mailbox, some guy named Nathan Green. Took a coupla days, but I followed him, found out he works over at Long-bottom High School. He's a high school counselor."

Baccara, hands in his pockets, stood watching Quinn.

Mickey's eyes were staring absently at the ceiling, thinking.

"Huh," Quinn said finally. "Find out what you can on this guy. How'd you find out he was bringing her groceries?"

"I saw him in her apartment one time. Coupla moments after he'd gone up the stairs with some grocery bags. It was dinnertime, and her apartment lights were on. She hadn't closed her curtains yet."

"Did they seem like they were, you know, together?"

"No," said Baccara. "At least, I never saw them doin' nothin'."

"Huh. Interesting." Quinn cocked his head in Baccara's direction. "You did good so far. Got anything else on this Nathan Green?"

"Not yet."

"Keep on him," said Quinn. "And check out the old lady, too. Send me her address so I know what part of town we're talking about. I'll be in touch."

Baccara moved toward the door, waved halfheartedly, and left.

Just then, Quinn's phone rang. It was Toby.

"Yeah?"

"Hey, it's me. Got a couple tidbits to share. First, I heard Rufus going around telling everyone how he pulled off the vote, to go to a town council. And somebody told me he was bragging about the demise of Open Town Meeting."

"Not good."

"No. And second, I heard that our nemesis, Anna Ebert, went in with some kinda citizens' petition to reverse the vote."

"Her again? Somebody oughta shut her up," said Quinn.

"Unlikely. Meanwhile, what about Rufus?"

"I'll handle him." Quinn rubbed his nose.

"I'll leave you to your charming ways, buddy. Signing off for now."

"Catch ya later, Toby. Thanks for the heads-up."

CHAPTER 32

Darlene lifted David out of his car seat from the back of her blue Volkswagen. He had gotten husky and strong in the few months they had been living at Joy Green's mansion. David routinely gurgled with delight. She lowered him into her baby sling and strapped it to her torso. He was a contented against her body.

The parking lot of the supermarket was moderately full, with a few carts adrift, blocking spaces. Darlene squinted in the sunshine, her straight blonde hair gleaming. She looked both ways for passing cars, then marched toward the store. She was so intent on getting out of the oppressive summer heat and into the cool, air-conditioned store, that she failed to notice a Cadillac backed into a space at the edge of the parking lot, under the cover of some skinny-trunked trees and their scant shade.

The Cadillac's visor on the driver's side was pulled down, casting a shadow on the person seated behind the wheel. He was careful to remain motionless as he observed Darlene and David. As they entered the store, he eased out of the car and stood alongside, staring at the entrance. He discreetly nodded to a second individual who was parked a few rows away. The second man was seated in a small, indistinguishable hatchback. The driver's window was open all the way, his left arm resting there.

At the discreet nod, the second man responded with a raised index finger.

The plan was in motion.

Darlene took her time shopping. For one, she was enjoying the air-conditioning immensely. Second, she hadn't quite decided what to make for Joy's dinner. She wanted something tasty and cool. The mansion didn't have central air-conditioning, just window units upstairs, and the kitchen could get astoundingly hot.

Darlene wondered why Joy Green, a wealthy woman, had never installed central air. When she'd made a bland comment about the hot kitchen one day, Joy had unexpectedly cackled.

"If you can't stand the heat, get outta the kitchen! Isn't that the saying?" She had smoothed back her snow-white hair, adding, "Now that I'm so old, I find the heat doesn't bother me. In fact, I rather enjoy it. Is the heat troubling you, dear? And how about Davy? He's not getting any heat rashes, I hope?"

Darlene had hastily assured her that the heat was no problem, but she had retrieved an electric fan from its storage place in the cellar. She'd stuck it square on the kitchen counter, where gusts of hot air blew toward her while she cooked.

Finally, Darlene had selected food for Joy, herself, and David, who had started eating soft foods. She really had no more excuse to linger, so she went to the row of cashiers, picked the shortest line, and waited. She paid with the credit card Joy had designated for household expenses.

In a matter of minutes, Darlene was pushing the shopping cart of bagged groceries toward her blue Volkswagen.

Standing on the passenger side was the man who had caused her so much trouble.

She shuddered.

"Hey, sweetheart," Mickey Quinn said. "Long time no see." He smiled, his uncannily white teeth looking voracious to her.

She was tongue-tied.

She eyed him. He had had a haircut recently; his blond hair had that just-cut, raw look. He looked thinner, different.

"I'm out, as you can see." He grinned. "Couldn't wait to see you." He stretched his hand toward her, across the front of the car. "How've you been?"

Something wasn't right. How could he look younger? Could he have been working out in jail? Just seeing him was giving her the creeps. She wanted him to get away from her car.

Darlene saw a shadow on the pavement beside her, and whirled around instinctively.

A man she hadn't seen before was right behind her, and seemed to be reaching for David, still in his sling, strapped to her chest.

"Get your hands off of him, you creep!" she shrieked. "Help! Help!"

She abandoned her cart and ran toward the store. "Get away from us! Somebody, call the police!"

When she reached the store entrance, she turned around to see if she was being followed. No one was chasing them, and no one was standing next to her Volkswagen anymore. In fact, no one was paying any attention to her whatsoever.

Great, she thought.

She didn't go inside to tell the store manager. He would insist on calling the police. They would want a report from her. She didn't want to wait for the police. If she made a complaint to them about Mickey Quinn, they'd think she was crazy, or trying to get revenge or something. It just wasn't possible. He had this town all sewed up.

She walked back to her car, still shaking.

Her grocery bags were still in the cart. Hastily, she stuffed into the back of the car, strapped David into his car seat, and drove home fast.

CHAPTER 33

As she entered the mansion by the side entrance near the kitchen, Darlene was still shaking hard. David was safe, thank God. That's all that mattered. She had driven away from the supermarket in a daze, scarcely noticing the traffic around her.

Her hands trembled as she lowered the bags onto the kitchen counter. Her heart was racing in her chest, and her entire body was quivering. Mechanically, she put the groceries away, barely aware of what she was doing.

"That was a close one, my sweet," she whispered to David, who looked up at her, wide-eyed, still in his sling.

Darlene went down the hallway to the spacious living room, where Joy was napping over a novel in her favorite reading chair. She was petite, even bird-like, curled over her book in the brocade armchair. Still trembling, Darlene tried to decide whether or not to wake her up.

"Are you coming in, or are you just going to stand there all day, like a bump on a log?"

"Oh, excuse me. I didn't want to disturb you. I thought you were asleep."

"I barely sleep these days."

"Not even over a good book?"

"Especially not over a good book." Joy smiled slightly. "So—something brought you into this room. I assume it wasn't to gaze upon my beautiful face."

"No—I mean, you look fine, of course—"

The elderly lady chuckled, and shoved her bookmark between pages. "Cat got your tongue?"

"Hardly." Darlene was looking grim. "I have a serious problem, actually."

"Oh?"

"Someone tried to take David from me. In the supermarket parking lot."

Joy blinked hard. "Oh, my." She lifted her head from the back of the armchair to peer intently at Darlene. "Really?"

"Yes."

In silence, they gazed at one another.

David began to mumble. He was drooling, and Darlene wiped his face with a tissue from her pocket.

"All I know is that David and I need to be somewhere safe. Someplace where I know he won't be taken from me."

"Why didn't you call the police, back at the supermarket?"

Darlene rolled her eyes. "The potential kidnapper has the cops in his back pocket."

"Aren't you being a bit melodramatic, my dear? Or overly paranoid?"

"No."

"What makes you think someone is going to kidnap Davy?"

" 'Cause a sleazy lawyer came to my apartment, while I was still pregnant, and told me that his client wants his kid—that David is his kid. But David is *my* child, pure and simple. His client is never getting my David. Ever!"

"And who is this client who warranted such extraordinary effort by his lawyer? You've been so tightlipped about who has been at the root of your problems."

"Mickey Quinn."

Once again, they gazed at one another in silence.

"You know that Mickey Quinn and his sleazy lawyer have this town all sewed up," Darlene said. "Justifiable paranoia, on my part, I'd say."

"However did you happen to have a child with that awful Mickey Quinn?" Joy fidgeted. "Not that I mean to criticize your taste in men, or anything—it's just, *him*? Of all people?"

"He raped me."

"Ah." The elderly woman's face fell. She closed her eyes. "Beastly. Just beastly." She wove her fingers together in her lap. "If you tell me, I'll listen."

It was Darlene's turn to hesitate.

She took a deep breath and walked over to sit down next to Joy, David on her lap, and quietly told Joy the whole story.

"But why didn't you call the police when all that nastiness happened?" Joy asked, when Darlene had finished.

"You don't understand. It's expensive as a single person. But it's more than that. I'm paying part of my grandmother's nursing home fees, the part not covered by Medicare. If I had called the cops, I'd've been instantly fired."

"Ah, I see." The elderly woman's eyes gleamed. Her faint smile appeared.

"You know the saying, 'God bless those who've got their own.' Well, we Bundts have only got each other. So we can't afford to lose our jobs.

"Indeed."

"So, what do I do about Quinn being after my David? I've been nervous whenever I leave this house that someone's after him. I've been too scared to visit my grandmother. I've been calling her from your house landline nearly every day, but it's not the same. Any ideas? I'm afraid to use my own cellphone, in case it's tapped."

"I'll think on it, long and hard."

"If I can stop shaking, I'll make a cup of tea for you while you think. Would you like a biscuit, too?"

"Make tea for both of us, and bring a bottle for David. We need to talk this out."

"I'm still nursing him. It's far cheaper that way."

"Yes, yes, of course. Silly me. Of course, nurse him as needed." Joy tilted her head toward David. "That should keep him quiet as we talk, I imagine."

God forbid you're interrupted by a baby's cries, thought Darlene. She often found herself impatient with Joy's notions that children should be seen and not heard; surely those ideas went out with the last century.

Darlene headed for the kitchen, holding David tightly in her arms.

In her imagination, she was still running from Quinn and his goon. If she could only run fast enough, she and David could escape his clutches.

CHAPTER 34

Rufus Fishbane was found by his cleaning lady, Maria Gomez, who came on Thursdays. His lifeless body was slumped sideways in his favorite armchair, an eye-bugging, teeth-gnashing expression on his face, a bloody line at his neck. Down his chest, his shirt was soaked with dark blood.

Maria screamed, and dropped the plastic kitchen bag full of garbage onto the hardwood floor. It sounded like some glass broke inside the bag. She began to shake.

"God rest his soul," she muttered, as she made the sign of the cross and retrieved the garbage bag. She turned and went to the kitchen landline to make the necessary phone call.

Police cruisers blasted their sirens and flashed blue lights all the way Rufus Fishbane's house, parting the traffic like a wave. Officers Mike Muratore and Shawn DuShane had arrived. The line of cars on the main thoroughfare had slowed way down, the better to view possible carnage with classic rubbernecking.

Officer Muratore entered the opened front door first, followed by DuShane. Silently, they viewed the scene.

"Have you noticed something weird?" said Muratore.

"This whole thing is weird. Who would kill the Longbottom town clerk?" asked DuShane. "Gives me the creeps."

"Who knows?" said Muratore. "Who'd ya think had a motive?"

"Huh." DuShane began to slowly scan the room. "No signs of a struggle, except in that chair. Nothing else has been disturbed."

Muratore sighed. "Guess we start by calling the coroner."

"The ambulance guys just arrived," said DuShane. "Let them call the coroner."

"Sure. We gotta question the cleaning lady, anyway," said Muratore.

The news spread through the police station like wildfire: The Longbottom town clerk had allegedly been executed, mob-style. But a big question remained. Who had done it, and why? Speculation ran the gamut. Maybe Fishbane had been into some kind of nasty business.

The coroner would determine the actual cause of death. She'd already said that she thought Rufus Fishbane had likely been choked, prior to having his head nearly severed from his body. Looked like it had been done by a wire, or maybe a knife, she said, which fueled the talk even more.

Rufus Fishbanc's distraught offspring had started in on the police. Shouldn't murder charges be brought?

Against whom? the police spokesperson had asked.

The children's' mother, long divorced from Rufus, made plain her bitterness. She announced she was glad to see him go before her. Yet the ex-wife still advocated that murder charges be brought.

"Something ain't right," she was heard to say. Maybe there was a victim-compensation-fund her children could tap into. She also wanted to know whether her children had inherited anything from him.

"Kind of ghoulish, wouldn't you say?" said DuShane to Muratore, sitting opposite his desk.

"Definitely. Sure is strange for the ex-wife to be so concerned about murder charges being brought. Ordinarily, she'd just go to the funeral with her kids." He scratched his chest as he thought. "The situation seems pretty funky overall, don't ya think?"

CHAPTER 35

"I know just the person to call," said Joy Green, flashing a sudden grin. Her teacup was poised halfway to her lips. Her eyes twinkled with anticipation.

"Who?" asked Darlene.

Darlene and David sat on the end of a long, velvet couch, facing the front windows. David's little face was tucked against her as he silently nursed.

Darlene kept looking out of the tall windows nervously, half-expecting to see a face peering in at her between the dense shrubbery that surrounded the mansion.

Joy's high-backed armchair was framed by golden sunlight slanting in from the west. The older woman's expression was hard to see against the light.

"Who?" repeated Darlene.

"A spunky young lawyer that I know," said the older woman.

"I don't have the money for a lawyer," said Darlene.

"I have a bit tucked away." The elderly woman paused. "I'm willing to help you and your David. *Our* David. He *is* Nathan's godson, after all, and therefore, part of the family. Interested?"

Darlene blinked, disbelieving. "I guess." She paused. "The thing is, I don't want to get started with a lawyer only to be left high and dry, halfway."

"Fair enough." Joy leaned forward to emphasize her words. "First of all, I won't leave you high and dry. That's not how I operate. And second, I believe this lawyer will do right by you."

Darlene exhaled. "I'll believe it when I see it."

Clasping her hands together, Joy leaned forward. "Why such distrust of lawyers, if I may ask?"

"Oh, well, it's a long story."

"I've got time."

"Okay." Darlene's eyes scanned the ceiling as she gathered her strength. "As you know, my parents died in a car crash when I was a little girl. I was eight years old, so certain things are a little vague, as if they were a bad dream, you know? After they died, my grandmother Luella raised me. She's the one in the nursing home now."

Joy was still, waiting. Steam rose from her teacup on the table beside her.

"The police decided it was the other guy's fault, not my parents." She shook her head slightly, as she corrected herself. "Not my dad's fault—he was the one driving. Even though this was the case, my grandmother never forgave him for being the one driving when her daughter, my mom, was in the accident that night. As if he somehow he should have foreseen it."

Darlene closed her eyes, reliving scenes from her childhood in her mind's eye.

"That's because my grandma *could* foresee things, back then, and still today. Maybe she'd actually known the accident was going to happen, and was angry when he failed to protect my mother."

"How terrible. Such a tragedy."

"Yes."

Darlene took a deep breath before going on.

"So, Grandma went to a lawyer to see about getting some compensation for their lives having been unjustly taken, to help with the task of raising me."

"Yes, of course."

"But the lawyer she consulted turned out to be a crook." Darlene's blue eyes blazed with fury. "The lawyer stole the money for himself. We never saw a penny of it."

"There's recourse you can take for that, you know. When lawyers turn out to be crooks."

"What kind of recourse?"

"People can complain to the licensing authority for attorneys. Here in Massachusetts, it's called the Board of Bar Overseers—the BBO."

"And then what?"

"The BBO can take away a lawyer's license to practice law. Put him out of business."

"Still doesn't get the money back, though, does it?"

"No," Joy conceded. "You're right there."

"As you can see, I don't have much respect for lawyers."

"With good reason."

"So, who is this hotshot lawyer you're so keen on?"

Joy smirked. "I'm glad you've dropped the excessive politeness. It was wearing on me."

Darlene tilted her head back to appraise Joy. "I've just been trying to be properly respectful toward a person older than myself. I never meant to be fake. I'm sorry if it seemed that way."

"Not fake, certainly not. Just entirely too cautious."

"Considering my family's history, it's not unreasonable to be cautious." Darlene looked down at David, still nursing. "However, I will never be too cautious when it comes to protecting him."

"Most admirable."

"Thanks. Okay, then. Who's this lawyer? He better be honest."

"She, not he."

"Huh." Darlene uncrossed her legs. She gave another swift glance at the windows around the room. The shaft of sunlight had moved to a corner where a profusion of begonias gleamed on the windowsill.

David unlatched himself from her breast and began to babble to himself.

"This lawyer's the one who protected the Jaston family from Mickey Quinn and his cronies, the ones who wanted to take Jaston Farm and turn it into a gambling casino—Anna Ebert, remember? It was in the newspaper constantly."

"Newspapers aren't my thing."

"You remember, surely."

"Yeah, I do." Darlene grinned. "Quinn was mighty exercised about 'that lady lawyer,' as he called her. Sometimes she was 'that lawyer bitch,' depending on how his day was going."

She chuckled. She held David upright and patted his back till he gave a resounding burp. "Attaboy," she said, kissing the top of his head.

"Anna did a fine job against Quinn," the elderly woman said.

"She paid a price, people say. Quinn sent some people after her. They trashed her office, I heard."

"Figures. Where'd you hear that?"

"Around. That's the thing, see?"

"What?"

"Quinn is tracking *me* now. He's determined to snatch David away from me." Darlene began to quiver again. "I'll never let that happen—even if I have to *kill* the creep! I'll claim it was self-defense. That could get me off."

"Please don't talk that way!"

"I mean it."

"There are other ways. The Jastons found one. Anna Ebert helped them devise a very effective strategy."

The two women sat, looking at one another, each waiting for the other to break the silence. The only sounds in the room were David's cooing and the ticking of the grandfather clock against the far wall.

At last, Darlene said, "Okay, I'll meet her. But only if you come with me."

"I'll call her office right now to make an appointment."

Joy picked up the phone. Darlene nuzzled David's head with its layer of blond baby hair as she waited and listened.

"Yes. Tomorrow at ten a.m. We'll be there." Joy put down the phone and smiled.

Darlene stopped trembling for the first time since she had come home from the supermarket. She felt a surge of hope.

With that, she lifted her teacup. The tea was utterly cold, but she didn't care.

Tomorrow she was going to the same lawyer the Jastons had used, with great success. Tomorrow, she would begin to fight back.

CHAPTER 36

Darlene and Joy sat in the lawyer's office the next morning at precisely 10:00 am. The office was situated above an antiques store on the Town Common. Because the building was more than a hundred years old, there was no elevator for its three floors. At least Anna Ebert's office was on the second floor, and not the third. Joy had climbed the stairs laboriously, utilizing her silver-handled cane and clinging to the railing with her other hand. Darlene had slowly followed, keeping an eye on her in case of a slip. Darlene was carrying David, and had found the slow pace tedious. She was jumping-out-of-her-skin-anxious to get there.

Finally, they were settled in two high-backed armchairs that faced an enormous wooden desk. Darlene perched forward on hers, David on her lap. He gurgled in appreciation.

Darlene studied the petite woman seated behind the huge desk.

Anna Ebert was well-dressed in a summer suit, and her glossy black hair fell to her shoulders. Her green eyes stared back at Darlene with obvious interest.

"Still no elevator," said Joy. "How are we old folks supposed to come and see you? I barely made it."

"I make house calls when necessary," the lawyer said, with a wink.

"I know. It's just that my young friend here needed to see you in your element."

"Oh?"

"Let's just say she needed to see that you're a regular person, with a regular office. You're not a pompous ass, like so many other lawyers we've had the misfortune to meet."

Anna Ebert laughed heartily. "I can always count on you, Ms. Green, to tell it like it is!"

Anna stood up and came around the desk, holding out her hand to Darlene.

"I pride myself on being an attorney for ordinary folks," she said, shaking Darlene's hand.

"I'm Darlene Bundt. And this is my son, David Bundt. He's the reason we're here."

"Good. Please tell me about your situation."

Darlene decided to not skirt the truth.

"David is my son, with Mickey Quinn."

Darlene held still, watching the attorney absorb this fact.

Anna Ebert was tried to hide her distaste..

"Yep," said Darlene, trying hard to remain nonchalant. "*That* Mickey Quinn."

Anna Ebert smoothed the skirt of her suit with open hands. She carefully kept her voice even.

"I notice that David has your last name, rather than Quinn's."

"Of course." Darlene took a deep breath, paused. "David is the result of a rape."

165

The attorney remained carefully expressionless.

Darlene's jaw clenched. She felt herself getting enraged all over again. "Quinn *raped* me. Why would I give my child his last name?" Her voice had gotten progressively louder.

"Yes, that's totally valid. How did you manage that?"

"I simply announced David's name to the nurse, when she wrote up his birth certificate."

Anna Ebert raised her brows. "And where was Quinn in all this?"

"Nowhere to be found. The person who helped me is Ms. Green's nephew, Nathan Green. We used to live across the hall from each other at my old apartment building. Now I'm Ms. Green's housekeeper and companion. She highly recommended you, by the way. That's the only reason I'm here."

Anna Ebert looked over at the elderly lady, whose hands were resting atop the head of the silver-handled cane.

"Thanks, Ms. Green. You've always been such a help, recommending clients, especially back when I was just starting my law practice."

"So, do you want to hear the rest of my story?" Darlene lifted her chin.

"Of course. Please go on."

"Yesterday, Quinn and his goon approached me in the parking lot, at the grocery store." Darlene heard her voice start to get shrill. She tried to calm down, but to no avail. "They tried to take David from me, in broad daylight!"

Anna Ebert, standing in front of her enormous desk, leaned forward. She stared directly at Darlene and said, "Do you have any witnesses?"

Darlene tried to control the quiver in her voice. "No."

"How do you know that they intended to take David from you?" Anna Ebert crossed her arms and sighed deeply. "I mean, I know what Quinn is capable of—believe me. But it's still necessary to have proof."

"How do I know his intentions? Cause I've watched him get what he wants, again and again. And he sent someone to tail me. Don't know if I'm still being tailed; I hope not. But it's made me afraid to go anywhere, including my grandma's nursing home.

"Did anyone else see the two men?"

"I don't think so. I ran back toward the store, screaming for help, but no one came."

Anna sighed. "And then what happened?"

"When I finally dared to turn around to look, the men were gone. Like I'd just imagined the whole thing."

All three women were silent. David began to gurgle and pump his legs against Darlene. She rubbed his back to soothe him.

"Pardon me if I question you in a tough way," said the attorney. "I need to see if there's any weaknesses or loopholes in your story."

"Okay."

"How do you know it was Quinn's *intent* to take David? Maybe he was just curious, and wanted to meet his son." Anna Ebert leaned forward as she posed the question. "Could that be it?"

"It was *way* more than just curiosity," said Darlene.

"How do you know that?"

"Because a while ago, Quinn sent his creepy lawyer to my apartment. It was right after Clarisse Quinn's funeral—remember her funeral, poor thing?—and I was still pregnant. Anyway, he showed up at my apartment to threaten me. He told me Quinn was gonna take my child for himself."

Anna Ebert's green eyes sharpened as she focused on David.

"That would've been Quinn's buddy, Tobias Meachum." Anna said. She began pacing the room in front of her desk. "I'm actually surprised that Quinn would be so bold as to plan a kidnapping that far in advance." She grimaced. "Well, maybe not."

David began flapping his arms in the air and babbling.

"Can't imagine ripping your son away from you at this age, but then, Quinn's generally pretty out of control." She continued her pacing. "Do you have proof that Meachum visited you at your apartment that day?"

Darlene discreetly unbuttoned her blouse and began to nurse David. "Not really. No one else was there."

"Hungry little guy, isn't he?" said Joy.

"No neighbors saw anything?"

"I don't think so. My landlady let him in, for some unknown reason. But I couldn't depend on her to be a witness for my side."

"Why would Quinn get the idea that he's entitled to custody of this child? Does he have any other children—or any experience with kids?"

"No," said Darlene.

"So where'd he get the idea?"

Darlene's memory of Quinn's musty office suddenly kicked in. She could almost smell the layers of dust, see the dim, yellow glow of the lamp on his cluttered desk. As she remembered, she felt gut-sick. Terror-stricken.

"I'm a fool," she whispered.

She remembered standing in the doorway, his eyes on her. His voice was gentle, promising he would give her all the money she'd ever need. All she needed to do was carry this child all the way to birth, and all would be well. She had somehow been convinced in that moment . . .

"It's all my fault," said Darlene, her voice barely audible. "I'm a damn fool."

CHAPTER 37

"What's that?" Joy said, leaning closer. "I didn't hear you."

"I said I'm a fool!" Tears were welling up in her eyes. They overflowed and ran down her cheeks. She swiped at them, and at her runny nose.

"Maybe so, maybe not," said Anna Ebert in a soothing voice. "Let's hear what you did first."

"When I first found out I was pregnant, I was gonna have an abortion, being unmarried and all. But then Quinn convinced me—begged me, actually—to keep the child." She sighed. "He had tears in his eyes, if you can believe it, big, tough guy like him, getting all weepy. I was surprised, for sure. But, eventually, it was my grandma who convinced me to keep my child. She'd had a portentous dream about my baby, which turned out to be David, wonderful David."

Darlene swiped at her nose again. "Can I have a tissue?"

Anna grabbed a nearby tissue box and handed it to Darlene, waiting while she blew her nose and wiped her eyes.

"So?"

"Quinn told me he'd sign an agreement promising to make payments to me if I kept the child. We both signed it. I've got a copy of it somewhere."

Anna Ebert's eyes sharpened. "We're going to need to take a look at that document."

"Okay. It's back at the house. I'll have to find it."

"We need to see if it grants any custody rights to Quinn as the father, in exchange for that promised support."

"See?" Darlene's voice had gone shrill again. "I *told* you I was a fool! I probably signed away all my rights as David's mother, when I didn't even realize what I was doing. I'm an idiot!"

"It may not be as bad as you think," said Anna Ebert. Her hands were clasped together prayerfully. "We'll see. I'll do everything in my power to keep you and David together. That is, if you'd like me to be your lawyer."

"Yes, please," said Darlene. "Only I can't pay you—"

"That's why I'm here," said Joy, cutting in. "Darlene is my employee, a very good one, and David is my nephew's godson. So it's 'all in the family,' as they say. I can pay a modest retainer, Ms. Ebert, and I ask you to proceed accordingly."

"I certainly won't turn away a paying client with a worthy cause."

"Thank you very much—both of you," said Darlene.

"Come back tomorrow with that document in hand. We'll look it over together, and go from there. In the meantime, you should be extra vigilant. That Mickey Quinn is a bad apple."

"I feel good knowing you're helping me. You certainly did a great job on the Jaston Farm case. Heard you whipped Quinn's butt in court."

"I can't take the credit for the great work of others. Including the crucial testimony of Clarisse Quinn. A very brave woman. She's the one who cracked the case wide open." Anna Ebert's mouth closed in a somber line. "May she rest in peace."

"Yes," said Darlene. She patted David on the back till he gave a slight belch. She peered over his head at Anna Ebert. "You seem to have a real heart." She raised her chin. "Never thought I'd meet a lawyer with one." She gave Anna a genuine smile, then stood up to leave. She helped Joy as she rose from her armchair, clutching her cane.

"Thanks again, both of you," said Darlene. "You've eased my fears some. We'll be back tomorrow."

Anna Ebert smiled and reached out to caress David's soft arm.

"I look forward to moving ahead with this case. In the meantime, look out for Quinn and his henchmen. Can't let anything happen to this sweet little guy."

CHAPTER 38

Darlene went to the cellar stairs and switched on the light. The bare lightbulb shone yellowish over the steep and narrow stairs. She gripped the railing firmly as she descended. The cellar corners were dark. Circles of light shone on the rows of steel shelves, piled high with boxes, wooden furniture, and mysteriously wrapped items. She was curious, but had no time to go exploring. The few boxes containing her papers were on the end of the nearest shelf.

Darlene tended to avoid paperwork whenever possible. She preferred work that required immediate action, rather than contemplation. Bartending had been her style; it just called for the immediate fulfillment of the customer's order. She only needed to know the correct drink recipe, and she could make it "sing." This usually meant using a heavy hand when pouring the spirits. She smiled. Quinn had berated her for being too liberal, said it was hurting his bottom line.

But she knew the customers liked her generosity, and kept coming back because of it.

She snorted at the memory of Quinn. What did he know about his customers? He was either in his back office, or sitting in the corner booth with his cronies.

She continued to sort through the sheaves of papers that she should've organized long ago, or simply thrown out. She hoped against hope that she hadn't signed a foolhardy agreement that was not in her favor. Knowing Quinn, however, it's likely it would be heavily in his favor. Tobias Meachum surely had made certain of that, since he was the one who'd written it up.

If only she could find the damn thing.

Ahh, here it was. Of course. He had presented it to her in a fancy folder, as if that made it more official. More palatable. More legit.

She opened it up, holding her breath. Maybe it wouldn't be as bad as she feared.

She scanned the document quickly. It did say that Quinn would provide "adequate financial support." That seemed good, she told herself. But as she read further down the paragraph, she noticed that it failed to state an actual dollar amount. Hmmm, not so good. She should've read this closer, back then, when she signed it.

She read further. Custody rights will be decided by the Massachu-setts Family Court, she saw. Oh, no. She felt her stomach drop. She and David would come under the scrutiny of a local judge. Quinn knew all of the judges personally. Justice would be dead and gone before she even showed up to the courthouse.

Why had she been so careless? So lacking when it came to pro-tecting her own interests, and David's?

What's done is done, she told herself. You were thinking of other things, like Grandma's health, and how you were going to be able to take care of her, and a baby. You weren't thinking clearly. That's the problem with jerks like Quinn; they were always three steps ahead, with their schemes. *Hopefully, Anna Ebert can rescue me from my own stupidity and naiveté.*

Darlene closed the folder. She couldn't look at anymore right now.

Scooping up all the other papers, she stuffed them back into the heavy cardboard box. The remainder of her papers could rot there, for all she cared.

She stood up and went upstairs, carrying the folder. Her chest felt heavy. If anything came between her and her David, her heart would break.

Please, please, dear Lord, let me keep me son. Let Anna Ebert succeed in helping me. *Nobody is taking David from me!*

CHAPTER 39

Today would be a good day to visit Beacon House, thought Mickey Quinn. The sun was shining, and he was feeling optimistic. He would shower and wear a suit, as befitting a member of the board of trustees—not to mention one of their best private donors.

Two hours later, Quinn drove over to a remote section of Longbottom that was sparsely settled. Beacon House was known in the area as a women's shelter that housed both women and their children who were on the run from abusive situations. Being on the board made him look good, and he burnished his public image whenever possible. He knew his public image was tattered now, but he'd behave as if everything was perfectly fine.

He parked alongside the road, about an eighth of a mile away. He'd walk.

Quinn set a leisurely pace; he didn't want to work up a sweat in his fine garb. There were no sidewalks in this part of town, so he had to step carefully. As he walked, he inhaled the sweet smell of rough, un-mowed fields and the sharp scent of pine trees. The weeds along the road grew waist-high.

As he approached the front steps of Beacon House, he took a moment to straighten his jacket and tie. He ascended the steps and rang the bell. He waved toward the camera that was aimed at him, sporting a jaunty smile. A buzzer sounded and he was let inside.

"Hello, Judy. How're you doing? How're things going around here?" Quinn kept his voice casual.

"Oh, hi, Mr. Quinn." Judy blinked rapidly. "Things are fine. Hope everything is all right with you, sir." She licked her lips.

"They are." Quinn smiled blandly, kept his voice light. "Bit of confusion lately, but things are working themselves out."

"I'm glad." Judy paused for a moment, her head bent discreetly over her paperwork, then looked up again. "Any reason you're paying us a visit today?"

"Nah—-no reason in particular. Just wanted to make sure everything is running smoothly. Thought I'd say hello to Martha, if she's around."

"Sure, she's still a resident here. I'll see if she's in the general hall. Or she might be on kitchen duty now, I'll check." Judy reached for her intercom and spoke. A reply crackled back. "She's on her way from the kitchen."

"Thanks."

Quinn took a seat in the front hall. Judy stayed at the front desk for another minute, then disappeared down a short hallway, into another office.

Martha appeared in the front hall after a long moment.

"Mickey! Long time no see!" she cried out.

"Yeah, it's been a while." Quinn stood up, and took her elbow. "Let's go chat in the garden for a bit, shall we?"

Martha shook her mane of gray-brown hair delightedly. "Let's go," she agreed, in a hoarse whisper.

"Heard your real voice there for a moment, Martha. Now you're back to whispering mode. What gives?"

"You know my story. My voice don't last for long, ever since my ex strangled me. He damaged my voice box," she whispered.

"Awful thing he did, with you being an up-and-coming singer 'n' all."

Martha didn't answer.

They walked to the back garden. Martha stepped onto the flagstone walk and shuffled along till they reached an iron bench.

"What can I do for my brave friend and protector?" asked Martha softly.

"You know, I didn't do all that much . . ."

"You pulled him offa me just when he was ready to strangle me dead out in your parking lot."

"Good thing I had cameras, so I could get out there in time." He chuckled.

"You saved my life, Mickey."

"All in a day's work. . . . Anyway, I'm here to ask for a favor."

"Anything."

"You remember my bartender, Darlene. She usta serve drinks to you and your ex, when you two still came around together in the old days. Well, it's kinda complicated, but the long and short of it is, I got her pregnant, and . . . well . . . you see, I *really* want my kid. He's my legacy. You know I've had a tough life. Successful, sure, but tough. I really want to raise my kid, and Darlene's not willing to share him with me. I really need to talk to Darlene and work out some kind of agreement with her, but she won't even see me, let alone talk it over with me. If Darlene ever shows up at Beacon House, will you let me know?"

"Sure," whispered Martha.

"Here's my card. It has my cell number on it."

177

Martha stuck the card in her bra.

"Call me anytime, day or night."

"On it!" whispered Martha.

———

"I don't know what to think about Mickey Quinn showing up here out of the blue like this," said Judy.

She and Gladie, the two front-desk people, were seated in the administrative office of Beacon House. "I'm afraid I don't trust him, ever since he killed his wife. Even if he's still on our board of trustees, *and* a big donor." She wrung her hands. "My radar is up. What about you?"

"Yeah," said Gladie. "The 'Curse of Quinn' is upon us—I can smell it."

CHAPTER 40

Another ten a.m. session in Anna Ebert's office. Joy and Darlene sat in their high-backed chairs in front of the enormous wooden desk, David in Darlene's lap. Behind the desk, Anna Ebert sat hunched over the document. As she read it, her scowls deepened. Everyone was silent, even David, as they watched her read. The grimmer her expression got, the more heartsick Darlene felt. Her stomach clenched as David's feet kneaded her legs. His toes felt sharp, like they could leave bruises on her thighs.

"Quinn didn't do you any favors, that's for sure."

"How bad is it?"

"Pretty bad. Or rather, pretty restrictive."

"What do you mean?"

"Well, for one thing, this agreement restricts you from taking David with you, if you were ever to move out of state. For you to 'retain custody' of David, you have to stay in Massachusetts. So much for taking a job elsewhere."

"I don't consider that a big deal, actually. My grandma is in a nursing home here, and I want to be near her. Plus, I'm not qualified for many things, so I don't really need to go out of state for a job."

"The second thing is, this agreement talks about 'competence,' " said Anna Ebert. "Quinn's side says he'll get permanent custody if you are ever proved incompetent. Incompetence can mean a lot of things. Physical, mental. On what kind of grounds would he try to go after you?"

Darlene hesitated. She didn't want her dirty laundry aired in front of Joy Green. She tossed back her long blonde hair as she considered the matter. The silence was broken by David's burbling against her neck.

She sighed. "Well, in the past—not now, not anymore—I used to smoke marijuana. It was already legal by then, with the voters' referendum, so I wasn't breaking the law. I was just being a little wild, I guess."

Joy's eyes were fastened on Darlene. It was impossible to know what she was thinking.

Will this cause her to fire me? wondered Darlene.

"Does he have proof that you continued to smoke marijuana, once you were pregnant?" asked Anna Ebert. "Or that you smoke it now, in the vicinity of your baby?"

"Of course not!" exclaimed Darlene. "I stopped cold when I found out I was pregnant! And I haven't smoked *any* since David was born."

Darlene squirmed in her seat; David started to whine in her arms.

"Oh, hush, sweetie. Mommy's got to talk to these people."

"I'm not judging you," said Anna Ebert, smiling gently. "That's not me, first of all. We're all human."

She leaned forward, peering into Darlene's face.

"A client's lawyer works *with* the client, from wherever the client is coming from. I don't want you to get the wrong idea about me, or about lawyers in general, despite your family's bad experience. Ms. Green explained your prior hesitation about lawyers."

The clock on the wall ticked loudly. Attorney Ebert folded her hands as she waited.

Darlene blinked. Did she want to have all of this come out in a nasty custody fight?

Who the hell did Quinn think he was, questioning her competence, her morals, as a mother? She ought to be questioning *his* instead. *How dare he?* She had been staring at the floor blindly, while caressing David's wispy blond hair on the crown of his head.

"It's just that if you *had* smoked marijuana during pregnancy, it could be argued that you endangered David's health."

"But I didn't!"

"And if you smoke it around your young child, they could make the same argument."

"But I haven't!"

"What proof do you have of both of those assertions? In case we need to defend you on those matters?"

"I'll take a blood test—and I'll come up clean! I haven't smoked weed since the day I discovered I was pregnant. And now I nurse him, so you could test David, too, actually. And Nathan Green is a witness that I didn't smoke while I was pregnant, or afterwards, and Ms. Joy Green, here, is too!"

"That sounds good for now. I'm just trying to anticipate things."

"Okay." Darlene shot a look at Anna Ebert. Did she trust this lawyer? She wasn't sure yet.

"Then there's the third item."

"There's more?"

"I'm afraid so. This says that if you ever marry, your husband is prohibited from ever adopting this child."

"Can Quinn even do that? Legally, I mean?"

"I'm not sure. I haven't encountered such a thing before in my practice. It strikes me as fundamentally unfair, reaching into the future like that, and thus, probably unlawful. I will have to research the issue."

Darlene sighed again. "That'll end up making this case expensive." She swiveled to look at Joy, who sat hunched over her cane. "Are you still on board with paying my legal fees?"

"Oh, yes."

"You sure?"

"Keep asking and you might talk me out of it."

Darlene shrugged and looked at Anna Ebert. "I guess it's a go."

"What choice do you have, dear?" asked Joy.

CHAPTER 41

"Why are you willing to pay my legal expenses? There must be something more to it than just the fact that Nathan is my son's godfather."

Darlene was seated on the brocade couch in the living room. David was in the old wooden cradle that had been retrieved from the cellar. The convenient foot pedal meant that Darlene was able to rock the cradle while seated, hands-free.

"Those old cradles kept many babies happy while their mothers were otherwise occupied," Joy commented.

"Not exactly relevant to my question."

"True."

"So, what about it?"

"Some other time." Joy flapped her hand. "Talking about Mickey Quinn is an unpleasantness I'd rather avoid. I wasn't surprised to hear the awful details of your situation, dear. He's thoroughly rotten."

Darlene continued to stare at Joy, as if she might discern the elderly lady's thoughts. It was midafternoon. They had returned from Anna Ebert's office with a raging hunger. Joy had even rocked David herself as Darlene made sandwiches. Both had devoured the tuna fish sandwiches, along with chips and lemonade.

Joy was noticeably sleepy after lunch, and would've happily dozed off, but for the presence of Darlene and David.

Darlene gave up watching Joy and began looking out the tall windows. After several days of gloom, the sunshine was very welcome. Lately, the weather had been oppressively humid, but today was much more tolerable.

Darlene's eyes fastened on a distant point in the side garden that featured an evergreen hedge. Something was moving in and around the hedge. Maybe someone's dog had gotten loose. On the other hand, it seemed kind of tall for a dog. Perhaps it was a deer. Although deer usually came out at dusk, not midafternoon.

Darlene sat up a smidge and craned her neck. *What was it?*

"So why did you smoke that wacky weed, young lady?"

Darlene swiveled back to face Joy.

"I wondered when you'd bring that up." She sighed. "The truth is, I enjoyed it. I felt it gave me inspiration. But now, David is my inspiration. I'm in a whole new phase of life now."

"Good."

"Are you going to fire me because of it?"

"No."

"Really?"

"Really."

"Huh." Darlene began wringing her hands in her lap. "I don't get you."

"Well, I've got a bunch of reasons to not fire you. First of all, I, too, was once young and wild." Joy smiled wryly. "If you can picture that." She raised her chin. "Second, I don't approve of ill-intentioned

184

men exercising their power over young women and children. That's always been unacceptable." She placed her gnarled hands over her knees. "Lastly, and most importantly, you're doing a good job. That's not something I can ignore. You're not someone to be casually tossed aside." She gazed at Darlene and smiled warmly. "So don't go worrying about being fired."

"Thank you. I mean that. Because I really need this job, with David."

"I know."

"May I ask *you* a personal question?"

"Of course."

"Why is it you never married, a bright, accomplished woman like you?"

Joy shut her eyelids and gave a slight smile. A long moment passed.

"I never found the right person."

"What would he have been like?"

"I needed the right *person*," repeated the elderly lady.

Her thoughts flashing to Nathan Green, Darlene suddenly understood.

"How brave of you, to live your life with honesty and integrity. May I say—you're awesome!"

"Thank you, dear." The elderly lady smiled with satisfaction.

"I have to say, I'm still curious about your connection to Quinn. But maybe I can guess?"

"You probably can. I discovered quite a long time ago that he has no regard for people of other persuasions. He once said some ugly things to my face, in a social situation. It was absolutely unacceptable." She smiled thinly. "By helping you, I'm having a little taste of sweet revenge. Speaking of tastes, if you'd bring me another glass of that lemonade, that would be very fine."

"Will do!"

Back in the kitchen, Darlene took another look at the evergreen hedge where she had seen activity earlier. Was someone or something hiding in the hedge?

She squinted, tried to make out details through the old-time windows. The glass in some of them was warped with ripples, so she couldn't be sure if she was seeing things or not.

Enough with the paranoia, she told herself. Just get the glass of lemonade and be done with it.

CHAPTER 42

Xavier Baccara waited impatiently among the tall weeds. They tickled his cheek and neck as he squatted. He planned to approach the mansion in the late afternoon, when everyone seemed to take a nap, or at least spent some time resting.

If I can score on this job, thought Baccara, *maybe I can get myself a sweet little bungalow. A place I can call my own, no more friggin' landlords.*

He told himself to pay attention.

The sounds emanating from the mansion had subsided. It was helpful that the old lady was too cheap to put in central air-conditioning. A person can hear everything through open windows.

Interesting conversation the two women had just had.

Baccara shook his head. He knew this Quinn was a shady character. He'd wondered whether he should even be doing this job, but he quickly squashed that thought. He had already come this far. And the payoff would be good.

He slowly stood up and crept over to a window with its sash pushed up all the way. Only a summer insect screen stood between him and the inside of the mansion. He pulled out large shears and began to cut a hole in the screen, large enough for him to fit through. He was a short, wiry fellow, and it was easy for him to climb into the side parlor in complete silence.

He stood utterly still, waiting. There were no sounds.

Baccara padded on the carpeted floor in complete silence, swiveling his head in all directions as he moved forward. As he moved deeper into the room, he spotted the infant in a cradle on the floor. The baby appeared to be asleep. The cradle was situated alongside a tall armchair turned away from him. He couldn't see if anyone was in the chair, next to the baby.

He stood stock-still, barely breathing. Finally, he made his move.

As Baccara bent over the cradle, a silver-knobbed cane came crashing down on his head.

He fell sideways with a cry. On his hands and knees now, he tried to stand.

The cane swooshed along the floor, undercutting his footing. Down he went again, this time hitting his head on the corner of an end table.

Baccara stayed down this time, groggy from the second blow to his head.

"Darlene!" screamed Joy. "Help! Come save David!"

Darlene came running into the room, full force. "What is it?"

Joy pointed to the man sprawled on the floor. "He tried to snatch David! I believe you now!"

"What should we do?" asked Darlene. "Besides calling the police?"

David seemed to be untouched, still sleepy. She gazed down at Baccara.

"I think that's the same man who tried to steal David earlier. I better tie him up before he comes to. You have any rope around here?"

"There's rope in the kitchen, in the utility drawer. I'll watch him. If he stirs, I'll smack him again with my cane!"

Darlene grinned. "Good work, Auntie Joy. Didn't know you were such a killer!" Her giggle had a hysterical edge. "Be right back with the rope!"

Baccara groaned from his position on the floor. Joy raised her silver-knobbed cane and held it there, poised.

Darlene rushed back from the kitchen with a coiled length of rope and a steak knife. She unwound a workable length and cut it, careful to place the knife out of the man's reach. She grabbed his hairy arms, pulled together his limp hands, and tied his wrists behind his back, with multiple knots.

Baccara's face was already showing bruises. His nose, flattened against the Oriental rug, was oozing a trickle of blood.

"Time to call the police, Auntie Joy. And you can lower your cane. He can't come after us now." Darlene cut another length of rope. She drew his legs together and tied them at his ankles. "Just in case. You know?"

"You sure have a cool head. Why don't *you* call the police?"

"No, thanks. This is your house. The call should come from you."

Joy reached for the telephone next to her chair and dialed 911.

"Yes. This is the big white house on Main Street, with the portico and carriage house. Yes, ten-oh-eight Main. We've got an intruder here. We're all right. Yes, he's subdued. Yes. Yes, *we* subdued him. But now you need to come and arrest him! Now, please."

Joy placed the receiver back in its cradle. "I guess now we wait." She glanced down at Baccara. "Should we sit him up?"

"Nope," said Darlene. "Let the cops see the scene exactly as it happened."

She plopped down on the nearby couch.

189

David gurgled and waved his arms. Somehow, he hadn't made a peep throughout the whole ordeal.

Nathan's cradle protected him, she thought.

"Thank you, Lord," she whispered.

CHAPTER 43

Officer Mike Muratore and his partner, Shawn DuShane, were sent on the call to 1008 Main Street.

"Don't usually see much happenin' on this side of Longbottom," said Muratore. " 'Less it's a burglary in one of these big houses."

DuShane was annoyed. "Our shift is supposed to be over in an hour. This call means overtime. I had plans for this evening."

"What plans?"

"I was takin' Sally out for dinner. It's her birthday."

"Aww."

"Yeah. I had reservations and everything."

"Maybe we can knock this call off quick."

"Not likely."

The squad car pulled up in front of the mansion and the two officers got out. As they approached the front door, it sprang open.

They were greeted by a thin blonde woman who quickly ushered them inside.

From the foyer, they looked into a huge living room filled with elegant furniture and paintings. The two officers gazed about, curiously, before focusing back on the blonde woman. She was pointing to her left, to a brocade armchair, where an elderly lady sat, holding a silver-knobbed cane. Near her feet was what looked like a twisted bundle of clothing, folded over, with an unruly mop of hair protruding.

"Ma'am," said Muratore, "can you please start from the beginning, and tell us exactly what happened?"

The elderly woman raised her chin in a dignified manner.

"Hello, officers. As you can see, we've apprehended an intruder in my home. We don't know who he is, but we've got him trussed up like a chicken." She chuckled, and caressed her cane with satisfaction.

The two officers glanced at the man lying on the carpet, then at one another, disbelieving.

"Okay," Muratore said. "Let's hear everything."

Joy Green recounted the incident from the beginning, with a certain glee, emphasizing the role that her cane had played.

"Kidnapping is a serious charge, Ms. Green. Are you sure that's what he intended?" said Officer DuShane.

"Yes!" said Darlene, joining the conversation.

"How do you know that?" DuShane took a harder look at Darlene. "Hey—don't I know you? Weren't we at Longbottom High together?" He hesitated. "You were one or two years ahead of me, so you may not remember me." He stopped talking suddenly, aware of the others in the room. "Whose kid is that, did ya say?"

"Mine," said Darlene.

He turned to Joy Green. "Are you the grandmother, then?"

"No. No relation. I'm her employer. She's my housekeeper, and her son lives here with her. A perk of her job."

192

Just then, Baccara groaned. He lifted his head, his face covered in livid bruises.

"Sleeping Beauty just woke up," said Muratore. "Perfect timing."

"Get him on his feet, read him his rights, and get him over to the station. They'll question him there," said DuShane.

"You got it." Muratore bent over to pick up Baccara by his armpits. "Come on, stand up!" He eyed the rope tied around Baccara's wrists and ankles, then shook his head. "You ladies did some job."

DuShane reached inside his jacket and plucked out his cheat sheet. "You have the right to remain silent . . ."

He read the Miranda warning rapidly, in a monotone. When he was done, he tucked the paper in his pocket and turned to face Joy Green.

"I'm sorry this dirtbag broke into your home, scaring you ladies," said DuShane. "We'll take him over to the station and charge him. He won't be bothering you—at least for a while."

"You might wanna get a restraining order," added Muratore. "Or you can go to the DA's office to press charges against him. You gotta do *something*, I'd say."

"Thank you, officers. You've been great," said Joy. "We'll be in touch as needed."

Darlene grimaced, saying nothing. She continued to stand over David in his cradle, waiting till the officers had removed Baccara from the premises. She was a she-wolf, standing guard. She'd *kill* anyone who tried to take David from her.

Darlene turned to Joy. "I need to see Anna Ebert, pronto."

CHAPTER 44

Maureen and Faith sat side by side in the front seat of Robert's pickup truck. Faith's backpack was at her feet. They had sort of talked about what to expect when they arrived at Faith's house, but even so, Faith was quiet, apprehensive.

They rode into Longbottom in silence. Maureen kept her mouth shut. *Sometimes silence is the only way to calm oneself,* she thought. Brave young Faith—going forth to meet her judgmental father—all that old-fashioned judgmental patriarchal shame imposed on young girls who "stray," with a moment's love and generosity to a lonely young boy. Then the resulting shame and judgments laid upon the shy, lonely offspring who know they've been born out of wedlock . . . not really wanted. And worse still, sometimes born into situations of neglect or abuse, situations of no-love and big hurt, hurt turning to hatefulness, hate turning into evil. Heaven forbid!

194

Maureen glanced at Faith, expressionless, staring out the truck window at trees and houses passing by. Who knew what the girl was thinking?

Maureen returned to her unsettling meditations, keeping her hands squarely on the wheel.

"Lord protect us from evil. Amen!" she whispered to herself.

Maureen wondered about Faith's father. She hoped he was a good man. Was he frightened, worried about "what others would say" about him, and his family? Was he concerned enough about conformity that he would cast aside his own family? Was that how conformity turned into the face of evil?

"Our Father, who art in Heaven, hallowed be Thy name," Maureen began to recite under her breath. She turned to Faith. "Do you believe in our Lord? Your name *is* Faith."

"I know. Kind of. I've been trying to live up to my name my whole life."

"Well, my girl, if there was ever a time for faith and prayer, this is it. We must pray that the Lord softens your father's heart. You, and your mother and I, we must remind your father that we are all blood-kin on this Earth, and he should suffer this little child—his grandchild—to come unto the bosom of his family. We are all children of the Lord."

"Thank you," whispered Faith. A solitary tear ran down to her chin.

"So let's go to your family's home with faith and a glad heart!" Maureen said, tapping the steering wheel emphatically.

She realized she'd been preaching at Faith, so she softened her voice. "It's okay to be a little afraid. Your dad's probably a little afraid, too, though he won't admit it." She grinned. "Dare to be brave, Faith. So much of life is just daring to be brave!"

They rounded a corner near the town hall.

"Which house is yours?"

Faith pointed to a small, neat, two-story wooden house. Its clapboards were painted light blue, and the house was embellished with white gingerbread trim and white shutters. Blue irises bloomed at the corners of the driveway.

Maureen pulled into the narrow double driveway, next to an orange Jeep.

"Ready for this?"

"Yep!"

"Lead the way!"

Faith's mother was waiting in the doorway, behind the glass storm door. She waved and her smile beamed. "Welcome home, sweetie!"

Faith approached awkwardly, then hugged her mother. "So good to see you, Mom!"

Faith and her mother walked arm in arm into the house. Faith turned back to look at Maureen. "It's okay, I'm home now. You can go."

Maureen had gotten out of the truck and was standing next to it, her hand on the driver's door handle. "You sure? I think I'd like a word with your father, just to be sure. That okay?"

"Sure," Faith replied, before her mother could make an excuse. "C'mon in and see our house." She turned back, steering her protruding belly around her mother.

"Hi, Dad. Come meet my guardian angel." Faith stood in the center of the living room, belly out.

Mr. Hammond's eyes narrowed. He was a medium-sized fellow with a ruddy complexion and a potbelly above his jeans. He was seated in a nubby armchair with legs outstretched, sneaker soles facing the door.

Maureen strode forward, her right hand outstretched.

"I'm Maureen Jaston. It's nice to meet you, Mr. Hammond. You have a lovely daughter."

They shook hands, and Maureen stepped back.

"Are you related to the Hammonds in town?"

"They're my aunt and uncle."

"Ah." Maureen took deep breath. "I married into the Jaston farming family, so I guess I'm still relatively new to the area. I don't know all the town connections and such. Would those be the Hammonds that were the foster parents for Mickey Quinn?" She blinked, wondering if her question had been out of line.

"Yep." He paused. "That was them." His face was carefully unreadable.

"Ah. I was just wondering."

"Yeah. I've been wondering, too. Like, how my daughter made her way out to your farm." He fidgeted in his chair. "Had me nervous. I kept worrying about whether Quinn's people would leave your place alone, considering the things that went on down there." He made a sour face. "Sure had me regretting shooting off my big mouth." He looked directly at Faith. "I'm sorry I yelled at you, baby doll. You're still my daughter. C'mere!"

He sat up in his chair, stretching out his arms. Faith went over to him and they hugged tightly.

Maureen looked around to see Mrs. Hammond, right at her elbow, clutching her hands to her chest, as if her heart would burst.

"Bless you, Mrs. Jaston! The Lord works in mysterious ways."

"He does indeed! Let's pray he keeps harm away from us all!" Maureen smiled lopsidedly. "I can get a little overdramatic with my prayers sometimes when I get choked up. Seeing them hug like that got to me. I hope you'll all be safe, well, and happy together. And happy. *Be happy!*"

With that, Maureen turned and left, leaving the reconciled family alone. She was so pleased with the day's outcome that she sang all the way home.

CHAPTER 45

"I understand you ladies had quite a day yesterday," said Anna Ebert, her eyebrows raised. "You hardly got home from my office when the proverbial horse manure hit the fan!"

"How did you hear so quick?" asked Darlene.

"I have a police scanner in my office. I only turn it off when I'm meeting with a client, like now. Keeps me apprised of the latest happenings in town, including this latest incident out at Ms. Green's house."

"Huh!" said Darlene, not much liking this information.

"I'll say this, that Mickey Quinn, he wastes no time in going after what he wants."

"He's a rotten egg, that one," said Joy. "Whatever he touches goes bad."

"So what do I do?" cried out Darlene. "How do I live my life like a *normal* person, without looking over my shoulder every minute?"

"Calm down, Darlene," said Anna Ebert. "I know you're feeling frantic and cornered, angry and confused. Ms. Green and I are here to help you find a solution."

"Like what?" Darlene's eyes flitted in all directions, as if looking for an escape.

"First off, let's go down to the DA's office and swear out a complaint against that joker who broke into Ms. Green's house." Anna Ebert stood, indicating she was ready to go.

"Oh, I don't know," said Darlene, twisting her hands into a knot in her lap. She looked down at David, who was mercifully asleep in his portable car seat.

"Why not? You want the guy prosecuted, right?"

"Yeah. I guess."

"Well, then, what's the problem?"

Darlene grimaced. "If the guy works with Quinn, the DA will drop the charges. Or never bring any in the first place. The Quinn I know is able to change the outcome of cases whenever he wants to. He used to brag about it, back at his pub."

Anna Ebert gazed at Darlene. "That's a defeatist attitude I'm not ready to accept, as your attorney."

Darlene remained silent.

Anna Ebert continued. "If you don't press charges, Quinn will know that he can get away with this crap. He'll know that you will fold at the first sign of a struggle, and he'll keep his hands clean. He'll have others do his dirty work for him. Next thing you know, he'll have made off with David for good, never to be seen again."

Darlene remained silent, twisting her hands.

"You need to press charges against this guy, what's-his-name, Baccara, so you can build your case against Quinn."

"How would that work?" asked Darlene.

"You press charges against Baccara for something serious, like attempted kidnapping. Not just a mere break-and-enter. You want the DA to go after him with the big guns, so he gets scared and has to either hire an expensive defense attorney, or get an overworked public defender who is assigned too many cases. Not good, either way, as he'll be on the hook for some serious charges. He'll get scared. When a defendant gets scared, he or she begins to divulge facts about the other people involved, to take some of the heat off themselves. That's when the evidentiary connection will be made to Quinn. You see?"

Darlene tilted her chin. "Suppose this Baccara doesn't spill the beans? Then what?"

"He'd be going to prison for many years. He'll talk." Anna Ebert's green eyes were ablaze.

Darlene was silent once more. David stirred in his car seat.

"You seem pretty confident the DA will charge this guy with something heavy, so we can make a connection to Quinn. But how does that help me keep Quinn away from us?"

"It will give me the basis to get a restraining order against Quinn, which will prohibit him from ever going near you, or, more importantly, David."

"Even if we get one, I've heard they often don't amount to much."

"Well, it's a place to start."

Darlene turned to look at Joy. "What do you think?"

"I think you need some serious help. I'd point out that going to the DA's office doesn't cost us anything. The DA is paid by the taxpayers. Anyway, I don't think you have any other choice."

"Yeah." Darlene sighed. "I guess."

"So, it's a deal?" asked Anna Ebert. "We'll head over to the DA's office tomorrow."

CHAPTER 46

Darlene lay in bed, going over the events of the day.

She and Joy had met Anna Ebert outside the DA's office. They had gathered in an anxious knot under the humid summer sun. Waves of heat shimmered up from the cracked pavement. David revealed his sweaty discomfort by wiggling in his sling.

Anna Ebert started to croon to David, blocking the worst of the sun's rays. She somehow managed to stay looking cool and polished in her summer suit, despite lugging a heavy briefcase.

Darlene had felt anxious going to meet the DA. Was he going to turn out to be a crony of Quinn's? Quinn was cozy with every two-bit politician in and around Longbottom. He knew their names, their spouses' names, their kids' names. His memory was unbelievable.

Darlene felt uncomfortable in the clothes she had chosen to wear, which seemed too casual next to her lawyer's attire. Carrying David in his portable car seat, which seemed to weigh more every day, was making her sweat. She had looked over at Joy, standing next to her. Brave old woman. *Salt of the earth*. All would be well.

They had gone inside, sat in the courthouse hallway on hard, straight-backed wooden benches. Darlene peeked at the other people there. Generally, they seemed a sorry lot. But then, they were all here on account of some sort of trouble.

Eventually, they had been called into a small, windowless room. A table with several chairs around it, and one chair behind, stood against the wall. A stooped young white man with a receding hairline was seated there, alone. His glasses reflected the glare of the fluorescent light. His mouth was neutral, making his expression unreadable.

Joy and Darlene took two seats opposite him, placing David's portable car seat on the floor between them. Anna Ebert had taken the final chair and began opening her briefcase.

"Hi, Bill," said Anna Ebert. "It's been a while."

"Hi, Anna. What can I do for you folks?"

"We're here to request that your office prosecute Xavier Baccara for the charge of attempted kidnapping. Currently, he is only up for assault. That won't do."

"Whoa. Our office decides the charges, and what we will prosecute."

"I know that's the purview of your office," Anna Ebert had said. "But we've got a unique situation here. Let me explain." She had gone through the litany of facts about Baccara, and how he was a henchman of Mickey Quinn's.

Darlene had been watching the young assistant DA's face for the slightest indication of interest or distaste. She was unable to tell what he was thinking. The fluorescent light reflected against his glasses, obscuring his eyes. His mouth was set in an even line that never wavered.

Man, this guy has perfected his stone-face, she had thought. *No telling which way he'll go.*

202

After Anna Ebert had finished, Joy Green had recounted how the accused had been subdued in her home, making sure that the DA knew she lived on the expensive side of town. She took particular relish in describing the role of her silver-topped cane, which she had conveniently brought along to illustrate her story.

The stooped young man dropped his pen when he was done listening.

"It sounds like you have a point. I'll discuss it with my boss." He pursed his lips. "We'll let you know if we need you as witnesses for the prosecution."

"Thanks, Bill," Anna Ebert had said as she stood up. "Come on, everyone." She held the door open for them to file out.

Once they were back in the parking lot, standing next to their cars, Anna Ebert had said, "I went to law school with Bill Laird. He's a straight shooter. I'm confident he'll do whatever he can to move the case along in the proper manner. We're still going to go for a restraining order."

Remembering her words, Darlene was finally able to relax enough to go to sleep.

———

As she slept, Darlene dreamed that her husband was a gentle, strong, green-faced man, with green hands and fingers, who worked as a gardener. His sleeves, rolled up to his elbows, revealed his sinewy green arms, and his green-trunk neck rose out of his collar. His green face beamed goodwill, and when he smiled, his teeth gleamed like pearls. When he spoke, his voice resounded like a trumpet. Although she couldn't make out what he was saying, the sounds were rounded and wild.

"Tell me again," she cried out.

"Hallelujah!" blared his trumpet voice.

Darlene was asking "What?"
"There will be justice for all!"
"How?"
"It is decreed in Our Lord's heaven. Amen."
"Amen," she had whispered in her dream.
She suddenly woke up. *If only my dream could come true*, she thought.
It took her a long time to go back to sleep.

CHAPTER 47

Darlene woke to the sound of raindrops falling softly on the roof. Sounded like it would be a long, slow, lazy-rain kind of day. The breeze coming in her open window was moist and cooling, a welcome reprieve. She recalled her unusual dream from the previous night. It created a sudden urge within her, to go and see her grandmother.

It was funny, how she often got a sudden urge to visit Luella. When she did, it always turned out that her grandma had been thinking about her, "summoning her up," so to speak. It was odd that she'd summoned her on a rainy day, since she so relished their walks on the grounds of the nursing home. There could be no outing today, Darlene figured.

She dressed herself and David quickly. He was still sleepy, and mumbled through nursing.

She carried David down to the kitchen, placing his portable car seat up on the counter, so she could feed him some baby cereal.

She made herself a cup of tea and poured a bowl of Cheerios. As she chewed, she pondered last night's dream.

"I don't even have a husband," she murmured, her back to the kitchen entrance.

"That's true, you don't," said Nathan Green as he entered the room. "I suppose I could oblige if I had to, as a marriage of convenience. Might be *very* convenient, actually."

Darlene twirled around on her chair. "Hey! What are *you* doin' here?" Her grin brightened her face to a rosy color, and her blue eyes shone.

"Just stopping by, checking on my two favorite ladies. Gotta make sure everybody is okay after the last few days." He reached up to place a hand on the doorjamb. "How are you, really?"

Darlene's grin abruptly vanished.

"It's been pretty hectic." Darlene crossed her arms. "First, the parking lot incident, then the attempted kidnapping here. The lawyer's office, the DA's office. I could use a little rest for my nerves! But I don't dare let down my guard." Her face crumpled. A single tear slid down her cheek. She swiped at it, angrily.

"C'mere, sweet thing. You've been through the wringer." Nathan held his long arms open.

She slid on stocking feet across the tile floor, letting his long arms engulf her, finding solace in her friend's arms.

"Nathan, you're the absolute best. Why couldn't you be straight, so I could marry you? I would love to find a man like you to be my partner." She hugged him vigorously. She began to mumble. "I dreamt of my fantasy man last night. Turned out he had green skin and strong arms. I guess I'll never meet my fantasy man, though. Too good to be true. Even if he is green."

"Heck, my last name is Green." He chuckled. "Doesn't that count for something?"

"Of course it does. You're just not *my* kind of green man." She sniffled.

206

"Just so those green men don't arrive on spaceships wearing weird helmets."

"I knew I shouldn't have told you about it. Never mind . . ."

"Listen, pumpkin," Nathan's voice was no longer amused. "I'm actually here to try to help you in advance of what might be coming."

"Like what?"

"In case you need to make a run for it, considering all of these attempts to grab David."

"Where would we even go—back to your apartment?"

"No. Beacon House."

"They take women with kids, right?"

"Of course."

Darlene withdrew from his embrace. "So things have come to that, have they?"

"Probably."

Darlene stood to one side and re-crossed her arms. "I suppose I better start packing stuff for David and me."

"Just what you can fit into a suitcase."

She eyed him, questions rising. "How do you know so much about this?"

"I'm the school guidance counselor, remember? The kids who get kicked out by their parents, or want to leave their foster homes, those kids come to me, and I find them places to stay. And of course, pregnant girls who are about to deliver . . ."

They both chuckled, remembering David's birth.

"I guess you've got some experience with that!"

"Listen, Nathan. It's really good that you stopped by. Turns out I need to see my grandmother today. I was hoping you could take me and David. I'm kinda nervous to go anywhere by myself."

"Does it have to be today? Can't you just lay low for a bit?"

"I really can't. I have this uncanny urge to see her, and when I get an urge like this, there's usually a good reason."

"Okay, I'll take you. But my little purple Toyota is hardly inconspicuous."
"Yeah. But the fact that I'm with a guy might put them off."
"Consider it done."

CHAPTER 48

The streets of Longbottom were moderately busy for a Thursday afternoon. Nathan drove with great care, checking his rearview mirror frequently to see if they were being followed. Darlene sat in the backseat with David. In an effort to instill calm, Nathan had turned on a satellite radio station that played all blues.

A purple car that carries all our burdensome blues, Darlene thought.

She gazed at the mom-and-pop stores that lined their route. So many nail salons. She had never had her nails done, despite her hands being on display as a bartender. She had always emphasized her straight blonde hair, her clear complexion, and her startlingly blue eyes.

"Let me know when we get near your grandma's place, okay?"

"Will do."

Darlene looked over at David in his car seat. He was angled so that he looked up toward the treetops and the sky. His eyes were round and watching intently.

She'd lost count of the number of auto repair shops and used-car dealerships. Sprinkled in between were tiny bars, pizza shops, and small, ethnic grocery stores.

"We're getting close. You wanna take a left at the light."

Nathan drove into the nursing home parking lot and parked his car opposite the main entrance. They emerged into the heat that radiated off the asphalt.

"I'll hang out in the main foyer while you and David have your visit," said Nathan.

"No! Come with us. At least for the beginning of the visit. Grandma has heard all about you, and how you helped me when David was born. She'd love to meet you!"

"If you say so." Nathan gave a half-smile.

They walked into the foyer and signed the guest book. Darlene gave a small wave to the other nursing home residents, most of whom were in wheelchairs. She could almost feel the residents envying David's innocent babyhood.

"Give a wave to everyone, son," she said, moving his arm up and down.

They walked to the nurses' station.

"Hello, everybody," said Darlene. "We're here to see Luella. This is my friend, Nathan."

"Welcome," said one nurse, reaching for the phone.

They went down another wide hall lined with medical supplies. Halfway along, Darlene darted into a room and called out, "Grandma! I brought someone for you to meet."

Luella lifted her head from her pillow to peer around the curtain that circled her bed. Her white hair was tousled and her nightgown was partially twisted around her torso. But her eyes were alert and curious. "Who's here?"

Darlene pointed to the tall man who stood behind her.

"This is Nathan Green. I told you about him. He's the one who helped me when David was born, and then he helped me get the job at his aunt's place. My dear friend, and guardian angel!"

"Of course! Your guardian angel *would* be disguised as your next-door neighbor." Luella lifted her hand to shake his. "Be not forgetful to entertain strangers, for thereby some have entertained angels unawares. Hebrews 13:2."

Darlene flicked her eyes at Nathan. "Grandma knows her Bible verses, for sure."

Nathan took her hand in his and bent to plant a kiss on her curled fingers.

Luella smiled. "Darlene and I cannot thank you enough for all that you've done for her and for our little David." Her eyes met his. "You are our angel, and our hero. Thank you."

Nathan withdrew his hand and smiled gently. "You're welcome. Your granddaughter is my dear friend. That's how real friends treat each other."

"And you'll be David's godfather, I hear. If we ever get around to a proper ceremony. Once that happens, you'll officially be family." She shrugged. "But who knows when we'll get to that."

"A privilege I look forward to."

"A gentleman too, I see," said Luella. "It's such a pleasure to meet you. Now, if I may, I'd like a word with my granddaughter, please."

"Of course. I'll wait in the foyer." Nathan withdrew behind the curtain, and walked out.

Darlene watched him turn into the hallway, then resumed their conversation.

"I had a sudden urge to see you this morning, Grandma. That usually means something's up." She bent to give her grandmother a big kiss on the cheek.

211

Luella smiled, delighted. Her bright eyes gleamed at Darlene from behind her tousled hair. "That's my girl." She reached for David. Darlene lowered him onto the bed.

David began crawling over Luella's legs, which were angled under the sheets. They both watched as he discovered the bed controller, and waited to see if he'd push any buttons. He lost interest, and began to crawl into Grandma Luella's waiting arms. She kissed him over and over.

"I've waited so long for the next generation of our family to come along. Warms my heart."

David squirmed away from her, raised his arms to Darlene. She picked him up, and placed him on her left hip.

"Sorry about that, Grandma. Guess he doesn't know you very well yet."

"Nonsense. Perfectly normal."

In silence, they both looked out the large picture window alongside her hospital bed. The morning rain had ended and cheerful sunshine was drying everything outdoors. Together, they watched a hawk circle and glide in the deep turquoise summer sky. When it passed out of sight, they turned back to one another.

"So, Darlene, tell me what's been happening with you and David. Then I'll tell you what's happening on my end."

Darlene eyed her grandmother for a long moment. "Okay. I'm good—so far, I guess. Although I've had a coupla close calls, lately. Can I be honest? It's been *terrifying*, actually. Some guy tried to snatch David in a grocery-store parking lot. Luckily, we got away, 'cause I screamed like a banshee. Then a guy broke into Ms. Green's place." She snorted. "Would ya believe that feisty old lady knocked him out cold with her cane? She's tough! Then I tied him up till the cops came and took him away. We think Quinn's behind it. In fact, I'm probably headed to a women's shelter with David, so we can be safe."

She paused, met her grandmother's eyes.

212

"Heavens, child!" Luella was astonished. Her hands fluttered in her lap. "Here you are, having to deal with that Quinn, scrapping and wrangling over your son. Now you have to hide away with David in a shelter. What will become of you both, with all this craziness?"

"I don't know, Grandma. All I know is, I can't let Quinn win. David is mine."

"How're you gonna outrun him? He and his people are everywhere."

"I've got help. Nathan is going to take me to Beacon House. And I have my lawyer to help me, too."

She looked at her grandmother again.

"You're probably wondering how I can afford one." Darlene pursed her lips. "Ms. Green offered to pay the lawyer's fees for me. I know how you feel about lawyers, Grandma, and believe me, I've felt the same way—although I think Anna Ebert is different."

Luella was silent, listening carefully.

"I don't know—am I being a damn fool to accept her offer, do ya think? Are they just using me, to somehow get back at Quinn?"

Darlene looked at Luella again.

"Whaddya think, Grandma?"

"Never mind their motive. You need serious help if Quinn is trying to snatch David away from you. Just accept their help and say a big 'thank you'!"

"You're probably right. Nathan knows about Beacon House 'cause he's a school counselor."

"That's good."

"My lawyer Anna Ebert is the one who's been helping the Jastons save their dairy farm from the developers. You remember that court case, and the Town Meeting attempt to rezone their land? It was in the papers."

"Hmph! Well, if there's *any* lawyer I'd trust, I'd trust that young woman. She seemed honest with the Jastons, and she's certainly a fighter."

213

Luella leaned back against her pillows and sighed. A noise in the hallway made them both turn toward the door. A nursing home patient, arm in arm with his younger visitor, shuffled down the hallway, heading toward the nursing station. Their shoes squeaked in unison on the linoleum floor.

Luella lowered her voice a notch, even though her roommate wasn't there. "You know I have trouble sleeping." She stretched her neck against the pillows. "But that's hardly news."

"Hardly."

"I had a funny dream a few nights ago."

Darlene froze. Waited.

"It was a walkabout dream." Grandma Luella's brown eyes, dark as olive pits, fastened onto Darlene's. Her voice took on an uncanny drone, as she began to speak.

"Once I was asleep, I awoke in an unknown place. I went walking, walking, to a desolate land that changed to prairie, then changed to forest. I met a man who lived in that forest. I didn't know who he was, what he did, or what his purpose was, so I asked him to explain. He called himself the Green One. I told him I was named Luella, and that I was looking for a gift for my granddaughter. He nodded and smiled, and said I was on the right mission, but that first I should warn you—I *had* to warn you about a fearsome beast that was tracking you and your bundled treasure. I had to journey all the way back here to warn you in time."

Luella looked up sharply.

Darlene had never before seen her grandmother go into a near-trance-like state and then emerge from it, seamlessly. What was going on? It wasn't like her grandmother to play make-believe games.

"You know I take my dreams seriously," said Luella, in her regular voice.

"I know."

"When the Green Man told me a fearsome beast was tracking you, I was filled with an awful dread. Then my dream continued, and I was

214

being tracked, same as you. As if you and I were the same person, or inseparable companions. I had a momentary view of Quinn's enraged face on the body of a huge wolf. The wolf had red-rimmed eyes and was about to leap onto me. Or us. I was frozen in place. I was so afraid that I just averted my head and squeezed my eyes shut. When I opened them, I saw the Green One standing nearby. His walking stick, which he gripped in his right hand, was a gnarled tree branch. He pounded it, once, on the granite rock on which he stood, and the red-eyed wolf slunk away. That's when the Green One told me I had to get back here quickly, to warn you."

"Spooky," said Darlene, thinking about her own recent dream with the green-faced man. The similarities were uncanny, actually. Did it come from a kind of women's intuition, brought about by their shared bloodline? Or did it stem from their years together in Luella's house? It was like they had shared the same dream.

"Of course, as it turns out, you've been having trouble in real life, just like my dream told me." Luella clasped her hands. "Why didn't you call me up and tell me what was going on?"

"Well, first, I didn't want to worry you. Second, I prefer to tell you these things in person, rather than over the phone. Does that make sense?"

"Not really. That's what telephones were invented for, child."

"I guess." Darlene brushed some loose hair off her cheek. "Why didn't you call me?"

"I don't like my business being discussed over the telephone, either."

Darlene laughed. "Look who's talkin', then. Good thing you and I have some telepathic communication going on."

Luella shifted her legs in her bed. "So you're takin' off somewhere, aren't you?"

"Yeah."

"Will I have any communication with you?"

215

"Maybe. I hope so. I'm not really sure what the rules of this place are gonna be." Darlene bent to down to place David in his carseat.

David, fastened into his seat, gave a loud squawk and waved his arms about.

"We'll find out soon enough, won't we, Davey-boy?"

"Ah, I hate to see you two leave, especially knowing I won't be seeing you regular."

"It's all for the best, Grandma—at least till Anna Ebert can figure out a way to keep us safe from that crazy, no-good Quinn."

"You take care of yourself and our baby boy. He's our future, you know."

"I know."

"I love you, sweet girl. And you, too, Davey-boy."

"We love you, too. And don't worry—I'll protect David with my life."

Afterwards, she wondered why she hadn't mentioned her own dream, so eerily similar to her grandmother's. Maybe because it sounded too outlandish. Maybe because she wasn't sure whether to give credence to her own dreams. Maybe she just didn't want to frighten her.

Nevertheless, the truth was clear. Trouble *was* coming.

CHAPTER 49

She had to pack as soon as possible. On the ride home in Nathan's car, Darlene began to make a list in her head.

Nathan observed her in his rearview mirror and smiled. "Just the one suitcase, remember."

"Got it."

"Nothing frivolous, y'hear?"

"Yep."

"I can hear the wheels grinding away in your head."

Darlene smiled fleetingly, then turned away and looked out the passenger window. The neighborhood was densely settled. Three-story wooden apartment buildings lined the streets. A Catholic church, with its next door parochial school, presided over the city block, its playground occupied by uniformed schoolchildren. Teachers chatted while their young charges ran around and shouted happily. Tree roots gripped the mottled-concrete sidewalk, beside the playground. The canopy of venerable trees swayed, and dappled sunlight fell on tiny front lawns.

"I see we're taking a different route home."

"Yeah."

"Why?"

"In case someone followed us. Don't have to be so completely obvious."

"I guess.

They arrived home without evidence of being followed.

———

Darlene carried David up to their room and stood in the doorway, looking around. They had a nice room at this gracious old mansion. She would be sorry to leave it. It was the finest place she had ever lived.

No use being sad or nostalgic. All good things seemed to come to a hasty end, somehow. Her life was a series of endings: from losing her parents and living with her grandmother, to several boyfriends who never amounted to much, to having her son out of wedlock, to being housekeeper for a rich old lady—her life had always been on the fringes. Now she was going on the run again. If only she could stop living her life this way. Would she ever have a normal life? Was there such a thing? She really didn't know.

She went to her closet and pulled out her large suitcase. She began tossing in underwear, bras, T-shirts, pants, socks, two nightgowns, a robe, toiletries. She paused. What else would she need? Books and music? Hopefully, they would have some there, as there was no room for such things in her single suitcase. Except for the family Bible, which listed her ancestors for eight generations back. She hadn't taken the time yet to add David's name to the list. She'd do it someday, but not today.

Now for David's stuff. She began with a package of diapers. They took up an inordinate amount of space. Well, that couldn't be helped. Next came a series of onesies and a half-dozen outfits, followed by a small hoodie. Weather was always unpredictable in New England, even in summer. She put in his favorite blanket and his two favorite toys, a squeaky rubber frog and a fuzzy teddy bear with an embroidered face. The frog invariably made David laugh, while the fuzzy teddy bear comforted him as he drifted off to sleep.

Darlene wondered what sort of accommodations they'd have at the women's shelter. Would there be a crib available for David? Would she have a decent bed? Time would tell.

A fizzle of nerves struck her gut. A sharp pain. Oh, dear.

She turned around and saw Nathan standing in her doorway.

"How's it coming?" he asked.

"Okay, I guess. We'll be ready in a bit."

She pressed down on the lid of the suitcase to see if it would close.

"It closes. So far so good."

She bestowed a smile on Nathan, though she felt like crying. She looked at the floor instead, and kept her face under control.

"Good. I'll be back tomorrow morning after I've made a coupla calls. You and David should be able to check in at the shelter tomorrow. Try to get some sleep tonight if you can."

"Let's pray we can get there safely tomorrow without any of Quinn's men tracking me. If my luck holds." Darlene held up crossed fingers, pointing heavenward.

CHAPTER 50

Xavier Baccara reflected on his recent charge of "criminal trespassing," which turned out to be no big deal. All his priors had been in New York and Connecticut; this was his first in Massachusetts. He had agreed to a court hearing date and was out the next day. He wasn't sure whether to credit Quinn for the easy disposition, but was inclined to let it go.

Baccara had parked his old blue van, with its barely readable inscription, down the street from Joy Green's mansion. It had been parked there for almost a week. It was impossible to see inside its tinted windows, and no one had been seen entering or exiting the van. But neighbors in that neighborhood didn't trouble one another about sketchy vehicles brought home by errant nephews or grandchildren; if one was patient, the vehicles were removed in due time, long before they threatened to bring down the value of the nearby properties.

Nathan had noticed the van the day he had driven Darlene and David to the nursing home to see Luella. He'd thought it looked familiar, but decided not to mention its presence to Darlene. It would only make her crazy. Correction: crazier than she was already.

Nathan had driven over to Joy's place again on Saturday, two days after their visit with Luella. He drove his purple car with the windows wide open in the blazing summer sun. The door scorched his arm where it was hanging out the driver-side door.

The van was still there. Something had to be done about it.

If all went according to plan, Darlene and David would be safely tucked away at Beacon House before the end of the day. Now, all they had to do was pull it off.

Nathan stopped in front of the mansion. The driveway that led to the mansion's service entrance wasn't blocked. That entrance had been constructed in the horse-and-buggy era, and featured a portico supported by tall wooden columns. The driveway continued on, out back, to the former stables, now the garage.

At eleven a.m., a medium-sized utility truck pulled into the drive-way at 1008 Main Street. It featured the insignia of an upholstery company on both sides, and the back. Two guys got out and walked over to the side door of the mansion. They knocked and waited.

Xavier Baccara was watching from his van down the street. He had spent the night alternately sleeping and staking out the mansion for activity. At last, something was happening. It had been hot and sweaty, spending the night in his van in this summer heat. He needed a shower, big-time.

The two guys disappeared into the mansion.

Baccara wished he had left a listening device in the house when he had been there, but his encounter with the two ladies had been regrettably short and unsatisfying. To say the least. That old lady! Jeez, she was a piece of work.

If only he could find out what was going on in there.

221

The two guys abruptly emerged from the house carrying a huge couch. They carefully eased it into the back of the truck. They went back into the house and reemerged, carrying a love seat. They went back inside a third time and came out with a large cardboard box. All of the items went into the back of the truck. The truck's rear door was rolled down and slammed shut. One guy locked it.

Throughout this transaction, Baccara observed that the tall, skinny man was involved in what was happening. Since he'd broken into the mansion, Baccara had discovered that the man was a school counselor named Nathan Green, the nephew of the old lady who owned the place.

He couldn't quite figure out what was going on, so he continued to wait, watching intently.

———

Nathan went back inside after the guys had loaded the furniture. He began making turkey sandwiches for himself and his aunt. He emerged from the kitchen with a tray of sandwiches and tall glasses of lemonade.

"Well done, Nathan," said Joy. "Very slick."

"I'm not quite done yet. But I want to eat first."

Joy looked at him quizzically. "What've you got up your sleeve?"

"You'll see."

After his last bite, Nathan wiped his hands with a napkin before reaching for his cell phone.

"Longbottom Highway Department, please." His eyes twinkled. "I'd like to report a nuisance vehicle on my street, license plate FT 4587. Yes, it's been here for a while. No, it's not owned by anyone on the street. Yes, I'm sure. Please tow it away today, if possible. Thanks so much. Good-bye."

"You're wicked, Nathan."

"Thank you, Auntie. I learned from the best."

"You're welcome."

"Oh, and thanks for lending your furniture. You'll have it back later this week."

CHAPTER 51

The two moving guys from the upholstery company had carried out the long couch with its back toward the street. Hidden on the seat, laying down, had been Darlene. The two guys had hefted the couch, plus Darlene, into the back of the truck.

Darlene had lain flat, silent and motionless during the transfer to the truck.

Next had come David, strapped into his car seat, safely wedged into the cushions of the love seat. Darlene had worried that David would give it away with a loud squawk, but miraculously, he had remained silent. Last had been their suitcase, hidden in a large box.

The driver had slammed shut the rear door of the truck. The other guy had gone over to have a word with Nathan, after which he'd shaken his hand and gotten in on the passenger side of the truck.

Now that Darlene was shut inside the back of the upholstery truck, it seemed airless. *It's hot as hell in here*, she thought. At least it wasn't totally dark inside, as a small window between the cab and the trailer let in a shaft of light. Thank goodness for small mercies.

"You okay, Davey-boy?"

She was met with a little whine for a reply.

"I know, son. It's wicked hot in here. I'm already workin' up a mighty sweat."

She wiped a trickle of sweat that was dripping into her ear. It was definitely bizarre being driven to Beacon House in an upholstery truck. Who knew life could be so strange?

The truck's engine had started, and they backed out of the driveway. Now they were picking up speed.

She felt nervous, being on the road, but both Anna Ebert and Nathan had assured her that Beacon House was in a safe location, properly protected by security.

They were moving through traffic now, stopping at red lights. The truck vibrated while they waited at a stoplight. A motorcycle had pulled up next to them, so loud that it rattled her nerves. She closed her eyes and tried to imagine she was on a carnival ride that would soon end; all she had to do was hang on for dear life and then it would be over.

Darlene's thoughts flashed to Mickey Quinn. She was in this outlandish situation all because of him. He was the reason she had to hang on for dear life. Why couldn't she just have a normal life as a single mother? Plenty of women did.

If it weren't for her grandmother, she'd leave this town. Take David with her and hit the road. Go someplace where Quinn and his creeps would never find them.

Maybe a stint at Beacon House would help her sort things out.

CHAPTER 52

The truck halted suddenly. The engine was turned off, and both doors opened and slammed shut. Next, the truck's rear door slid upward with a grinding noise.

Dazzling sunlight hit Darlene in the face. She squinted. David gave a loud cry.

"Hey, Davey, looks like we're here."

The burly truck driver was standing there, waiting.

"Okay, ma'am. We're at Beacon House. Let's get you and the little guy inside with all your stuff."

Awkwardly, they clambered down onto the blacktop driveway. Darlene, holding David, was ushered inside an old building, built on a fieldstone foundation of stone. It had once been an inn, before the Civil War, she had heard. Then it was used as a farmhouse, with various extensions added on. It had been converted to a women's shelter a few decades ago.

Darlene stood in the entryway, opposite a small desk with a middle-aged woman behind it. She sank gratefully into a nearby chair. It felt good to be there, with David safe in her arms.

He's already almost too heavy to hold, she thought. *He's gonna be a big guy someday.*

"Hi, sweetie," the woman said. "I'm Gladie. Everyone's on a first-name-only basis here. We do everything we can to maintain an extra layer of privacy and protection."

Darlene nodded. The entryway smelled vaguely of bleach. *At least it's clean.*

Gladie smiled warmly at the two of them. "What is your little one's name?" She reached for the pen that was tucked above her ear, ready to write their date and time of arrival in the logbook. Her salt-and-pepper hair was crisply cut, her face accented by laugh lines.

"David. And I'm Darlene."

"I'm gonna take you two to room five to get settled in. I'll come back for you in a bit, before dinner."

Darlene was led down a hallway to an adjoining wing of the building. She followed Gladie closely, till they suddenly halted in front of a closed door.

Gladie put her hand on the doorknob. "It's nothing fancy."

Darlene felt a swell of gratitude. "I don't need much. I'm just so happy to be here."

"Great. Get yourselves settled, and I'll see you soon." Gladie blew a noisy kiss at David, who was snuggled in Darlene's arms. David hid his face in his mother's shoulder. "Shy one, huh? Well, that's okay."

"He hasn't been around a lot of people."

"One good thing about this place, he'll have other kids to play with here. Not that you want to be here in the first place, but that's one silver lining." She waved her fingers at David, who buried his face again. Turning away, Gladie left them alone.

Darlene entered the small room and looked around. It was a bit cramped, with just one dormer window. Here she was, being judgmental about a bedroom in a women's shelter, when she was damn lucky to be here. Who the hell was she, the Queen of Sheba? Grandma would have asked that question in a deliciously acidic tone. Of course she and David would share the full-size bed. David would go on the inside, against the wall, under the slanted ceiling of the dormer. She just hoped she wouldn't roll over onto him at night.

Darlene's suitcase was deposited outside her room with a thud. The young worker left without a word.

"Thanks," Darlene called out.

David had begun to crawl toward the door.

"Yep, let's collect our stuff."

Jeez, she missed her grandma, even though she'd just seen her two days before. Already, that seemed ages ago. So much had happened since then.

Darlene was tired of being on the run, on the defensive, having to protect David from the brute force of Mickey Quinn and his cronies. She didn't know how long she'd have to stay here at Beacon House—probably at least until Anna Ebert could come up with some sort of plan. She'd have to be tough and hang tight.

CHAPTER 53

Morning sunshine beamed into the tiny bedroom. Darlene began to stretch in bed. She and Davey were *safe*. The fierce tension that had clenched her heart had eased, thankfully.

Breakfast in the common room, next to the kitchen, turned out to be haphazard. Each family stayed together, gathering food items on their trays. Then the next family grouping would move up, breakfast trays at the ready.

Darlene was curious about the other occupants, but knew enough not to stare. Personal questions were off limits, too. Nevertheless, she furtively stole glances at the other women, wondering what tale of misfortune had brought each of them here, children in tow. She was glad to see two other babies near David's age.

At the other end of her table was a mother who kept her bruised face down, while her sad-eyed young daughter draped herself against her mother's hip. She looked to be around six years old. The older brother, perhaps ten, sat silently across from them, hunched over his cereal bowl. He gave off an aura of anger that seemed more akin to that of a teenager. Darlene could see they were related; all three had pale, freckled skin with unruly coal-black hair. The three of them didn't speak, yet seemed to be attuned to one another.

Darlene looked down at her own David. He was staring at her unabashedly, with big, round baby eyes. Darlene grinned at him.

"That's right, kid. You're no slouch, either."

Darlene ate her scrambled eggs. She put tiny pieces on David's plastic plate that sat on the tray of his high chair, where he perched crookedly. He ate eagerly. Next came a handful of Cheerios. More eager hand-to-mouth munching.

"Hmmm," said Darlene. "Wonder if we should be done with nursing, once and for all. Your teeth hurt like the dickens, you know. Time to start you on a sippy cup."

David chortled in agreement, waggling his hands as he picked up individual Cheerios.

"Can I sit here?" whispered a hunched-over woman holding her tray of food. She stood next to Darlene, unnervingly close.

Darlene smiled slightly. "Of course! Please." She ducked her chin. "Sit down. Make yourself comfortable."

The woman looked at her sidelong. "Thanks, but I haven't been comfortable in years," she whispered, but sat down next to Darlene, all the same.

"I'm sorry to hear that."

"Yeah, everything went downhill when I realized my marriage was a terrible mistake."

"When was that?"

"Oh, probably right after I threw the bouquet."

Darlene chuckled softly. "Ha! Good one! At least not everyone here is doom and gloom."

"Just most of 'em," the woman whispered. She nodded toward the others in the room.

"How long have you been here?"

"Sad to say, for quite a while. I'm a damned slow learner," she whispered.

Darlene waited for more.

The woman bent over her tray and began to eat.

Darlene turned back to David, watched him grab more Cheerios.

"Lots of these women have been here a bunch of times, sometimes because of the same guy," the woman whispered. "Sometimes it's diff'rent guys. Everyone's got a story."

"I bet."

"So what's your story?" the woman whispered.

"What's yours?" countered Darlene.

For a moment, Darlene thought she recognized the woman, but then realized she was just imagining things.

The woman eyed her from behind a gray-brown scrub of hair.

"I asked you first," she whispered, more loudly.

"Are you able to use your voice normally, or only whisper?"

"Bad case of laryngitis.

"How long have you had it?"

"Six years," she whispered, with a certain fierceness.

"Huh. Unusual." Darlene scratched her scalp. "So, what's your name?"

"Martha. Yours?"

"Darlene." She gestured. "This is David. Do you have kids? Tell me about your no-good husband . . ."

"I asked you first," Martha whispered. "Remember?"

Darlene laughed. Several heads in the room turned to look at her. Darlene ducked her head when she realized people were staring. "Getting me in trouble right away, huh?"

"Trouble's already gotcha, or ya wouldn't be here," whispered Martha.

"That's the damn truth," Darlene said. "I mean, the rotten truth." She nodded sideways toward David. "I find myself swearing a lot these days. I have to clean up my language in front of the kid, here. Makes a person finally grow up, huh?"

"I see you're as good as me at avoiding talking about it." A glimmer of a smile reached the woman's red-chapped lips.

"Yep. Gotta get my bearings. Trying to let Old Man Trouble slide away from me right now."

Darlene swiveled around to scan the room. The other families were leaving their tables, trays in hand. The threesome with the coal-black hair stood silently in unison. The boy piled their dishes and silverware onto the top tray, and took the pile to the kitchen window. He disappeared into the kitchen.

Perhaps he was on kitchen duty, thought Darlene. I'm sure I'll be assigned to something soon.

A tall, toffee-skinned woman with a brunette braid faced them, hands clasped together.

"May I have everyone's attention, please? I need to make an announcement. For the newest arrivals here, we're going to have Group Session this morning at ten-thirty in the meeting room. Every-one is welcome, all ages, according to personal discretion. See you then, and have a peaceful start today to your morning."

The woman retreated behind a door that said "Staff Only."

"Who was that?" Darlene whispered to Martha.

"Look who's whisperin' now?" Martha snorted. "That's Reverend Renee. She's the head honcho of this place."

"What does she do? I mean, aside from praying?"

"Lots of stuff. You'll see."

"Huh."

"She's got a whole team workin' with her," whispered Martha.

Darlene picked up David from the high chair and slung him onto her hip.

"Okay, Martha. David and I are gonna chill for a bit. We'll see you later this morning."

"I'll save ya a seat in Group Session," whispered Martha, her eyes twinkling through her mass of wiry hair.

CHAPTER 54

The Beacon House meeting room was situated in the finished cellar of the building. The massive beams of the former inn, built in the pre–Civil War era, supported two floors of rooms above the cellar. Big windows in the back looked out on a generous yard surrounded by a tall fence. Outside the fence was a thick screen of evergreens and trees, and the property sloped down a hill in the rear.

A little before ten-thirty, Darlene had come down the carpeted stairs to the meeting room, David in her arms. When she walked inside, she was struck by the open view provided by the back windows. She thought immediately about their safety; that's why she was here in the first place.

She began eyeballing the premises. She noticed the tall fence, and the small cameras positioned in discreet corners of the yard. The yard was split into different areas: One corner had a swing set; another, a picnic table. There was even a small vegetable garden in one corner. Very good. They seemed to have their act together here.

She relaxed slightly. Darlene scanned the meeting room next. There were sagging couches around the entire perimeter of the room; some folding chairs and two rocking chairs completed the group seating. There was a bin of jumbled toys in the corner, along with a pile of folded blankets.

"You're early," Martha whispered, loud enough to be heard across the room.

"Yeah, old habit of mine."

She picked a couch that looked more comfortable than most and quickly plopped down, David in her arms. Instantly, her butt dropped nearly to the floor.

"Yikes." She put David down while she clumsily got to her feet. "That's a helluva couch. Coulda warned me or something."

"Nah. That'd take the fun outta watchin' the newbies try it out! We call that couch 'the Great Deceiver,' 'cause everyone new—and I mean, *everyone*—goes for that one first. The others look like hell, but are actually in better shape."

Darlene couldn't keep the annoyance out of her voice. "Since you're such an expert, what do you recommend?"

"See for yourself," whispered Martha. She smiled, mouth clamped shut.

"Whatever," said Darlene. "You can tell me sometime. Or not. I got my own problems, Martha. I ain't in the mood."

Darlene moved to another, high-backed couch and sat down, positioning David on her lap. She closed her eyes. She would practice avoidance. Lucky for her, David was in his morning sleepy time. He snuggled in her arms, almost ready to drop off to sleep. She slivered her eyes to monitor the goings-on in the room, but studiously avoided eye contact with Martha.

Martha reminded her of someone from long ago. Very strange. It was nagging at her memory.

Other women, some of them with multiple children, had started filing into the room. Darlene surveilled them from the corner of her eye. Several young girls, teenagers, each arrived with a child balanced on a hip. She realized that she was a bit of an odd duck here: a thirty-six-year-old with her first child, never married, and not in any kind of relationship. But everybody here was escaping somebody—husbands, boyfriends, stepfathers. Who knew? Some low-life abuser who was hurting them and their children.

A hush fell over the room as a young woman wearing a white medical coat entered from the side door. Darlene raised her head and stared. The woman was white and slender, with wispy black shoulder-length hair. Her smooth face, pale blue eyes within black-framed glasses, and serious expression made her look no-nonsense.

"Good morning, everyone," said the woman. "For those of you who've just arrived, I'm Dr. Sasha Locander. Call me Dr. Sasha. I'm the in-house psychologist. We have group sessions here, where we talk our way through to the other side. No one is ever required to speak. It's all voluntary. And children are welcome to contribute to the discussion."

She gave a rueful smile.

"I know it's tough to think about sharing your family's personal business in public. But sometimes, just the act of telling can really help. It helps the others who've had similar experiences, but haven't been able to speak yet. By telling the hurtful truths, others see that they are not alone. They see that it's possible to air one's own dirty laundry, and the world won't collapse. It can lead to breakthroughs, and newfound bravery."

Dr. Sasha paused.

"Is there anyone who would like to start?"

The room was quiet, but for the soft chattering of a toddler against his mother's chest.

Darlene saw the downcast women's faces, eyes gazing at the floor. She wondered how long the painful silence would last. She furtively looked around the room, waiting to see who would pick up her head to speak.

She smiled inwardly at their shyness. Then a moment later, she felt deeply saddened. Each woman here had been terrified into seeking refuge, just like her.

Dr. Locander called out, "If any children want to play games or do some coloring, they can go now with Ms. Connie to the playroom." No one moved.

A skinny teenager, who bit on her fingernail before she spoke, said, "Guess I'll tell my sorry-ass tale." She lifted her sallow face toward the ceiling, and said in an even tone, "My name is Marie Therese. I've got an evil stepfather—don't know why my mama married him. He doesn't work half the time, barely pays rent. He's a lazy-ass bum.

"Anyway, when he was outta work for a long time, he was just hangin' around the house—it was during the summer, when I was off from school. I was workin' second shift at Burger King, and he'd be after me, the shifty-eyed bum, in the mornings. It was after my mama left for work, but before I left for my shift. He would start pawing on me . . ."

Marie Therese paused.

"How much was done by force?" Dr. Sasha asked gently.

"The bastard knew how to hurt me where it wouldn't show."

"How much was physical, and how much was psychological?"

"He didn't bother with mental games. He was very direct."

"There *had* to have been mental games, like, We won't tell our secrets to your mother, or We'll make sure you don't get pregnant."

Marie Therese gazed at the ceiling, her eyes filling with tears.

"Yeah, I guess you're right. It was filled with those mental games, but I ignored them, 'cause I was so disgusted with it all, and so afraid of the daily hurt he put me through. Those physical things happening

237

to me distracted me from the mental side." She shook her head, a tear flying off her cheek. "Believe me, things got pretty creepy, pretty sick."

"What can we learn from this?" asked Dr. Sasha.

Silence filled the room. Darlene was struck by how even the children were quiet. Perhaps a sign they were from abusive homes? They dared not utter a sound in this situation.

She looked down at David. He was being unusually quiet, too. Could he sense the situation from the other children?

"We learn that we are in denial of how deep the damage really is. We make bargains to try to keep other parts of our lives 'normalized.' And we *go along to get along*, as the saying goes," said Dr. Sasha. "This makes us ashamed of ourselves and our weakness. Once we have been shamed into weakness, it's just a matter of our abusers, our tormentors, triggering our 'weakness button' whenever possible, whenever they want."

Oh, boy, thought Darlene. This sounded too damn familiar.

"But, of course, we don't want to spend our lives subjected to our 'weakness button,' now, do we?" Dr. Sasha raised her voice. "That's why each and every one of you women were brave enough to get out, get away, get safe. For that, I say, each of you is a heroine, to yourself, and to your children. Bravo!"

She smiled broadly and said, "Children, you should be so proud of your mothers. They are so brave!"

There was a stirring of gladness in the room.

Darlene thought about being a heroine to herself and David. She hadn't thought of it that way before. She straightened up a bit.

"Children? Would any of you like to go and play now?" Dr. Sasha motioned to an older woman seated along the wall. "Ms. Connie, will you show the kids who want to play the way to the playroom?"

When the clatter of exiting children died down, Dr. Sasha sat down to resume the discussion. "Now where were we?" She looked around at the circle of faces. "Anyone?"

238

"Weakness button," said Marie Therese, with a tilt of her chin.

"Thank you. Now, when it comes to those 'weakness button' triggers, who in your life would do those things to you if they really loved you?" asked Dr. Sasha.

She slowly scanned the faces that were riveted to hers, seeking answers, seeking wisdom.

"Or could it have been someone who had a mean streak ... maybe something worse than a mean streak—a streak of evil."

She turned her head once more to scan the circle.

"Who here believes in the possibility of evil?"

A few women raised their eyes to meet Dr. Sasha's gaze.

Absolute silence.

"I turn you over to Reverend Renee."

The stately woman of color was seated in a rocking chair in the corner. Her thick braids framed her broad face like a crown. Reverend Renee, carrying a red leather Bible with verses preselected with a satin ribbon, rose and stood next to Dr. Sasha. She delicately opened the Bible's pages.

"This is from the book of Isaiah, chapter thirty-five, verse three, which says, 'Say to them that are of a fearful heart, Be strong, fear not; behold, your God will come with a vengeance, even God with a recompense; he will come and save you, and the ransomed of the Lord shall return and come to Zion with songs and everlasting joy upon their heads.' "

Reverend Renee folded her hands on her Bible. She scanned the upturned faces, looking to her for answers.

"What does that mean to you, when trying to discern the Word of the Lord? When trying to understand and feel the inspiration and glory of the Holy Spirit upon your immortal soul?" Reverend Renee's large black eyes were half-closed.

"It means that we shouldn't be afraid," said a squat woman seated by the tall windows. "I finally got brave enough to leave." She compressed her lips, looked down.

239

"Praise be," said the reverend, smiling. "Anyone else?"

There was a stirring in the room, but no one spoke up.

"Each of you has found the light of the Lord in yourself—in your heart, your soul—in such a way that you knew you had to find the road to freedom. You had to search for that elusive road to personal, individual freedom. Blessed freedom! Bless each of you and keep you, and keep your loved ones, too. Amen."

Reverend Renee lowered her chin to her chest, her hands clasped around her Bible, and fully closed her eyes. "Let us each pray in silence for a bit as we ponder our own trials and tribulations, and how the Lord will give us the strength to overcome."

"Hallelujah," Martha whispered, loud enough to be heard by all. Their subsequent silent prayers were incongruously filled with sighs, knocks, and bumps

"May your prayers be answered," said the reverend, lowering the red leather Bible clasped in her long fingers. "Amen." She chuckled. "You brave ladies are dismissed. After all that pondering and prayer, it's time for lunch, so head on upstairs."

Darlene stood up, David resting heavily in her arms. Despite his weight, the weariness upon Darlene had eased slightly. Perhaps she and David would emerge from this place, strange as it was, with some chance of a life of normalcy and peace.

CHAPTER 55

Lenny Starbird sat in a booth at the back of Beacon House. From his desk, he could watch all the monitors, as the cameras scanned the grounds. He especially kept an eye on the tall brick wall which surrounded the backyard. That seemed to be the point where intruders tried to breach the compound—as if they wouldn't be noticed creeping in through the shrubbery and low-hanging trees as they came to the brick wall. He just hoped no one ever tried with a grappling hook and rope.

Today, he noticed a new woman passing time in the playground area of the backyard. She was sitting on the corner of the sandbox, hunched over, while her son crawled on the sparse grass at her feet. She looked tired,, and her golden hair drooped over her shoulders.

The phone rang at his desk.

"Hello?"

"New party coming in this afternoon. Be ready for a quick intake. Three kids and a mother."

"When are they arriving?"

"In the next two hours."

Lenny ran his hand through his dark, curly hair and frowned. These intakes were always problematic. He had to hustle them and their stuff inside, all the while making certain no one had followed them here. The last thing he needed was some raging guy confronting him or chasing down the woman and her kids.

He stood up. A navy blue uniform concealed his wiry strength. In his few months here, he'd had to use his martial arts instincts, some wrestling moves, and even a couple of brute moves to stave off two lowlifes who'd come around. Management had decided they didn't want him armed; liability reasons, they said.

Nonsense. As if the lowlifes wouldn't come armed? Who're we kidding?

Originally, he'd had to decide whether it was foolish to even take this job. After a few days' thought, he decided he'd be doing a good service for these women and their kids. Anyway, the risk was probably small. He hoped so, anyway. It only took one crazy son of a bitch to take a person out. The job brought its own good karma with it, he told himself. Plus, he needed the paycheck.

Lenny glanced at the monitor that showed the backyard playground. The new woman and her son were still there. He liked the way the sunshine highlighted white-gold on her blonde hair. It tumbled over her shoulders as she reached down for her son, who kept crawling. She was saying something. Lenny wished he could hear her voice.

"Lenny?"

His daydream broke. "Yeah?"

"The new intake will be here in ten minutes. The driver just phoned."

"On it." He turned away from the bank of cameras and reached for his set of handcuffs.

Although management wouldn't let him carry, so far no one had objected to this extra bit of hardware. Twice it had come in handy, till the police had arrived.

———

It was late when Lenny Starbird finally sat down to dinner. Evening came on quick, and the women and children lingering in the backyard had gone inside. Since everyone was now safely inside, he could relax just a tad.

He decided to take this chance to gobble down his refrigerated premade dinner, once he had zapped it in the microwave. It was quite the healthy alternative. His landlady's homemade meatballs were pretty damn good, actually.

He took another bite. His mouth watered over the sauce, thick, spicy, and savory. Meatballs firm, yet soft.

He thought back to earlier in the day. This afternoon's intake had been the usual messy affair. A woman and her three terrified kids had been driven to Beacon House by another woman. The friend's car had clattered and rattled as it nosed down the road.

A man—the abusive boyfriend, or husband, an arrogant jerk if there ever was one—had openly followed them in his large black truck, which towered over the woman's low-slung vehicle. Lenny had seen them cowering inside, covering their faces, peeking between fingers, except the harried driver, of course.

The driver had pulled up to Beacon House, with no attempt to be discreet.

Leading an abuser to the exact location of Beacon House was not helpful, to say the least. Distinctly ill-advised. This would lead to long-term problems, which tended to come up at later points, usually unexpectedly, which is why he was on high alert at all times.

Today, this jerk had just lurked from across the road.

Lenny watched him from the front entrance as the woman and her three children scurried inside. He watched as the abuser checked out the sparsely settled neighborhood, the lonely street, the solitary building, and finally, him. The abuser made eye contact with Lenny and then looked away.

The truck's engine roared as the abuser sped off.

Lenny stood there, stock-still, till the truck was out of sight, just in case the abuser was watching Lenny as he drove away.

It was psychological warfare with these jerks. That, and maintaining good karma.

The woman driver also finally drove away.

Lenny turned, went inside. The golden-haired woman with the baby boy was filling his mind's eye as he returned to his closet-sized office. She had captured his imagination. He wondered what her name was.

Soon his 3:00 to 11:00 p.m. shift would be over, and he could go crash back in his RV, which he'd parked at Jaston Farm. How that all happened was strange, but good. Strange that his good luck had stemmed from Robert Jaston's misfortune.

It was also sad, considering that it was his farmer-landlord who had been shot in the leg earlier this year, and was now recovering from the wound. He wasn't able to do many of the chores on the dairy farm, so their son, Jacob, was covering the milking at five a.m. and five p.m.

When Maureen heard Robert accepting Lenny's offer, she had said, "You're the answer to my prayers." Her eyes filled up with tears.

"You're welcome, Mrs. Jaston." He nodded. "And you, too, Mr. Jaston."

"Don't be silly. If you're gonna be hooked up to our farmhouse, and in and out of our kitchen, it's Maureen, and Robert." She smiled through her sniffling.

"You'll always be Mrs. Jaston to me, after what you folks have been through."

"Whatever . . . just call me Maureen, okay?" She grinned.

"Okay." Lenny scratched his forearm. "You remember that I've got a job at Beacon House as a guard, thirty hours a week. So I won't be here all the time as your personal security."

"Yes, that's okay. Just knowing you're here on the premises will be a deterrent. We're grateful for however much you can contribute."

To seal the deal, Lenny and Robert had shaken hands across the kitchen table.

———

Just like that, Lenny had found himself an extension of the Jaston family, which felt good.

Tonight, he drove back from Beacon House to Jaston Farm, where his RV was parked behind the farmhouse, at the end of the building's long curved driveway. Extension cords and hoses connected the RV to the farmhouse. The RV was actually out of sight from the road, but he preferred it that way. He wanted to be a lookout. He liked to be sensitive to what was happening in the area.

He was going to recommend that the Jastons get a decent guard dog. He'd keep the dog in his RV. He could tell Maureen was a stickler who didn't want a dog underfoot, getting her kitchen muddy. She made everyone take their work boots off right at the door. No barn muck was ever allowed inside.

Lenny parked his Ford truck next to his RV. Tupperware in hand, he stepped out, crunching over the gravel driveway as he strode toward the farmhouse. The fields were aglow in the moonlight.

Approaching the door to the kitchen, he rapped the wood frame with his knuckles.

Maureen came to unlatch the screen door, then returned to the kitchen sink, the water running.

"Come on in, Lenny. The kids are still up, since it's Saturday night. Don't mind them."

As he stepped inside, Lenny saw Robert standing with his back toward him, leaning on the kitchen counter.

"Standing pretty strong there, buddy," said Lenny.

"Yeah, thanks."

"Need a hand with that cup of coffee?"

"Trying to see if I can get this cup over to the table in one piece," said Robert.

"Don't go breaking my cups! You've got people here to give you a hand," said Maureen with a trace of asperity.

Lenny gently took the full cup from Robert and placed it at his kitchen chair.

"How's your leg feeling?"

"Gettin' better, day by day. The doctors did a great job."

Robert limped over to his chair and slumped into the seat. A heavy silence fell.

Maureen looked at Lenny and rolled her eyes. She noticed her eleven-year-old twins, Layla and Shaina, standing in the doorway that led to the dining room.

"What's up, girls? Getting ready for bed? We've got Sunday prayers to get to in the morning."

"We just wanted to ask Mr. Starbird a question," said Layla.

"Not now," said Maureen. "Another time. Mr. Starbird is tired; he just got off work," she said, retrieving the Tupperware container from him.

Lenny looked past Maureen at the two girls. He winked. They giggled.

"I got time for maybe one quick question, but it's gotta be quick."

"Sucker!" whispered Maureen, shaking her head.

Shaina twisted a lock of hair with a finger.

"We just wanna know if you have a girlfriend."

She stood on one leg, then the other, back and forth, twisting her hair.

Lenny made a gesture like he had been heart-struck.

"You girls are wicked, a question like that!"

"Well, do you?" asked Layla. Her expression was solemn.

"Why do you want to know, anyway?" said their older brother Jacob, who had just swung into the kitchen. "It's not like either of *you* are gonna be his girlfriend."

"Jacob," said Maureen, "lay off the girls."

"That's a question for another day, I'm afraid," said Lenny. "I'm off to my shack."

"It's a shack?" said Shaina.

"It's an RV," said Jacob.

"Good night, Lenny," said Maureen, diverting the kids from the beginnings of a squabble.

"Girls, get upstairs and get ready for bed! Sorry about the inquisition, Lenny. We're still working on our social graces."

"I'm happy to learn *some* youngsters are learning social graces these days," said Lenny. "Thanks again for the meatballs. Dinner was great."

"Stop by tomorrow before your shift. I'll have something for you to take along."

"Sounds great. Thank you again, and good night, everyone."

Lenny waved as he left the warm kitchen.

CHAPTER 56

Mickey Quinn was shaving when his cell phone rang. He answered, even though he didn't recognize the number.

"Mickey!" a voice whispered through the phone.

"Yeah, who is this?"

"It's your friend Martha."

"Yes?"

"Well, she's here, with the kid, David."

"David! So that's his name." Quinn gulped. "Any idea how long they'll be there?"

"Don't know nothin' more."

"Gotcha. Great. Hey, thanks. I'll catch ya later, babe."

Mickey Quinn looked at himself in the mirror and grinned.

My smile still has the same old glint, he thought.

———

Last week had been truly epic.

Quinn had gone over to Rufus Fishbane's house. He'd told him he wanted to talk about the future of Longbottom. Rufus, feeling grand, had said, "Sure, c'mon over!"

Quinn had worn a windbreaker with zippered pockets. He had listened to Rufus brag on himself, and had indulged the talk, nodding slightly, smiling. They both had had a tumbler of bourbon on the rocks, with Rufus drinking his quickly.

Rufus had downed his second bourbon, and had started in on a beer.

Quinn had waited to make a trip to the bathroom, down the hallway.

Once Quinn was behind the bathroom door, he'd stuck his hand in his pocket. A coiled wire lay flat inside. *Might as well take a piss while I'm here*, he'd thought.

He had taken his time, methodically washing and drying his hands.

As he opened the door, he slipped his right hand into his pocket. The wire was thrice wrapped around his right hand, the other end loose.

Quinn quietly walked down the hallway. He could see Rufus, sitting in an armchair with his back to him.

Quinn lunged toward Rufus, his arms outstretched. He pinned Rufus to his armchair by the neck, tightening the wire as he pulled it deeply against his throat.

Rufus's arms went to his throat, trying to claw off the steel wire that was choking him.

"Argh," gurgled Rufus, his legs kicking out futilely.

Quinn waited a long time, pulling the wire as taut as possible, his arms and wrists aching from the prolonged exertion.

"Sum'bitch is strong," he muttered. "Now, that's the end of his bigmouth ways. Bragging how he rigged the ballot questions! The fool could've triggered an investigation of the vote—-the last thing I need...."

He slipped the wire back into his pocket, coiling it up. Briefly, he wiped down all the surfaces he had touched, including everything in the bathroom. Then he had let himself out the back patio door and started a solitary trip back to his own house, a mile away.

On the way home, he had stopped in at McGillicuddy's for a beer.

A fierce rival of his own establishment, he thought he'd see how *this* place was doing. Make an appearance. Not to mention establish a plausible alibi, he mused. He'd made sure to go there every afternoon for a week before killing Rufus. Especially similar times from day to day. Patterns made good alibis.

Who did he see there after leaving Rufus's but his old buddy, Toby, perched on a barstool, skinny knees jutting out.

Quinn had slipped up alongside him, sat on the next barstool. He waited till Toby turned to see who was there.

"Man! What're ya doing here?" asked Toby, clearly astonished.

"Looking for a new lady friend." Quinn grinned. "Now that I'm a widower."

Toby peered at him. "You doing okay?"

"Never better."

"Where ya been?"

"Out and about." Quinn signaled the bartender. "A whiskey sour, my man."

"Glad you're enjoying your newfound freedom. Just don't do anything outta bounds, buddy. I'm a genius, I know, but there'll come a point when even *I* can't help you. You know that, don't you?"

"Yep." Quinn drank. "What are you doing here? Why aren't you in court this afternoon?"

"Case was dismissed. I got out early. Came here to see and be seen."

A young redheaded woman had plopped down on the stool on his other side.

"Buy you a drink?" said Quinn.

"No, thanks. You're old enough to be my father."

Quinn smiled lopsidedly. *I'm better off concentrating on my kid,* he thought. *Time to split this joint.*

"Catch ya later, Tobe." Quinn waved and walked out.

Next door to McGillicuddy's was a used-car lot. This was where Quinn had parked, hiding his car among the others.

That night, after leaving McGillicuddy's, he had thrown the coil of wire under one of the beat-up used cars. Then he'd walked further to his own car, got in, and drove off quietly.

He was pretty sure no one had seen him.

Rufus had gotten plenty of people mad at him. Hell, half the old-timers in town felt cheated and outraged when the Open Town Meeting was ended.

Who knows what might have happened? Maybe some crazy old codger had attacked Rufus. Plenty of people for the cops to check out, he thought.

Now he just needed to get home and shower off. He smiled in satisfaction.

All is well.

CHAPTER 57

Quinn stood at the entrance to Beacon House, paused, poised, ready to enter.

It was a Wednesday afternoon, almost three o'clock, on a cloudless day. He was dressed in his casual-smart attire, as if going away on a business trip. His Cadillac was waiting outside, door unlocked, nose in a getaway position.

Gladie greeted him at the door.

"Why, hello! Mr. Quinn, what brings you here? Our next board meeting isn't for another two weeks yet. Is there anything I can help you with?"

"I'd like to see my friend Martha, if I can?" he said, tapping a toe impatiently.

"I'll see if I can locate her. If you'll wait here a minute, please," said Gladie, turning and heading down a short hallway. She gave a silent warning beep to the security guard while she searched for Martha.

Quinn craned his neck around the stairwell, to see if he could peer up to the second floor.

Where in this huge, rambling house would Darlene and David be?

The security guard, Deke, was just ending his shift. Good. Better to have stuff happen at change-of-shift time. Who was on duty now? Lenny Starbird? Right. He'd heard Lenny was generally late.

Gladie had located Martha in the basement lounge and gestured for her to follow. Martha, thin and hunched over, with her mop of gray-brown hair, scurried up the stairwell behind Gladie.

When they reached the foyer, Quinn was nowhere to be found.

Gladie spun around, wild-eyed. She told herself not to panic. No doubt Quinn was just in the guest bathroom, or had stepped back outside to go to his car.

"Mr. Quinn! Where are you! Guests are not permitted upstairs!"

Gladie was getting more riled up each moment that Quinn remained out of sight.

"Mr. Quinn!" she yelled. "Come back to the front desk immediately!"

Gladie whirled around to face Martha. "Why does Mr. Quinn want to speak to you?" Gladie glared down at the shorter, hunched woman. "Didn't he talk to you when he stopped by a while ago? What was that all about?"

"I don't remember nothin'," Martha whispered.

"Let's hope it was nothing."

Lenny Starbird appeared. "What's going on, ladies?"

"We might have an intruder on the premises. Don't know where he's got to, exactly, or who he's after. I don't know whether he's armed."

"Any idea who it might be?"

"Yes," said Gladie, hands on her hips.

"Who?"

"Mickey Quinn—Longbottom's notorious wife-killer!"

253

CHAPTER 58

Darlene faced Mickey in her bedroom in Beacon House.

David had crawled behind her, against the wall, on the queen-size bed. He cooed.

Mickey stood in the doorway, blocking any possible escape.

"Whaddya want, Mickey?"

"You know."

The silence between them grew. Neither would break their glare on the other.

The baby noises behind them subsided.

Quinn's mouth curled into a sneer, while he continued to stare.

Thump. A surprised, angry cry, as David fell off the bed. He began bawling.

Darlene swooped to pick him up, but Quinn shoved past her. He scooped up David, held him tightly in the crook of his elbow, like a football.

"*Nooooo!*" screamed Darlene.

Quinn made for the door, but was waylaid at the threshold by Judy and Reverend Renee.

Quinn tightened his grip on David, who was wailing.

"Get outta my way! This is my kid!"

He shoved forward and began running down the stairs.

"Stop him!" screamed Darlene. "He's kidnapping my son! Stop him!"

Just as Quinn reached the foyer, intending to dash out the front door, Lenny Starbird stepped forward, arms outstretched.

"Whoa! Hold on here, buddy. What's going on here?"

Lenny shifted to block Quinn from passing him.

"Whoa, slow down, now. Let's put these on, now, just in case."

Lenny snapped a handcuff on Quinn's arm that held David.against his body. Quinn lashed out with his other arm, missing Lenny's face. Lenny gripped Quinn's other arm fiercely, but lost his grip as Quinn twisted his arm free..

The reverend and Judy came running down the stairs and stood right next to Quinn.

"Judy," Lenny said, keeping his voice professionally calm, "could you take the little guy away from our agitated friend, please?"

Lenny fought to keep Quinn subdued while Judy took hold of David, and tried to remove him from Quinn's grip.

She couldn't. "He won't let go!"

David was screeching at full voice, while Judy tugged again.

"Let go of the kid, or I'll arrest you!" said Lenny, wrestling with Quinn.

"Ha! You got no authority to arrest me, and you know it! Let go a' me! Punk!"

"I'm still a cop in Longbottom, even if I'm laid off. By the power vested in me, you're under arrest. Hell! You belong back in jail. goddammit!"

Judy swept in at that moment and took David, just as Lenny grabbed Quinn's other arm and cuffed his hands together. He shoved Quinn face-first against the wall.

"You're the big shot who shot his wife dead last year, right? Shiiiitt." He looked around, saw a throng of people. "Is that poor kid back in his mother's arms yet?"

Darlene had emerged from the group of onlookers. She raced over to Judy and grabbed her son, clutching him fiercely.

"Clear out, everybody!" said Lenny Starbird. "This guy's under arrest. Judy, call 911!"

CHAPTER 59

"How did you know to come up to my room?" asked a still-shaken Darlene. They were sitting in the chairs near the desk in the entry-way. She was clutching David so tightly that he continued to whimper softly.

"I knew something wasn't right when the silent alarm went off," said Reverend Renee. "I figured I better get up to the women and children's quarters."

"We coulda been down in the meeting room," said Darlene, "or out in the garden."

"No. The guard's got the meeting room, kitchen, dining area, and garden all covered on his cameras. I figured on trouble up here, where y'all are, individually."

"Wow! You are truly amazing."

"Nothing to do with me. Our Lord guides me to where I need to be at a particular time and place. That's the truth, I say. It's our Lord that's all-seeing!"

"Reverend Renee has been involved in some of the most amazing interventions and rescues," said Judy. "It's like she's psychic."

"Really?" said Darlene.

"Yep. She's the spiritual leader of our community—but you knew that."

"Don't give me credit I don't deserve," said the reverend. "It's all the Lord's work."

She paused, looked closely at Darlene.

"Are you a person of faith?"

"Not really," said Darlene. "But I suppose I should be—after your rescue of me and David. My grandmother took me to church every week. I guess it never fully took."

"Start coming to church where Reverend Renee preaches on Sundays," said Judy, hovering.

"I should. Whenever we get settled somewhere . . . soon."

"Why wait?" asked the reverend, with a broad smile. Her gleaming teeth accented her clear, tawny skin. "We welcome all newcomers at our Sunday services, as well as our Bible study sessions, on Wednesday evenings and Saturday afternoons. Children are always welcome, as well as singers for the choir."

"Great. I could use some peace and spirituality. We'll be over to your church, I promise," Darlene said. She'd almost stopped shaking. "I think David needs a diaper change after all this excitement, poor thing. And I need a cup of coffee. My nerves are shot!"

"C'mon, girl," said Judy. "I'll take care of you."

She grasped Darlene's free hand and helped her up, and they made their way to the kitchen.

———

"Where you at, girl? You still with us on Planet Earth? How're ya feeling, honey?"

The questions in the kitchen were coming at Darlene from all sides. An array of lunch items were strewn across the countertops. The women ignored the mess, waiting to hear the details of what had happened.

Darlene sat there, dazed, still clutching David. After the diaper change, he had fallen asleep on her shoulder.

The circle of faces hovering around her was confusing. Someone placed a glass of water in front of her. She absentmindedly took a few sips. Her head was spinning.

She knew one thing for sure: She felt tremendous relief. The worry was gone. Amen!

———

The first person Darlene called once she'd collected herself was her grandmother.

"Grandma. I'm so glad to be able to talk to you. Something wonderful just happened! David and I were *rescued! By the staff here at Beacon House! Just like you've always said—trust in the Lord. The Lord finds a way through good people around us!*"

Darlene paused as Grandma asked more questions.

"Yes . . . yes, David was almost kidnapped by Mickey Quinn. It was a miracle! True justice, that doesn't come very often in life."

Darlene's voice was quavering.

"No, it's okay. Really, we're both fine." Darlene paused again to listen. "Yes, there's someone here you can speak to . . . hold on a moment."

Darlene turned the phone over to Reverend Renee. Darlene smiled at Judy, who was holding a sleeping David in her arms as they sat comfortably in the kitchen's sole armchair.

"Hello? This is Reverend Renee speaking." A pause. "Yes, your granddaughter and great-grandson are safe and sound. Praise the Lord for these good tidings, yes?" Another pause. "Yes indeed! Amen!"

There was another lengthy pause as the reverend listened.

"Darlene is *fine*. Just a little shaken up. It sounds like you raised her to know the Lord—well done there! Okay. I'll give you back to Darlene. All is well! Blessings!"

The reverend handed back the phone to Darlene. "We'll give thanks for our blessings later today," she murmured. The reverend put the kettle on to boil.

Darlene and Luella continued to chat.

"You were right, Grandma. Things work out for a purpose. Thankfully, Quinn is under arrest, which means he won't be tailing David and me anymore." Darlene sighed. "Funny how things work out in ways we can't foresee. As you've often said, only unshakable faith can make us brave enough to get through the craziness of life."

Once the teakettle whistled, Reverend Renee brewed a pot of black tea for everyone. The group sat around a group of mismatched plates. They had pulled out an assortment of food from the refrigerator: two kinds of cheese, apples, grape jelly in a squeeze-top jar.

"How come we just got Saltine crackers here?" complained Judy. "Can't we ever get something tastier?"

"Speak to management about it," said Gladie.

"Who can eat?" muttered Darlene. "I still feel sick to my stomach."

"Here. I'll make you a cup of this herbal tea with ginger. It'll settle your stomach," said Reverend Renee. She pulled a teabag from a tin on a shelf and poured the hot water into the cup.

260

Darlene felt the warmth of the teacup, tasted her first sip. The tangy heat of the tea soothed her throat, settled the pit of her stomach. A warm glow spread in her belly, toward her heart. She relaxed a bit, for the first time in months.

CHAPTER 60

Officers Muratore and DuShane had sped over to Beacon House as soon as the 911 call had come in. They stopped at the front intake desk.

"Where's the perp?" called out Officer Muratore.

"Downstairs. In the guard's office," said Judy. "Follow me."

She hustled forward and they clattered down the stairwell after her.

From the hallway outside of the guard's office, they took in the scene: Mickey Quinn was perched awkwardly in a chair, his hands handcuffed behind him, his legs outstretched before him.

"Hello, boys!" Quinn called out jauntily. "We can always count on our men in blue!"

"Shuddup, Quinn!" said Lenny Starbird. He was scowling.

Muratore and DuShane flanked Quinn in his chair. DuShane pulled out his cheat sheet once again, and read Quinn the Miranda warning.

Quinn sat there, a smirk on his face.

Finally, DuShane was done.

"Okay, Mr. Quinn. You're coming with us."

Quinn awkwardly stood up, and he and the officers moved as a unit toward the door.

The crowd of women, along with a few of their children, stood back from the entrance, watching Quinn. Everyone was silent as Quinn walked past them, and out the front door.

Quinn called out, "Hey, can somebody call my attorney, Tobias Meachum? He needs to come and pick up my car. My car keys are in my pocket. I can't reach them with my hands cuffed behind my back." He smirked, wiggling his fingers.

Muratore bent over to dig in Quinn's pocket, wearing an expression of massive distaste. He fished out a keyring full of keys, and tossed it onto the sidewalk.

"Somebody take the keys and follow up on this," he said.

Judy stepped forward to pick them up.

Muratore grabbed Quinn by his elbow and shoved him into the backseat. Then he and DuShane slipped into the front seat and drove off.

A feeling of tremendous relief washed over Darlene as she watched the officers drive away with Quinn.

CHAPTER 61

"What have we learned from today's incident?" asked Dr. Sasha Locander.

The meeting room was overly warm from body heat. Everyone at Beacon House was there, turned toward Dr. Sasha, ready to listen.

"The reverend would like to read a poem that a friend of hers wrote. It gives us food for thought. The poem is called 'The Answer.'"

Everyone watched as Reverend Renee stood up, a small index card in her hand.

"My friend Nancy wrote this. It goes like this:

Prejudice has an ugly face,
it isn't pretty, it's a disgrace.
We are all sisters and brothers,
created to love, not hate one another.
Beneath our skin and deep within,

understanding must begin.
Color, race, and shape of eyes,
matters naught if we are wise.
Look deeply now at one another,
learn from sister and from brother.
Find the peace and find the love
that rains upon us from above.
If each of us is to survive
we as people must decide,
A change of heart and mind
to erase prejudice from mankind.

The reverend looked around the room, making eye contact with many of the residents.

"It's actually kinda ironic, isn't it? People of color, people of little means, whatever your circumstances are—others use it as a reason to stop you, to question you, while Longbottom's high and mighty walk right through!" Her jaw was set. "Guess we at Beacon House have learned a valuable lesson!" She shook her head, disbelievingly.

Dr. Sasha stepped forward again.

"We learned that people in positions of authority are sometimes not as pure-minded as we would hope. That sometimes these people in authority have personal interests that they put *first*, ahead of their public duty."

Dr. Sasha slowly surveyed the room, gauging people's reactions.

Reverend Renee stood shoulder to shoulder with Dr. Locander.

"We must all have faith that the Lord holds us in the palm of His hand. Justice somehow prevailed, through unforeseen circumstances. Let us all silently pray."

She bowed her head, clasped her hands. A few moments of silence passed.

"Lastly, let us all remember to be vigilant. That has been the key to success here. Go in peace," said the reverend.

CHAPTER 62

"What the hell were you thinking, Mickey?" said Toby. "You were gonna take your kid, flee the country, screw me, screw everybody— *what the hell?*"

They were staring at one another through the cell bars at the Longbottom police station. There were four cells, and three of them were filled. Mickey occupied the one on the end, nearest the station desk.

Tobias Meachum was so angry, he didn't bother to lower his voice. Apparently, he didn't care who heard him.

"*Damn you!* I thought we were buddies from way back, but it seems you don't mind screwing an old buddy if need be. You know you're going back to jail now, to await your murder trial. I can't get you out on a dangerousness hearing this time, not after the *bullshit* stunt you just pulled at Beacon House. You're a goddamn fool!"

Toby slapped his hand against his leg.

"You really thought you'd get away with that?" He snorted. "Fat chance. You can try to bullshit the judge, but it ain't gonna work this time. I'm telling you the hard truth. You realize that you're jeopardizing my law license? That ain't cool. I want no part of this, Mickey. It's time for us to part ways. Good-bye, my friend. Good luck with the rest of your life."

"I know I'm an asshole, Toby. Always was," said Quinn.

"Yeah. And now you're an asshole on your own."

———

Mickey Quinn was headed back to the county jail. The Longbottom cops had already told him he was due to be transported that evening, along with two others.

Quinn thought back to his prior stint in the county jail with his cell-mate, Dooley.

Great, he thought. *Just what I need. More time in a cell with a psychopath.*

Quinn reflected on Toby's words. They were unexpectedly harsh, but not unreasonable, considering. Quinn punched the thin mattress he was sitting on. He'd have to get another lawyer. But where would he get one like Toby?

"Dinner," said the Longbottom cop, shoving a tray through the slot in the bars.

Quinn picked up his tray. A thin bologna sandwich. An apple. A packet of cookies. A bottle of water. Pretty uninspiring.

Well, he was hungry, so he might as well eat.

———

"Let's go," said the county sheriff.

It was still light outside after their dinner.

Quinn and the two other prisoners were handcuffed and led to the waiting county van, which was long and blue, with reinforced locks. They found seats in the back, while the two sheriffs took their seats in front, one turned around to face the prisoners. The prisoners were separated from the two guards with a metal grille. A third sheriff followed the three detainees in another vehicle.

"Here we go, boys!" announced the driver. "Off to the county jail. Good times ahead."

Quinn rolled his eyes. The other prisoners were silent.

The van left the police station parking lot and swung out into Longbottom traffic. It was muggy in the van, thought Quinn. He was still in his business suit, wrinkled by now. His tie had been lost. Soon he'd be back in those jailhouse scrubs. *Great.*

He peered out his window. Just yesterday, he'd been a free man, pending his upcoming trial. He watched the neat houses go by, wondering when and if he'd ever see a regular neighborhood again.

That made him think of his own house, which had been taken care of by Toby, the last time he was in the clink. Who'd watch his house this time? Who knew if he'd ever get back to it anyway? Damn. And what about his car, abandoned in front of Beacon House? Had Toby managed to collect it? Quinn didn't want his car ending up in the junkyard.

That damn Darlene. Keeping his son away from him. This was all her fault.

The van made its way through downtown Longbottom, crossed the railroad tracks, and proceeded toward the Massachusetts coast. Twilight was setting in.

The van driver drove with a heavy foot, making the van sway on curves. The local highway was two lanes, going through farmland, mostly cranberry bogs. An occasional car's headlights shone brightly as it flashed by.

Quinn watched the passing miles with a sense of foreboding.

Would he ever walk freely again?

The cranberry bogs were situated below the highway, maroon-colored in the near-dark, with sections carved into the landscape. One bog's lone shack had a small light. A three-quarter moon was hanging in the sky. It glowed, too, across the bogs.

Pretty desolate out here, Quinn thought.

The van driver sped up on a straightaway portion of the highway.

Quinn looked over at the two other prisoners. They were both staring forward, unseeingly. Neither was looking out their window at the passing landscape. The guard facing them was slumped against the headrest, apparently asleep.

Typical state employee, Quinn thought. *Mean, incompetent, and lazy. Just like those damn social workers who stuck me in foster care.*

The van driver suddenly slammed on his brakes, halting with a screech. The van's nose spun to the left, sending it askew on the road. Ahead, in the sweep of its headlights, were two Hummers, blocking the highway. There was no getting around them. They stretched from edge to edge of the narrow, two-lane highway. On either side of the road was a steep drop-off into the cranberry bogs.

"*Shit!*" yelled the van driver. "What the hell is going on?"

The other guard woke up, groggy, and started looking around.

Two men dressed in dark clothes and facial masks leapt out of the Hummer on the right. They carried long guns and pointed them at the sheriff's van.

One of them came closer, peering in at the group of prisoners. Standing at the front, he yelled, "Quinn!"

"Yo!"

"The masked man strode forward, opened the door, and yanked Quinn out of his seat.

Quinn lurched, stumbled. The masked man gripped him by his arm and pulled him toward one of the waiting Hummers.

"Hurry up! Get in!"

Quinn dove head-first into the door nearest him. He crawled onto the backseat, again in handcuffs. The door was slammed shut behind him.

As Quinn tried to sit up, the Hummer sped forward, tossing him back. The vehicle roared down the highway, in the opposite direction they had been driving.

"Where are we going?"

"Never mind. Here's some stuff. Courtesy of your friends in high places."

Elation flushed into Quinn's limbs.

He still had the juice, baby.

He pawed through the contents of the small briefcase he'd been handed. Inside, an envelope of cash. Quinn grinned. His passport. Toby somehow must've gotten his car and retrieved his stuff quickly, before his vehicle was seized and impounded.

Wonder how he managed that one, he thought.

"Where are we headed?"

"Local airport. Private airplane."

"Great. Thanks."

"Tell it to your buddy."

The Hummer sped down the highway in the dark. Quinn gripped the briefcase against his belly and waited to see what would happen next.

CHAPTER 63

Quinn and the two masked men drove up to a small airport out in the countryside of southeastern Massachusetts. The fields surrounding the airport were lit along its two perpendicular runways. With the wind picking up, a four-seater plane waited, engine running, and pointed southbound.

"You guys are great!" Quinn grinned. "Any way you can get these damn handcuffs offa me? I don't wanna get on the plane with them. Not a good look."

He was feeling jaunty.

"When we stop the car. We got something to cut them," said the one not driving, who didn't turn around to look at Quinn.

These guys don't say much, thought Quinn. *Wonder how Toby connected with these two so quick. Maybe as a Friend of the Kennedys?*

The Hummer pulled up alongside the small plane and stopped. The driver shut off the engine and unlocked the doors. The other masked man got out and opened Quinn's door.

Quinn skooched out, arms outstretched. His feet landed on the tarmac.

Just then, four other cars rushed onto the tarmac and surrounded the Hummer. One car pulled right alongside.

Police lights flashed. Sirens blared. More blue lights swept across the night sky, blindingly out of sequence. Night shadows skittered.

"Shit!" screamed Quinn. "What the hell is happening?"

He looked around wildly.

"You're under arrest!" shouted the nearest officer. "Everybody get down on the ground! Now!"

Quinn groaned. He hung his head, then began to drop to the ground.

"Goddammit," he muttered under his breath as his knees touched the tarmac.

He swiveled his head to the cop standing nearby, gun drawn.

"How the hell did you guys know to come here?"

The officer growled, "We have our ways." He snorted. "The van driver was on the radio to us in seconds, with an APB out on the Hummer. Its license plate was on the camera!"

The officer kicked away the briefcase and grabbed Quinn, pulling him up to a standing position. He shoved him against the side of the police car and patted him down, then pushed Quinn toward the police car rear door.

"Get in!"

Once again, Quinn was shoved headfirst into the backseat. He was still handcuffed, and fell in, scuffing his nose.

"Shit," groaned Quinn.

He heard three gunshots, but saw nothing, since his face was still pressed against the rear seat. He wondered what was happening.

Outside the car, under the frenetic flashing blue lights, a battle was taking place.

One of the masked men was lying on the tarmac, facedown. A black pool of blood oozed from under his torso, gleaming under the airport lights. The other masked man crouched behind his Hummer, gun drawn, waiting. A semicircle of officers crouched behind their vehicles, also waiting. It was going to be a standoff with this guy.

The radio crackled. Quinn heard: "Status of escaped prisoner . . . report in . . ."

He heard the officer in the front seat reply, "Prisoner secured. Unsecure location. Request to proceed with transfer to county jail immediately."

More crackling.

"Request granted. Proceed immediately."

Quinn felt the engine start. His heart sank.

Toby had almost pulled it off.

Somehow, somebody had gotten wind of it and snitched on the plan for his escape.

Damn.

Now he really *was* going to jail—no bail this time—and then to trial for the murder of Clarisse. He had almost gotten his son free and clear of Darlene. But now he was going to prison.

Prison.

Who knew if he'd ever get to see his son again.

He sighed. At least no one suspected him in the killing of Rufus Fishbane—not even Toby. Some things are best buried deep, then forgotten.

He laid his cheek against the backseat and settled in for his ride to the county jail.

So much for being an FOTK.

CHAPTER 64

Darlene and the women at Beacon House heard the news the next day.

How Quinn had been on the way to the county jail when he'd been whisked away by unknown men. How he'd been recaptured by law enforcement and taken to the county jail to await his trial for murder.

Darlene's heart leapt for joy. He was behind bars again. And would be for years.

Beacon House had been a steadfast, worthy refuge. Even though she and David had been singled out for attack here, the guard at this place had been stellar in his defense of them. She had to find out who he was.

Now that the drama was over, she and David could leave Beacon House.

But what was she going to do about finding a place for them? She had effectively abandoned her apartment mid-year. They had taken her last-month's rent and simultaneously rented it out to a new person. No going back there.

Pity. She had *loved* living across the hall from sweet and funny Nathan.

"Whatcha thinking about, girl?"

A new resident at Beacon House was at her side.

"My son's father has just been arrested and put in jail. And I'm really happy about it." She smiled wide. "Now I can get on with my life, without looking over my shoulder, worrying about whether he's gonna get all up in my business."

The woman chuckled. "Sounds like he got what he deserved."

"Yep." Darlene scratched her head. "And the guard here rescued my son yesterday. He was awesome!"

"That hullabaloo yesterday was *you*?"

"Yep. That was me and my boy."

"If I was you, I'd check out that guard. He's kinda cute."

Darlene tilted her head. "Really? I don't know. I'm kinda off men."

"Whoooeee, girl! At least go up to him and thank him. He did you a righteous turn!"

"You're right. That's the right thing to do. Good advice."

———

Darlene rested David on her thigh as she sat on the iron bench in the garden. She was still thinking about what to do next, where to go. It was weighing on her mind.

She sighed.

David cooed and reached for her chin.

"Hey, Davey-boy. We did all right yesterday," she whispered. "We gotta go find that guard and thank him, don'tcha think?"

She nuzzled the top of David's head. She was still surprised that he had been born with a full head of hair, and blond, to boot. She combed his hair with her fingers.

"Yeah, let's go find that guard."

275

She stood up, David in her arms. She walked along the flagstone path to the back door of the shelter.

Darlene blinked as she entered the building, waiting a long moment for her eyes to adjust, so she wouldn't stumble with David in her arms. Looking the length of the room, she saw a tall, thin man standing at the far door. Looking closer, she recognized it was the guard.

She walked up to him and said, shyly, "I wanted to thank you for what you did yesterday for my son and me."

Lenny Starbird looked at her and smiled, gave her a little salute. Then he placed his hand over his heart and took a deep breath.

"Ma'am, I'm breaking protocol to say this, but when you get out of here, and go back to your real life, I wondered—may I take you out on a date? You don't need to worry—I'm a gentleman. And your son can come with us, too, if you'd like."

He inhaled sharply.

"I sure hope I haven't made a damn fool of myself."

He began to turn red, and ducked his head. His black curls covered his ears.

"Of course I'll go out with you," Darlene said softly. "It'd help to know your name first, though!" She laughed, jiggling David up and down in her arms. "Why don't you tell me a little about yourself."

"Yes, ma'am. I'm Lenny Starbird. I'm just a local Longbottom guy. And a cop. At least, I *was* a cop, but I got laid off when our department's budget was cut. Took this job here. I can tell you more on our first date." He looked around him. "I'm on duty now . . . May I have your number?"

"Got your cell phone on ya?" she said with a smile. She tapped in her number on his phone.

"Thanks. Your name's Darlene, right?"

"Yeah. Sorry I forgot to introduce myself. This is David." She took David's arm and waved it at Lenny. David gurgled and waved some more. "I think he likes you! That's a good sign." She smiled again. "I gotta go now, Lenny. I look forward to seeing you again!"

She gave a little wave as she turned away.

Lenny Starbird returned to his office humming. Things were looking up. He grinned to himself.

CHAPTER 65

Darlene had finally gone to sleep in her little room at Beacon House, with David lying next to her, between her and the wall. Even though she knew Quinn had been arrested—and therefore, that they were safe—it had taken a while for her body to stop quivering from the extreme adrenaline of it all.

She eventually calmed herself by thinking about Lenny Starbird. He seemed like a really nice guy. He'd even offered to have David join us on our first date. How many guys would do that?

———

In the morning, Darlene woke up simultaneously tired and full of excitement. She hadn't had enough sleep, but she was eager to get started on the rest of her life.

278

But first she had to secure a place for herself and David to live, and quickly. She didn't want to stay at Beacon House a moment longer than they needed to.

She decided to make her first call.

"Nathan, my friend, are you busy at this exact moment?"

"Never too busy for you, pumpkin. I heard about everything on the news—it was on all the Boston channels! This Quinn fellow sure knows how to make a splash!"

Darlene could hear the glee in his voice.

"Yeah, it was quite a scene here, that's for sure."

"And what about the chase and the take-down at the airport!"

"I missed that part. You'll have to fill me in." Darlene paused for a moment. "I have a question for your first, though. Do you think there's any chance I could get my job back at your aunt's place? It was pretty perfect. And Auntie Joy is a sweetheart, even if she likes to come off as tough."

"Not a problem. In fact, that would be *great*, actually. She got so used to having your help that she demanded I fill in during your absence. I can't wait for you to get back on the job, so I can get back to my own apartment, and my life. How soon can you get back here?"

"As soon as you can come and pick us up!" Darlene said, grinning.

CHAPTER 66

"I couldn't *wait* to come back to this job," said Darlene. "Want to know why?"

Joy Green raised her elegant profile to gaze at Darlene and David. "Please tell me," she said, taking a sip of her steaming tea.

"First off, it's the beginning of our new lives, in freedom! No more Mickey Quinn breathing down our necks, sending people after us. I'm free to raise David, clear of all of his father's bad influences.

"And did I tell you, I met someone? I know, funny place to meet a guy, at a women's shelter, right?"

Darlene grinned hugely. She leaned back as David plucked at the brocade couch over her shoulder.

"And you'll never believe it, but the guy I met—he's a cop, named Lenny Starbird—he said I should bring David along on our first date. Ha! We'll see if he really meant it."

"I imagine he did, if he said it," said Joy. "That's wonderful, Darlene. You've been so devoted to David . . . it's time you got out a bit."

"Yeah, you're right." Darlene giggled. "He did seem like a curiously old-fashioned kind of guy. He called himself a gentleman."

"Don't you know, my dear?" Joy straightened in her armchair to peer at Darlene. "Gentlemen never go out of style."

"Now that's something my grandma would say," Darlene murmured.

"Smart woman, your grandmother."

"Yeah, she is. Any smarts I've got came from her. But my second reason for being grateful, is that working here, while keeping David close by me, is so comforting. Just being here, in this house, around art and books—I haven't even started reading all those books in your library, but I'd like to, if I may."

"Of course!"

"And I know I can learn from you. You're truly kind. And wise. I'm so grateful to you for introducing me to Anna Ebert, who got me into Beacon House, which, in turn, helped free David and me from Quinn's shackles."

"Quinn did that himself, with his own audacity and recklessness." Darlene grinned.

"But mostly, I like your take-no-hogwash attitude. You're much like my feisty Grandma."

Darlene let out a belly laugh. It felt so good to be safe, and to be back here.

"And you're dear to me, too, just like my grandma," Darlene said.

She reached for Joy Green's hand and gave it a squeeze.

"For now, we're family of the heart. But when Nathan becomes David's godfather, we'll *officially* be family. As Grandma would say, *Hallelujah for that!*"

ACKNOWLEDGMENTS

To my fellow TaleSpinners, fine writers all:

Nancy Gay, Phyllis Goldfeder, Anna Votruba, T.J. Herlihy, Donna Ryan, Joyce Thorne, Christine Muratore, Mark Linde.

May your words always shine!

ABOUT THE AUTHOR

Adelene Ellenberg was born in Kentucky, raised outside of Chicago, and now lives in the countryside of Massachusetts. As a lawyer and a person of faith, she has advocated for the downtrodden and disrespected from all walks of life. Having seen the law used as both a weapon and a shield, she wrote *Eminent Crimes*, followed by *The Killer's Kid*. For more, see AdeleneEllenberg.com.